MERMAID STEEL

JAY HARTLOVE

Published by Water Dragon Publishing
waterdragonpublishing.com

ISBN 978-1-953469-61-8 (Trade Paperback)

10 9 8 7 6 5 4 3

FIRST EDITION

*I dedicate this book to Sheri Hand-Fager,
my biggest fan and most ardent supporter. Sheri, you've been there
for me when there was literally no one else on my side. You even
helped me with this book back in 2015 when it was still a dream.
Well, that dream came true!
Thank you from the bottom of my heart.*

MERMAID STEEL

1

S TEN HOLDSMITH DID NOT SEE IT COMING.
He braced a sandal against the sailboat's wood foot rail and grabbed the rope net with his strong hands, focused on unraveling the tangled mass. He had thrown out the net, but it hadn't spread in the water. He hauled it up for another try, only to find it now tangled and heavy. His pleasant little excursion was rapidly turning into a lot of work. The sea was thankfully calm, with a clear midday sky, warm sun, and only a light breeze. It would rain later. It always rained in the afternoons. He could stay out as long as he wanted to. He was just waiting for this to become the fun time he had hoped for.

Half a dozen sea gulls circled patiently overhead. He smirked. "Sorry, boys. Nothing yet."

He mopped his tanned brow and three-day beard with his loose white sleeve and returned to the nets. He barely heard the wind snap the sail full. Not being an experienced sailor, he didn't connect that the snap meant the sail had come untied, and was coming his way. He caught the movement out of the corner of his eye just in time to twist his head out of the yardarm's path, but it still caught him square in the chest, toppling him over backward. He flailed to grab any handhold, but only got the net that was wrapped around his feet. "Oh for Atlan's sake!" he blurted out as he fell, followed by the net sliding over the rail.

As heavy as it was on deck, it felt much heavier in the water, and it was on top of him pushing him under. He needed to keep calm and focus on freeing his feet. He couldn't get any stroke to the surface with his feet bound. His lungs were not as full as he needed, having been struck by the sail. He wriggled and pulled in directions that seemed logical, but felt no loosening. He started pulling with his hands, but couldn't find a rope that didn't tighten the mass. Calm didn't stand a chance as fear and anger fought to take him over.

One rational thought managed to form. What had possessed him to think he could go fishing, with no experience and no teacher? So what if he lived in a fishing village? He was a blacksmith, and should be in his shop wielding a hammer, not dying, caught like a fish. Not a helpful thought.

Maybe if he let the net roll over and fall below him, maybe he could see an opening. He pushed the rope mass with one hand and tried to row himself in the opposite direction with his other arm. Movement! Encouraged, he pushed harder. Once on top of the bulk of the net, though, he saw how far he had sunk below the surface. His chest felt like it would burst. His courage dissolved in the warm water.

A flash of silver streaking by caught his eye and his heart skipped a beat. Great, now he would be eaten. Maybe he could use the net to defend himself from the shark. He twisted and searched but couldn't see past his tangled prison.

Something tugged on the net hard. He braced himself for the sensation of teeth ripping flesh, but it didn't come. Another powerful tug, and he felt one leg come free. He squirmed around to see what was happening, and came face to face with a mermaid.

She smiled at him with her overbroad mouth, flashing a full array of sharp teeth. She had a carved mother-of-pearl knife in her hand and she was cutting him free. He smiled back in utter relief. One more tug and his other leg slipped loose. As happy as he was to be free, he looked up and was not sure he would make it to the surface. She must have seen the desperation on his face, because she did something completely unheard of for merfolk. She seized him under the armpits and flicked her tail in fast tight strokes.

The water rushing past his face was so forceful it roared in his ears. He marveled at how her muscular tail shot them through the water. He clearly outweighed her, yet she dragged him like a toy. She swam so fast they breached the surface and arched up into the air. All he could think about was that first delicious breath.

When they splashed down, she kept a hand on him. He was exhausted and shaking and glad for her steady grip, despite the social taboo. He was so relieved and so grateful, he had to let her know. He reached up and squeezed her webbed hand on his shoulder. When he had caught his breath, he looked at her earnestly. "Thank you."

"You're welcome," she said with an understanding nod.

He had never seen a mermaid this close before. Her gills, which had been expanded in flowery petals underwater, now lay closed and smooth on the sides of her hairless head and neck. She looked quite a bit more human this way, like a teenaged girl with short, curly, albeit oddly silver colored hair. With her full lips closed, he almost forgot about all those pointed carnivore teeth behind. What really caught him were her eyes. Maybe it was the shine of her silvery skin, light, almost white in her face fading to dark gray around the back, but the deep aqua color of those eyes that seemed just a little too big for her head — something about that color just wouldn't let him go. He caught himself staring and looked away.

"Are you all right?"

"I'll be fine. Now that you saved my stupid hide."

She turned and looked at his boat. "I assume you did not throw yourself overboard in a fishing net on purpose."

"Not on purpose."

"Can you make it back onto your boat?"

"I think I can manage."

Without another word or gesture, she disappeared back under the surface. He looked around and waited, but she was gone. Merfolk had a reputation for not being socialized. He shrugged and swam to his boat.

Once back on board, he took the sails down to stop the boat from being blown around randomly. He shook his linen clothes so they could dry hanging loose on his body.

He was just deciding his next move when the mermaid popped up alongside, holding his net. "I thought you might need this."

He reached over the rail and took the end she handed up to him. "Thank you, again. I would need it more if I knew what I was doing with it."

She gave him a curious look. "Were you trying to teach yourself to fish?"

"I thought I should know, coming from a fishing village. I borrowed the boat 'cause I wanted to see for myself."

"I cut up the net pretty badly getting you out. It will have to be mended before you can use it again."

"I'm sure I'll have no trouble finding someone who can fix it, for a price."

"I would be happy to mend it for you."

"No, you don't have to do that."

"Please let me repair the damage I made. I have some talent with weaving rope."

He regarded her, bobbing in the water, with her earnest expression. "If I let you fix the net, you will have to let me pay you back somehow. Some metal fixtures or something."

"Metal is always a welcome gift." Then she frowned. "I do not understand what you mean by, 'pay me back.' I just want to do what is right."

"I appreciate that, but I should pay you for your work."

Her frown became almost comical as she twisted her lips to the side and rolled her large, glassy eyes trying to comprehend what he was saying. "I will accept whatever gift you want to give me as thanks for doing you this favor. Is that what you mean?"

He blinked and rubbed his short, rough beard with his hand as he thought over her offer. "Yes, that works for me."

She waved her hand in a shooing motion. "Then please step back from the edge."

He did, and she dove beneath the surface. A second later she flew up out of the water, twisted around and landed smoothly on her bottom with her tail hanging over the edge. Her strength and agility again surprised him.

She pulled her thin, rainbow-colored shell knife out of a belt she wore over one shoulder and went to work on the net straight away. Now that he could see all of her, he realized she was clothed in a light blue woven tunic that clung to her shape, covering her down over what would have been her hips, with a slit down the back for her dorsal fin. He caught himself staring at her long, bare, dolphin-like tail, the fluke of which she flipped in the air in what he guessed was boredom. As she dried off in the sun, he realized her skin wasn't silver, but shades of gray and white, white all down her front and almost black down her back. She was really quite beautiful. He surprised himself with that thought.

However fascinating she was to look at, what she was doing was just as amazing. He knelt down next to her to get a closer look. She glanced up and smiled at him. "You look like you've never seen anyone mend rope."

"I guess I've never watched it done." She unraveled a length from both ends of a cut piece, then twisted sets of pairs together, holding each pair as she twisted the next. Once she had four pairs, she twisted the pairs together in the opposite direction to form a healed rope. What made this bit of workmanship all the more magical was watching her do it with her long, thin fingers that were webbed together up to the last joint. "You're really good at this."

She lowered her head modestly and said, "This is what I do in my village. I'm a weaver."

"And you made this, um, shirt you're wearing too?"

She smiled. "My erda? Yes."

"Doesn't the fabric slow you down in the water?"

"Not this fabric. We weave it so all the fibers run longways and don't hold onto the water." She pinched the cords. "See, it's almost dry already. Unlike yours," she added, indicating his white shirt which still clung to his broad chest, showing the ample hair underneath.

He stood up and stepped to the back of the boat. "Well, if I am going to get you an appropriate thank you gift, I'm going to need to sail back to my shop. Will that be all right with you, going back to the human village with me?" He started pulling up the sails.

"I should be done with this before we get there. I can always hop in and swim alongside to stay out of sight."

"Oh, I don't care if anyone sees you on the boat."

"I wouldn't want to make any trouble for you," she said.

"Don't worry about me. The villagers all think I'm crazy anyway. I just don't want anyone giving you a hard time." He finished tying off the sail lines. "We'll see if there is anyone around. My shop is on its own pier, so we may not run into anyone anyway."

"Your shop? What do you make?"

"Oh, I'm sorry, I didn't say. I'm a blacksmith. You probably figured out I am not a fisherman." He tied down the rudder, stepped up to her and held out his hand. "My name is Sten. Sten Holdsmith."

She shook his hand. "I am Chielle Mmava." She pronounced her first name in a piercingly high pitch and her second in a low deep breath. It was not like anything he had ever heard before.

"Chee-el?" he attempted.

"Very close," she nodded. "Certainly good enough, given how different our throats are. How lucky for me to have rescued a blacksmith. I don't have to tell you how important your craft is to us."

"Important enough to have given your race a bad name from thefts. I have never understood why we can't sell you the metal you need. Or exchange gifts, or whatever you want to call it. Merfolk shouldn't be reduced to stealing. It destroys any chance of our peoples ever patching things up."

"Merrow."

"Pardon?"

"We call ourselves Merrow, not Merfolk."

"Really? I've never heard that. I wonder why not." He returned to steering the boat.

"You are a trusting person, Sten Holdsmith, to take a Merrow to a blacksmith shop."

Caught off guard, he remembered Atlan's scripture, 'Always know how lucky you are, and always be ready to help the needy.' How many times had that motto gotten him into trouble? "Oh, I don't think your people are thieves. In fact, I would say most humans don't really believe that. I've tried to sell hardware to Merrow, but human law forbids direct commerce."

"Merrow law forbids it too. It is an ancient law that must be respected."

"Well, I don't mean any disrespect, but it doesn't make any sense. It leaves your people at a disadvantage."

"The only disadvantage my people feel is not being able to make steel ourselves. It can't be done underwater. We are left working with your cast offs."

"That's the problem. Even if it's stuff nobody wants anymore, they still see it as stealing. The fact that you can disappear under the surface and reappear suddenly makes people nervous to begin with."

She stopped weaving and looked back at him. "You seem to be having trouble understanding how our two villages relate."

"You're right. I've only been here a year, and I see a lot of suspicion and resentment, and it doesn't make sense to me. You all have been neighbors for generations, yet no one wants to reach out and even learn about your people. I had never heard the term Merrow. I honestly didn't know what to expect back there when you freed me from the net."

"Did you think I might harm you? I'm glad I could be an honorable example."

"Me too!" He interrupted himself. "Wait a minute. I was going to give you some stakes and jump rings to take back with you. I figure those are pretty useful. Only thing is, if you show up back in Celidan with such a bounty of stuff that is obviously not found, aren't you going to be accused of doing business with a human?"

"But it is a gift."

"I have a feeling there are just as many suspicious people on your side of the surface as on mine. These hatreds run deep, not to make a pun. I'll have to think of something that won't get you in trouble."

The afternoon breeze blew them towards shore without needing to tack. Standing there just steering while she worked on the net gave him time to think. This underlying mistrust between the villages had been eating at him for months, ever since he was told he couldn't sell to them. Maybe meeting her was a chance to bridge the gap in some small way. He caught himself. *Justice issues? Again?* He straightened up involuntarily with a twinge of pain across his back.

"Are you all right?" she asked.

"Yeah. Just an unpleasant memory. Hey, you're making great progress there."

She held it up and showed only a couple of cuts left.

As the afternoon wind blew them passed the palm tree lined beaches of the harbor of Saint Rochel of the Sea, the piers and wharfs of the town came into view. The sky clouded up and the air became thick with humidity. Right on time, he thought. The seagulls that had been following them gave up and went ashore.

As he watched her working, suspicion crept up on him that maybe she knew he was a blacksmith all along. What a coincidence that she was right there to save him, him with skills her people needed so badly. "We'll be there soon."

"Just finishing up." She held the net up to show him.

"Very nice. You saved me a pretty penny and an embarrassing story. Thank you."

She swung her tail up onto the deck and did something Sten did not expect. She walked aft toward him. Or rather she wriggled. She extended her set of long flippers from what would have been her thighs and bent her tail into a hump shape that placed the flat of her tail fluke against the deck. She then scooted in a rolling motion between the flippers and her tail.

She caught his amazed expression. "You can't tell me you've never seen a Merrow walk."

"I'm sorry, I didn't mean to stare. I didn't realize your tail is so flexible."

She pulled up next to him and cocked her head playfully. "I can do all kinds of things."

He cleared his throat and took half a step back. Flirting? She must have known he was a blacksmith.

More frankly, she offered, "May I help with the rigging when we pull into the dock?"

He looked around at all that needed to be done. "Sure. My dock is on the inside of those piers, so I'm going to need to swing the sail around as we tack. Do you know what I mean by that?"

She smiled and nodded. "Yes, I am familiar with how sailing works."

"You've sailed before?"

"No, but I watch humans sailing all the time. I like to watch and learn whenever I can."

Oh. Maybe he was wrong to suspect her motives. Or maybe she felt she needed to lie to gain his confidence. In either case, this was a chance for him to do the right thing. "That's good you like to learn, because I've decided my gift to you will be to teach you something."

Indeed, Chielle's sailing skills were handy as they navigated around the piers and pulled up to Sten's berth. They both watched for anyone looking out of the bamboo and woven mat buildings on the piers that might see her, but there was no one. The barking seals on the piling cross beams under the piers covered any sound they made.

Sten was taken by the smells of the harbor, the seaweed and barnacles that clung to the pier pilings, the smell of cut fish. He never noticed these when he was home. Did it always smell like this? He guessed a few hours out on the open ocean had cleared his head.

Chielle sighed and smiled as they pulled up to the floating landing platform. He started to ask why, then saw it was the ramp she was relieved to see. Everywhere else on the piers there were only ladders to climb. She may be flexible, but a ladder would be a real challenge without two feet. She had no difficulty walking up the ramp to the wharf topside.

She turned around at the top and pointed to the name on the prow of the boat. "Why is your boat called, 'The *Back Forty*?' Forty what?"

"She belongs to a friend of mine who is a rancher and a farmer. He owns lots of land. We measure land in acres, which is a pretty big piece. I guess it's a joke among ranchers that you never get to tend your furthermost acreage. Norn doesn't get to sail as often as he would like so he named his boat after that *back forty* acres of land."

"Thank you. I never would have figured that out."

As he led her into his shop, she stopped and her big eyes went even wider as she looked at all the tools and metal fixtures around the hearth, hanging on hooks and stacked in piles. He watched her for a moment as she took it all in. "The tools of my trade."

"These are what you use to form things from metal?"

He pointed to items as he spoke. "Yes. I hold the metal with these tongs and beat it with these hammers, around these forms to make shapes. The key is the heat." He turned a wheel on a box next to the stone pit and the sound of rushing air flooded the hearth. The embers glowed brightly red.

She pulled back in surprise.

"That's what you're missing underwater. But," he held his hand aloft, "but, you can still do a lot with metal that is cold. That is what I want to show you today."

She pried her gaze up from the red glow and smiled at him. "Really?"

He looked her square in the eyes. "I don't like it when life is unfair. That's gotten me into real trouble in the past. But fair is fair. You saved my life. This is the least I can do." He picked up a short length of steel bar and handed it to her. "Besides, this will be fun. Try to bend that. Metal is stiff like that because it is actually made up of crystals. When you bend metal, you are shifting the crystals over one another. You can use force and vibration to loosen the crystals as you go. He took the rod from her and picked up a hammer. He held the bar with a pair of tongs and positioned it on an anvil.

When he struck the bar, she jumped at the ringing sound and covered not only her ears, but the whole sides of her face with her webbed hands.

"Sorry. I should have warned you. This gets pretty loud. I'll go softly. Even light tapping will show you what I mean." He smacked the bar repeatedly as he turned the ends up with the tongs. "See, the beating is actually stretching the metal, like clay." In a couple of minutes, he beat the bar into a circle and handed it to her.

"You can feel it is warm from the beating."

"All that beating doesn't break anything?"

"No, it's almost as strong as when it was straight. Now if I really shaped it a lot, and I needed it very strong, I would heat it up to a glow in the hearth and beat it into its final shape while red hot. That sets the shape to a rigid strength. That's not necessary for making small fixtures like rings or stakes." He picked up another bar and handed it to her. "Here, you try."

She took a hunching step over to the anvil, then stood up on her tail fluke. Sten looked down at how she did this and saw she rested her weight on the bend in her tail. Her dorsal fin, which he had not really looked at before, stuck out from what on a woman would be her buttocks, and now pointed straight out behind her with the curvature. This posture brought her up to his same height. She picked up the hammer and started to put the bar on the anvil holding it with her other hand.

"No, you can't hold it with your bare hand. I can't even do that with my grizzled paws. The vibration is way too much. Hold the bar with the tongs. See how the handles are wrapped? It saves your hand." He helped get her set up. "Bring the hammer down in the middle until you see a dent."

She smacked it but made no mark. She tried again harder and made a mark, but winced at the sharp sound. "It's too loud for me," she said, disappointed.

"I plug my ears with cotton when it gets too loud for me. Let me get you some." He pulled a couple of tufts from a bag on a shelf and handed them to her. She stuffed them in her ears, which fitted in front of the first folds of her gills, and bravely tried again. Again the ringing made her wince.

"It's hurting my face as much as my ears. Merrow use the whole side of our head to hear vibrations in the water. I'm afraid that makes me pretty sensitive to this banging."

"Hold on a second," he suggested, undeterred. He stepped through a door into his living quarters and returned with a long thin bolster pillow and a knit cap. "Now, this is going to look funny. Obviously you will have to find some other way to do this on your own. If we bend this under your chin and up to cover your cheeks and temples, then we can pull the hat down to hold it in place."

She looked at the items doubtfully. "Go ahead and try."

He stepped up but then hesitated when he realized this meant handling her face. "Sure. Um, I'll bend this up. Can you hold the ends up to cover what you need? Then I'll pull the hat down and tuck these up here." Her skin was smooth and soft, yet felt dense and firm. He didn't linger, but he was intrigued.

All the while he fussed, she smirked at him like this was some silly game. "You have a funny way of getting close to a girl."

He ignored the comment. "There, see if that works."

She assessed the makeshift headgear with her hands. "Why not?" She picked up the bar with the tongs and hefted the hammer. She brought it down with gusto and made a significant dent. "Look at that!"

"Excellent. Now keep doing that until you get a feel for how the metal responds to the hammer. Lots of impacts while bending it down onto the anvil. Keep repositioning the bar as you go, so your strike is always straight down on the anvil."

She made several more strikes and smiled at the results.

"The key is to keep hitting it. Once you start, you want to keep it up, keep shifting those crystals, keep creating that heat inside the metal that lets it bend. Once you get the hang of this, I'll try you on the shot bag. That makes a more muffled sound."

"Shot bag?"

"Instead on an anvil, if you want a concave bend, you can use a leather bag." He hefted one off the bench. "It's filled with lead pellets. You have to hit the metal harder, but the bag absorbs a lot of the sound. Go ahead with the anvil and see what you can do."

She started pounding until she found a rhythm, and with it the metal began to bend. She beamed up at him. "Look at that! The pillow and the cotton are working too!" she said too loudly.

2

"WE ALREADY KNOW ABOUT POUNDING METAL to shape it." Chielle could tell her older brother Thymon was about to dismiss her, in that casual manner older siblings learn from years of pestering. He even feigned disinterest by smoothing his gill flanges against his neck.

She forced the air through her sinuses to add urgency to her underwater song. She didn't care if the townspeople of Celidan all around them overheard. "Oh no, do not turn away from me. I'm telling you he showed me a secret, a technique you do not know. Look at this ring."

He glanced around to see if anyone was listening. The shopkeepers and their customers on the busy avenue continued about their business without looking their way. When Merrow continued swimming in and out of the organically shaped, hollow coral buildings, he turned back to his sister. He took the iron bracelet with that raised eyebrow half-smirk Chielle had faced too many times.

"I made that. By myself on my first try. In a matter of minutes."

The disdainful eyebrow came down and he pursed his wide lips as he examined it with his wide-set glassy eyes. "All right, what's the trick?"

She lit up at having gotten through to him. "You have to strike the metal many times, without stopping, all around where you want it to bend, to heat it up inside. The metal becomes softer for a moment as you hit it, so you can bend it at the same time."

Thymon eyed the little dents all over the surface. "What about something thicker than this?"

"You'll have to hit it harder, but the secret is to keep hitting it while pushing it where you want it to bend."

"Won't that make a tremendous noise? It's going to deafen the Merrow doing the work, and scare off all the fish for miles around. What was the hammer made of? These dents you made are all the same size. Didn't the hammer flatten out with all this pounding?"

"Well, no. It kept its shape the whole time." She struggled to find an answer, lest she lose his hard-won attention. "Oh, it must have been hardened in the fire. He talked about how you can harden a finished piece by heating it up until it glows and then letting it cool down."

"If you have a fire."

"Can't we make our hammers above the surface?"

He handed the ring back to her. "Maybe. Let me think about it."

Disappointment sent a shiver down her spine. "There must be a way to use this technique."

He frowned and cocked his head. "There are a lot of details to work out. I don't know if we can make this work on any practical scale. Then there's the question of whether Rorra would want us doing this human work. Thank you for bringing this to me."

She didn't try to hide her emotions as she let her fins droop.

He glanced around again at the Merrow going about their business. "It's really a good thing you brought this to me. Anybody else, and you would have been severely punished for consorting with a human. Why in all the swells is this man helping you in the first place? What is he after?"

"I told you, he was going to drown."

His disapproving eyebrow climbed back up. "Not our problem."

"You would let a blacksmith drown, with all those skills we need so badly?"

"Did you know he was a blacksmith when he fell in?"

"Well ..." she hesitated, but then decided the truth was better than lying. "Yes, I did."

Thymon didn't hide his surprise. "You were following him around, hoping for a chance to talk to him."

"I'm not proud of it, but yes."

"Are you sure you didn't push him in?"

"Very funny."

"I'll bet he has no idea you were hunting him."

"No. I needed to build his trust."

"I have to say, little sister, I didn't think you had it in you. At least you won't have to keep up the rouse. He gave you his technique, and you gave it to me. You have no need to go back."

Chielle scanned his face, hoping to find some hesitation, some hint that he was not commanding her to stay away from Sten. She didn't find it. "Right. I have no need," she said before turning and swimming away.

Chielle sat on top of her family's coral home, weaving sea grass fibers into a fine mat. The curved dome of the roof was her favorite spot for this kind of boring handwork, since it afforded her a view down the canyon over most of Celidan. No one else was up on their roofs, and she was used to that. The roofline of the cultivated hollow shapes of the homes had changed very little since she first came up here as a young girl. It took years to grow a house.

The constant slow downshore current brought with it the smells of folks in the upper town preparing supper. She opened her mouth and gills wide and let the smells fill her head. All the predictable comforts of home, as assuring as they were, only reminded her of how nothing ever changed, nothing ever got any better.

Off in the distance she spotted three swimmers coming into town. Something about how they were grouped together looked odd to her. She set her weaving down and swam up to get a better vantage. As they approached, she saw it was her brother and two of his friends, one of whom was being held and helped along by the others, as if he were injured. They swam rapidly up the street and into the front of the house. Chielle swam down the back of the house and slid in a portal. She caught up with them in the front common room. When she coiled up in a back corner of the curved chamber to watch, her pet octopus found her and wrapped himself around her arm.

The eldest of the three, Serool, was cradling his left hand and breathing hard, obviously in a lot of pain. Her brother Thymon swam quickly to the kitchen to get supplies, while the youngest, Kriish, was fussing over Serool, too nervous to be of any real use.

Serool looked up and noticed her in the back of the room for the first time. He grimaced awkwardly, averted his eyes, and turned away enough for her to not see well.

"Stop twisting away," complained Kriish.

Chielle knew why Serool didn't want her to see. She ignored his embarrassment, lifted the sunstone out of its wall sconce, and set it down on the floor next to them so they could get a better look. Thymon came back with a couple of jars. When he peeled back the rag Serool's hand was wrapped in, Kriish gasped, which did not help matters. The skin from the back of his hand all the way up his forearm was blistered and peeling. There wasn't very much blood, but the flesh was mutilated. Chielle thought it looked cooked.

Thymon dipped his fingers in one of the jars and started to smear a waxy paste on the wound. "This is going to hurt, but we've got to seal it or it's never going to heal."

Chielle asked quietly, "Is that Mama's ambergris?"

Thymon glanced up at her as she drifted above his shoulder. "Yes. I'll only use a little. It goes a long way."

Serool winced at his touch. "What's in the other jar?'

"Jellyfish nettles for the pain."

Kriish asked, "Doesn't that stuff hurt even more when you put it on?"

"Only at first," Thymon assured. "Then it kills all the pain. It's kind of extreme, but then, so is this burn."

Chielle observed quietly, "The only thing hot enough to burn someone like that is the lava vent."

"What of it?" her brother said without looking up from his work.

"What were you guys doing messing around with lava?"

Kriish reached into his shoulder pouch, pulled out, and proudly held up an iron spearpoint as long as his hand. "Ain't that a beauty?"

She recoiled in surprise, then frowned and snatched it from him. "Gimme that." She held it close to the sunstone on the floor. "This was beaten while it was hot." She flashed a glare at her brother, who avoided her look. "This is what you do with the technique I brought you? Make weapons? What are you going to do with weapons?"

Serool answered through teeth still clenched in pain. "Defend our fishing pools. The humans have been dragging their nets through Parker's Meadow again, which the treaty says is ours alone. Thymon tried talking to the fishermen, and they threatened him with their steel weapons."

"The guy pulled a gleaming knife on me as long as your arm," her brother added.

Serool continued. "I told my dad, who asked Jeljing. Even the Shaman didn't think there was much we can do."

"It's their law too," Chielle tried.

"The humans don't enforce the law on their own kind," Thymon insisted. "No, we have to defend ourselves and our waters."

She drifted back, staring down at the viciously pointed tip in her hands. "There hasn't been bloodshed with the humans since before we were born. You tried to make me feel guilty about using human skills. How is Rorra going to feel about us taking up arms? Rorra abides and provides. We've always found ways to keep the peace."

"That's right," Thymon barked. "We, we have always been willing to compromise. We have always given them a little bit more to keep the peace. Now they grow greedy. They figure we'll just keep giving up more territory. They've taken everything the law allows them, and now they want more. Enough is enough."

Serool nodded. "That piece took me less than an hour to make. Your trick about continuous pounding really works. And with the lava, that thing is harder than anything I've ever handled."

"I drove it right through a coral head," Kriish said proudly. "Didn't even scratch the metal."

"You guys are going to boil yourselves working with lava."

"I just slipped," Serool dismissed. "It was my own fault. It's worth the risk. Besides, the more I make, the better I'll get at it. I figure I can make a dozen of these a day once I get going."

"A dozen a day? What, you're going to arm the whole town?"

"If we need to."

She looked down at the spearpoint, shaking her head slowly. She dropped it onto the coral floor and swam into the back of the house.

Chielle wasn't trying to sneak up on him, but Serool jumped when she glided up behind him. "Headed home?"

"*Pkwee,*" he chirped. "What, are you following me?" He tucked his wounded arm up as if to hide it from her.

"Look, you don't have to be embarrassed for my sake. Yes, I think it was stupid, but I care about your well-being a lot more."

"Aren't you afraid your brother is going to notice you caring a little too much?"

"Seriously? You still worry about that, years later? We're grown-ups, and he never suspected."

"Well, forgive me for having a guilty conscience," he said humorlessly.

"Wait." She pulled up and he stopped to face her. "I did not know you've been carrying that around inside you. Yes, I was pretty young at the time, and I was every bit as reckless as you. You may have been older, but it's not like you had any great elderly wisdom. We were young and living on impulse. There's a first time for everything."

"Yes, but your brother's best friend should not have been your first."

She blinked and looked away. "I would like to remember it for the fun we had, and not regret it as a mistake."

He continued to swim toward home.

She followed. "We make enough mistakes without having to regret ones in the past."

He just kept swimming and did not respond. She swam alongside him, but he kept pulling ahead.

"If you want to talk about mistakes to regret," she said, "you can start with taking up weapons against the humans."

He shook his head and muttered something she couldn't make out.

"I'm serious. You may have hurt yourself making spears, but that's nothing compared to what the humans will do to you if you take them on in battle. They're vicious and they have had steel weapons a lot longer than we have. I'm sure they know how to use them better."

Still no response.

"Dammit Serool, I still care about what happens to you, and I don't care who finds out. Don't throw your life away."

He finally stopped and turned. "Fine. But if we don't fight for what's ours, what do we do instead? You know what will happen if Harper's Meadow falls to them. Our people will have to find new hunting and harvesting."

She frowned at him, not sure what to say.

"Let that sink in. Moving away. Abandoning our homes."

"Is food that scarce?"

"Yes, it is. We cannot afford to give up any more. If you come up with some other plan, you let me know, and I will back you up and not go to war. But until then, you don't have to remind me how dangerous this is going to be."

He swam off and she floated there, feeling her heart sink.

Jacio Bilboa wished he could remember where he left his hat. It had been cloudy that morning so he didn't think he would need it as he left his mother's house to come to work with Sten on the docks. Now, as he labored at unbolting the sail rigging on their customer's sloop, the clouds dissipated, and the sun bore down on his dark brown neck. The fourteen-year old apprentice swept his long, straight black hair off his face and wished he had taken a little more time to look for his hat.

"Jacio! Heads up!" Sten yelled as he threw a towel down to him from up on the dock. "Wrap that around your head,"

"Thank you!" he yelled back up. That was probably the thing he liked most about working for Sten. The white blacksmith was always looking out for him.

He bent over and started wrapping it around his head in a turban when he was interrupted by a cheery female voice calling out, "Hello there!"

He looked around and couldn't place it.

"Hello up there! I'm down here."

He stepped to the railing and there was a mermaid bobbing in the water. "Oh. Hello."

"Hello. We haven't met." She was frowning, like she was upset, but forced a smile. "I'm Chielle. I'm a friend of Sten's."

"Oh." Sten hadn't mentioned anything about befriending a mermaid. "All right."

"Are you a friend of Sten's also?"

"I work for him."

"Oh, that's nice." The forced smile gave way to the frown again. "Can you please tell him I'm here?"

"Uh, sure." Jacio started to just yell up, but thought better of it. "Wait here."

He picked up the wrench he had been using and slipped it through his belt. No reason to leave such a valuable tool out where the mermaid could get it. As he climbed up the ladder he wondered when Sten had started talking to them, let alone befriending one. Or maybe she had only said she was a friend.

Sten was inside the shack stoking the hearth. "Boss, there's a mermaid down by the boat asking for you. She says she's a friend of yours, named She-oll or something."

Sten brightened at her name. "Really? Did she say what she wants?"

"No. She just asked for you."

He put the logs and tongs down and wiped the soot from his hands on his heavy leather apron. "Well, let's find out."

Jacio followed Sten out to the ladder, watching his boss carefully, trying to figure out what he thought of his visitor. Jacio had only been working for Sten two months, and they had never talked about the merfolk. As he followed Sten down the ladder to the landing, he couldn't help but think a mermaid would only want to befriend a blacksmith to steal steel and tools.

"Chielle! How are you?" Sten greeted her as he hopped out onto the boat.

Jacio noted how Sten stretched out her name like he was trying to sound like a merman.

"Have you had any success with the bending?"

She shifted her big blue-green eyes around and wouldn't make eye contact. "Well, yes. The technique works fine. Thank you again. The Merrow men already knew about the pounding."

Jacio stayed back on the landing but watched and listened carefully. She was clearly hiding something. Why couldn't Sten see that?

"They also already knew about using heat. You know the volcano down at the end of the peninsula? Well, it has a lava vent underwater. It is extremely dangerous, but, in spite of that, some of our men have used it to smith metal."

Sten shook his head and shrugged. "That's great. You sound like this is a problem."

She blinked and sighed and finally looked him straight in the eye. "Sten, they're boiling their own flesh to get this done. They've started making weapons. Weapons they are going to use to defend our fishing pools from your fishermen."

"Attacking humans doesn't sound right for your people. Why the sudden change? Don't they know how much trouble they are going to cause picking a fight, an armed conflict, with humans?"

"They aren't starting the fight. My brother told a fishing crew to stay out of our waters and the fishermen threatened him with a knife."

"Has there been any bloodshed yet?"

"Not that I know of. You know that will change if both sides bring weapons. Sten, can you talk to the fishermen? I tried to talk to my people, but they won't back down."

"I doubt they would listen to me. I tried talking to them in the pub after you and I spoke two weeks ago, and they wouldn't have any of it."

"There must be something we can do to head this off." She seemed genuinely upset.

"I'll tell the town constable. Do you have a law officer in Celidan?"

She blinked and nodded. "Yes, and I will go to him as well. My brother will be furious with me. He'll have to see this is for his own good. It's for all of our good."

"Go do that, and let's meet back here tomorrow and talk again."

"Thank you, Sten." She smiled what Jacio was sure she thought was a sweet smile. He found it kind of frightening.

She dove away and Sten started for the ladder. Jacio swallowed hard and considered holding his tongue, but decided this was too important to let it pass. "Sten, did you teach her how to smith?"

Sten stepped up onto the wharf and turned to face him. "Yes, but apparently it's something they already know how to do."

"If that's true, then why do they still steal our metal?"

Sten stopped and turned his dark brown eyes on Jacio with an intensity the boy had never seen in his boss. "First of all, they are not a race of thieves. They are actually quite happy with our cast offs. They have been for decades. Second, she just said the lava burns them. I can't imagine using a lava flow to smith metal, the idea is insane. They're only doing it because they think they have no other choice. There is always another choice besides taking up arms. It's what makes us civilized."

"My mother says they're not."

Sten did a double take. "What, let me guess. She says they're savages? Would a savage come warn us of a brewing fight, to try to keep the peace in the face of anger? I know what savage and uncivilized looks like. That's not what we've got here."

He started to climb the ladder but stepped back down to face him. "Wait, your mother speaks ill of them? Your Indru people were native to this land before my Alcan tribe came here. Your people lived side by side with the Merrow in peace. I thought only my white people hated them. What made that change?"

The skinny, brown-skinned boy had no idea. He raised his eyebrows up to the towel around his head and shrugged.

Sten frowned and shook his head. "I'm asking a child to explain adult stupidity. Sorry." He headed back up the ladder. "Please keep working on that rigging while I run into town. I've got to go find the constable."

As he watched Sten climb, Jacio knew what he felt in his gut, but he did not know what to think.

Eleven committed, able-bodied Merrow with hardened spears should be plenty to make a stand against the four fishing boats headed toward Parker's Meadow. Thymon kept telling himself that. He had hoped for a lot more men at his side. This would have to do.

As the lead vessel turned into the bay, Thymon motioned for his men to surround it. They surfaced all around, spears raised at the ready. Thymon was pleased at how shocked the fishermen were. "These waters belong to us!" the Merrow called out. "You are not allowed to fish here! You must leave now!"

The two humans at the rail, one white and one brown, were too surprised to move. The rhythmic sound of the boat hulls sloshing in the gentle waves punctuated the tense silence. Then a very broad-shouldered white man with a full grey beard stepped up and yelled back. "How're you gonna stop us? I ain't afraid of those pig stickers! You don't have the guts to harpoon me and my men!"

Serool, next to Thymon, caught his eye with a questioning raised eyebrow. Thymon gave him a nod. Despite his bandaged hand and arm, Serool hurled his spear on target, right passed the bearded man's head. He flinched out of the way as it stuck in the wheel house wall with a loud crack.

"That's your last warning!" Thymon yelled.

"Fuck off!" the man fired back. The two men on either side of him did not look so sure. As if to make himself clear, the man marched over to the net rigging and grandly flipped a lever that dropped the net over the side.

Thymon caught Serool's eye. "Cut the net."

Serool vanished below and Thymon continued to engage the man, who was becoming more and more irate. "Whatever happens, you will have brought it on yourself!"

"I don't take lightly to being threatened, you filthy fin! The gloves are off! You lift a finger to stop my men and I will strike you down!"

One of the other fishermen pointed down and said something Thymon couldn't hear. The bearded man looked down, then up at Thymon with a sneer. He stormed into the wheel house. A moment later he stepped out holding a long metal stick with a wooden handle at one end. He pointed it down into the net and a burst of smoke exploded out the end with a roar.

Now it was the Merrow who were shocked. They exchanged confused glances before diving under to see if Serool was all right. Thymon was relieved to see his friend swimming back up to meet him. "He barely missed me," he sang underwater. "What was that thing?"

"I don't know, but he's not afraid to use it again."

They were interrupted by the sound of another explosion up on the surface. One of the Merrow had thrown another spear which stuck out of the boat's railing. A fisherman stood holding one of the weapons, a cloud of smoke hanging in front of him. The Merrow was thrashing about in the water, wounded.

Thymon noticed the other three fishing boats were not slowing down. The sailors on those ships all looked fearfully at what was happening, and steered around the melee and back out to sea.

"Come back here, you cowards!" the bearded man bellowed at them. When they did not turn back, the man had angry words with his own crew. The other men started pulling up the net and raising the sails to leave. The bearded man shook his fist at Thymon. "We'll be back! And with more guns!"

3

“THERE MUST BE SOMETHING YOU CAN DO to head this off.” Sten leaned forward onto the table at the back of The Pied Cock pub, pressing his point.

Across the table, Constable Arum Blaine sat resolute and impassive. He folded his heavily muscled arms across his broad chest and leaned back in his chair. “I can’t arrest anyone for a crime that hasn’t happened yet.”

“I’m not talking about arresting anybody. These fishermen need to be reminded of the law. They need to know you’re there to support them if the Merrow step over the line, but also to punish the humans if they overstep.”

“You’re calling them Merrow? Isn’t that what they call themselves?”

“Are you going to wait until this blows up?”

“Challenging the treaty is not by itself a crime. I’m here to keep the peace, and that means punishing whoever starts a fight. The merfolk have backed down whenever our fishermen have moved into new territory. If they want to stand up for what they see as their rights, then they can do that. Whatever boundaries the two sides work out, that becomes the new norm. I don't set those boundaries, they do."

"Both groups see this as fighting for their livelihoods. Nobody's going to back down without a fight, and there goes your peace."

Blaine unfolded his arms and leaned forward. "Why are you suddenly so fired up about this? Frankly, this is nothing new. And I've never heard you even talk about it."

"It's been itching at me for a while, actually. Ever since you told me I couldn't sell metal to them. I've been watching and listening, and it recently just all fit together for me. This is bad, and it's getting worse. You don't want to let this get out of hand."

They were interrupted by half a dozen fishermen noisily entering the front of the pub, laughing and cheering each other on. The last one in, Roff Collum, was much quieter. He sat at a table off to one side while his fellows crowded against the bar and ordered drinks. Paulbert Caron, the longhaired Indru barkeep attended them wordlessly. Caron was usually a chatty gossip. Sten watched and wondered. This did not seem to be the usual return from the sea.

"Did you see the looks on McDonagh's face and his crew when they saw the muzzle smoke and those spears sticking out of the deck rails? I thought he was going to hand out oars to get out of there faster!"

"If you don't stand up for yourself, then nobody else is gonna do it for you."

"Damn straight. If Atlan taught us nothing else, it's to stand up for yourself."

"Just think lads. If McDonagh and the others don't want to upset the natives ..." the full bearded sailor paused dramatically, "then we'll have Parker's Meadow all to ourselves!"

The other five men at the bar roared with laughter. The speaker was their captain, one Selric Boole, all five-foot five, and 200 pounds of broad shouldered, loud-mouthed meanness. Sten had learned not to try to reason with Boole. Every time he tried to discuss anything with him, the sailor shouted down any point he disagreed with.

Boole continued. "Hey, what're we doing over here drinking while Roff sits over there under a cloud." Boole grabbed a bottle and another glass off the bar and walked over to Collum's table. "You should be celebrating too." He turned back and raised his own glass. "To Collum, who had the guts to fire back, and blast the bastard fin back into the depths!"

"Back into the depths!" the others yelled in unison.

Sten caught Arum's blue eyes and held them.

The Constable raised his eyebrows and cocked his closely shorn blond head, but did not get up.

"You said you had to wait until a crime was committed," Sten reminded him.

Arum turned to watch the fishermen.

Sten noticed Collum was not looking very celebratory. He drank the whisky Boole brought him. Sten recognized it as drinking to drown memories.

Sten got up. "Excuse me, Constable." He walked casually into the thick of them and leaned against one of the many heavy bamboo posts that held up the beamed ceiling. "Hey fellas. Did I hear you say you've been firing those new flintlocks? How are they working?"

"They work great." Boole eyed him suspiciously.

"You know you have to clean them with rags and oil every night after you fire them. You can use the ramrod. The black powder burns the inside of the barrel down to the bare metal. In this humidity, that will rust overnight if you don't treat it."

Boole's frown spread into a grin. "Listen up, lads! Words of wisdom from our smithy. Take good care of those rifles. We're gonna need 'em."

While the others laughed at Boole's antics, Sten stepped over to Roff. "Mind if I join you?"

He glanced up from his drink absentmindedly. "Suit yourself."

"Sounds like things got pretty exciting out there today. They started throwing spears at you and you shot one of them?"

"I did." He paused and then said quietly, "I panicked. Lost my head."

"You're not proud of yourself? They're sure proud of you."

Roff looked down at his drink. "Shooting a man for defending his farmland is nothing to be proud of."

Sten smiled a half grin. "I'll let you in on a little secret. I'm proud of you for feeling that way. That treaty has made good sense for both villages for a hundred years. If someone wants to change it, firepower is not the way."

Roff looked up at him. Even his golden fisherman's tan seemed somehow grey. "Sten, you're not helping."

"Oh, I know. Regret will eat your guts. How badly do you want to make up for it?"

"What are you talking about, some kind of payback?"

Sten pointed to the back of the pub. "Blaine is sitting right over there. If you want to get it off your chest, he's the man you should talk to."

"What, so he can throw my arse in jail?"

"No, Roff. It's not about your arse. It's about stopping arses like Boole from getting the whole town up in arms and starting a war. Blaine's got to know that not everyone thinks like Boole."

Roff looked sideways over at Blaine.

Sten pressed his point. "Besides, they say confession is good for the soul."

Roff's gaze drifted from the constable in the back to the captain by the bar. "You make a good point. I think I will talk to Blaine." He looked Sten in the eye. "Later."

Sten understood. He was still disappointed. He took in a deep breath and let it out slow, then pushed his chair back and stood up. "Enjoy your drink."

Sten's thoughts were so dark he didn't notice the nearly full moon lighting his way home. As was usual for late summer, the afternoon rains blew away leaving a clear evening sky. He hadn't taken a lantern with him, since he hadn't planned on staying so late at the pub.

The clouds swirling this time were in Sten's mind. The rhythm of his footsteps on the wharf planks gave him some much-needed order. He always liked that rhythm. It was like the song his anvil sang when he pounded steel. It comforted him. Or at least, it usually did. Tonight, he found no comfort. His village was headed for a pointless, unjust war, and no one cared to hear his warning.

Blaine had said this was nothing new. Were things always this bad? Was he boxing at shadows? This wouldn't be the first time he let himself get carried away. If he made a stink, he'd have to live with the enemies he'd make. He let that sink in. It took him two years to find Saint Rochel, and he'd only been here a year. He really did not want to move again.

As he approached his shop, he noticed the lapping of the waves on the pilings below was especially loud. He looked over the edge and indeed the tide was very high. He turned back to his door and startled when he saw someone standing there. He could see their outline against the woven panel walls of his shop, but the bright moon cast a strong shadow from the thatched roof over the stranger. "Who's there?"

"It's me, Sten. I didn't mean to surprise you. You don't see very well in the dark, do you?"

"Chielle? What are you doing out here in the middle of the night?"

"We need to talk about what happened today." He had never heard her voice so tense. He couldn't make out her features, but she sounded angry.

"How will you find your way home in the dark?"

"I'll use the moon. Never mind about me. A Merrow was shot today."

"Yes, I know. It was horrible. Did he live?"

"Yes, he'll live."

"I'm sorry this went badly."

"That's not good enough," she said flatly. "We want the man who shot Komoa."

"Oh, wait a minute. That's just going to fan the flames."

"What does that mean?"

"Handing him over to you will push the villages into a full-scale war."

"How?"

He tried to explain. "Whatever punishment you give him, the humans are going to see it as unjust, and they will attack your people all the more viciously. Then you'll want retribution, and the whole thing will spiral out of control."

"Our punishments are very just. We would punish him the same as we would one of our own, no worse and no better."

"You know what, I believe you. But my voice doesn't count for anything up there," he said pointing back to the town. "I just spent the evening trying to convince our law man that his town is about to erupt in violence, and he ignored me. He sat there and watched the fishermen celebrating their victory."

"You saw the men from the boat? Did you see the man who shot Komoa?"

Sten paused and thought about not telling her, but the pause gave it away.

"You did! You know who he is!"

"Yes, I know him. I spoke with him, and he is very sorry for what he did. He says he panicked and fired without thinking. He's miserable with regret."

"Well, that's good. It will make it that much easier for everyone to get over his punishment."

"Chielle, you've got to give up on that idea. It's just not going to happen. They will never give him up to you."

"If your fellow villagers would listen to you, would you tell them to give him up?"

"Please don't put me in a spot like that."

"Would you?"

"Probably not. I just don't see that leading to anything but more hatred and violence."

She made a hollow grating, choked off sound that left him imagining how angry she must look. He was glad for the darkness. "You are so infuriating!"

He stepped towards her, but then he heard a loud splash.

Sten left his curtains open to wake himself with the first light of day. He tore open the remains of yesterday's loaf of bread and ate it with a block of cheese while he got dressed. He had no time to waste. He gathered up the raw materials and tools needed to repair a large two-chamber water pump, stacking everything neatly on the main work bench. He had everything ready when Jacio came walking up the wharf.

"Good morning!" he called out through the open window. "Come on in. I've got something I want to show you."

"Good morning," Jacio said as he walked in. He stopped when he saw the array of items.

"A couple of days ago Norn Tureck brought this pump by," Sten explained. The flapper valves are rusted out and need to be replaced. You know what that involves?"

Jacio nodded and described the job. "That means taking the whole top off, making new flappers and putting it all back together."

"Exactly," Sten said with some pride in him. "We did a smaller one of these a couple of weeks ago. It's a whole day's work, and I haven't had a big block of time to devote. I'm giving the job to you."

The boy blinked and looked up at him.

"I trust you to do this right. It's a big job, but only because there's lot of steps. Each step is pretty simple."

"Are you going to help me?"

"No. I'm not going to be here today at all. I've got business up in Silverton."

"The capitol is three hours away on horseback. You don't own a horse." He grimaced. "You're not going to hitch a ride on the fish wagon?"

"I'm hoping to borrow a horse from Norn. I'm leaving you in charge. If you don't get it done today, that's fine. We can finish it together tomorrow when I'm back."

Jacio took a deep breath and looked rather dubious.

"You have the skills to do this. Nobody else is scheduled to come by today, so you'll have no distractions. If you need a hand or if you get hurt, Gerb is right down the wharf. He'll be there all day sewing sails."

"Just like every day," he finished for his boss. "Well, thank you for having faith in me."

"You're a smart kid." Sten pointed at his chest. "It's time you let your inner Atlan shine."

Jacio smiled. "All right. Have a safe trip."

Norn Tureck owned a ranch that stretched from the edge of town all the way back to the foot of the mountains. By the time Sten got there, a score of men and women were busy working the rice paddies and tending animals. Norn wasn't so sure about letting Sten take one of his horses for an all-day trip. He changed his mind when Sten offered to make an even trade of the use of the horse for the repair of the pump. For that generous a trade, Norn threw in a bag of grain to feed the horse for the day.

On the first half of the thirty-mile trip, Sten and the tall brown stallion named Flash had the road to themselves. The road wound its way up over the coastal mountain range, with no villages along the way up to the pass summit. It gave him time to think about what was happening in Saint Rochel and Celidan. At the highest rise that still faced the ocean, he stopped and turned to look. Saint Rochel looked so peaceful from up here, a little gem tucked up against the coast. He imagined Celidan just off the coast, peaceful too, a gem of its own kind. From here all he could see was the fruits of history, with no hint of the future. The morning drizzle at the coast didn't make it up the mountain. The warm sunshine, the gentle breeze, and the smell of flowers wafting off the hillsides did nothing to lighten the weight of his thoughts.

What had changed that had brewed such tension and unrest between the two villages? Sten had only been here a year, and although the humans already did not trust the Merrow when he arrived, people had worked themselves up to the point of war. Unless it had been like this all along and meeting Chielle just brought it into focus for him. Were the fishermen just being greedy? The self-congratulatory joy he had seen in the pub looked more like a score being settled. Had the Merrow done something to so enflame them?

Whatever the cause, something had to be done to stop the violence. If Arum Blaine didn't think it was his job to steer the fishermen away from mayhem, then some other authority would have to be brought in.

Just past the summit, Sten was pleased to see a settlement. Flash was sweating and looking parched. It was actually just a group of four small farms alongside the road. As he turned into the common yard, he noticed two teenagers digging in a vegetable patch. The Alcan boy had bright red hair and freckled white skin, while the Indru girl had dark skin and wavy black hair. They hardly noticed Sten's approach, as they were flirting with each other as much as getting any work done. Sten hesitated and watched them for a moment. He recognized that look. He'd gotten that look from Chielle that first day. She certainly wasn't in a flirting mood last night on the wharf.

"Excuse me. I am Sten Holdsmith, from Saint Rochel by the Sea. Could I get a bucket of water please, for my horse?"

The boy said, "Sure, mister."

The girl grinned at the boy and provoked him, "Race ya for it!"

They braced themselves to sprint, but Sten interrupted. "Isn't that the water pump, right there?" he said, pointing across the front yard at a standing hand pump.

"Oh, that's broke," the boy explained. "We get water from the spring back in the canyon," he said pointing away from the road.

"Did this well run dry?"

"No, sir. The lifter inside is broke."

"Well, that's easy enough to fix. It's just a rod."

"My dad has a rod to fix it. We just can't get the top off."

Sten got off the horse and tied the reins to a fence post. He walked across the yard and examined the pump. It was covered in a thick patina of red rust, except where someone had scratched and dented it. "The top unscrews. You can't just pull it off."

"Oh." After a moment's hesitation, the boy followed up with, "Are you sure?"

"I'm a blacksmith. I know how these things are made." It was badly rusted, but seemed otherwise intact. He tried the handle and indeed it was not connected inside. He considered tapping it to loosen the joint, but didn't want to do any more damage to the threads.

He noticed the fence that surrounded the yard was split rails sitting in notched posts. He pulled a rail out of its cradles and slid one end up under the spigot, wedging its length against the vertical barrel to form a lever arm. He gave it a shove, but it did not budge.

The boy and the girl stood by watching him. Sten reached his hand out to the boy. "I'm Sten."

The boy shook his hand, "I'm Cam."

"Nice to meet you, Cam." Sten looked at the girl, and then back at Cam, and waited.

Cam didn't take the hint.

Sten extended his hand to the girl. "And what would your name be, my dear?"

She blushed and took his hand gingerly. "Mada."

"Very nice to meet you as well." Turning back to Cam, he continued. "Can you come over here and grab this end of the rail? I'll hold this still here at the pump, so we don't accidentally break the barrel off." When Cam had taken up position, Sten told him, "Now push as hard as you can." Sten pushed against the barrel to aim all of Cam's energy into twisting. Cam leaned into it and grunted his extertion, but the top of the pump did not budge.

"Alright, let's try something else," Sten offered. He walked over, untied Flash, and led him into the yard and over to the pump. He took a length of rope out of the saddlebag and tied one end to the saddle. The other end he looped around the end of the rail that Cam still held. Sten turned to Mada. "Come on over, I want you to meet someone. Mada, this is Flash." He handed her the reins. "Can you please lead him away in that direction?" he said pointing straight out from the rail.

Mada and Cam exchanged smiles of understanding and seemed happy to be caught up in the sudden adventure. Cam held the rail up in place, Sten leaned into the barrel to hold it upright, and Mada beckoned Flash to pull. The horse resisted when he felt the rope go taut, but upon the girl's encouragement, Flash leaned into the task. Sten had to grab and push the pipe and the short end of the lever with all his might to keep the horse from snapping the whole pump off.

Cam looked down at how Sten was holding the barrel vertical and arched his brows in amazement at Sten's strength.

At last the top twisted, slowly at first, with an earsplitting squeal of dry metal on metal. Once they had it a quarter turn around, the sound subsided, and the rope slid free. Sten dropped the rail and turned the top around and round by hand.

"There you go," he announced with quiet triumph. "Now your father can repair the lifter."

Mada beamed. "No more hauling water all the way back from the spring!"

Cam grinned at her and shook his head. "One last trip Maddy! We still owe Mr. Sten here his bucket of water."

She pouted and slumped her shoulders, but then brightened. "Said I'd race ya." With that the two took off running.

Sten smiled at their sheer joy. He wound up the rope and put it away, and started brushing the sweaty salt off Flash's hide. A few minutes later the two returned with a full bucket of water. Sten took a handful for himself and Flash sucked up the rest.

"My dad will be back from town soon," Cam said. "You can talk to him about what we owe you for getting this open for us."

"You don't owe me anything. I got my water. We just had to work for it."

Cam blinked and rolled his eyes in thought. "Are you sure? Farm hands sure don't work for free."

Sten smiled as he explained. "I have a friend who feels that paying someone for something is really just trading gifts. You needed a hand getting that loose. I was willing to do it for nothing, as a gift, because it was the right thing to do." Why was it he smiled whenever he thought of Chielle? "You gave me and my horse water, even though you had to run all the way back into the hills to get it. You were going to get it for me even before I helped you. That was a gift too. We traded gifts."

"Like we're celebrating something?" Mada ventured.

"Absolutely. Happy … Wednesday!"

Sten had only passed through Silverton once on his way to Saint Rochel a year before. He had been excited to see the seaside village and hadn't stopped to really look around the regional capital. Now that he had grown accustomed to the heat and the bamboo architecture of coastal life, he noticed what a blend of styles this city had adopted. Stone and pine stood alongside palm and reed. He put up Flash in livery and walked into the center of town.

Even more than the buildings, the way the people dressed spoke of a deep cultural blending. The light-skinned Alcan wore heavier clothes than at the shore, but of a similar style. The men wore shirts, vests, and trousers. The women wore dresses over corsets. On the other hand, the dark-skinned Indru men wore loose tunics and long shorts, while their women wore dresses of wrapped soft fabric. He had only seen a few women in Saint Rochel dressed like this. Most of the Indru women dressed in much more structured Alcan clothes. If the wrapped soft look was the Indru cultural style, why did Indru women in Saint Rochel dress like Alcans?

His musings were cut short when he reached his destination. The last time Sten had to deal with a court, it was against his will and it did not end well for him. Even though these circumstances were very different, he still had to purposely calm himself as he approached the bright white, massively beamed annex behind the provincial palace that was the Courthouse. On top of his apprehension at coming here, Sten did not do well with crowds. He did even worse with waiting. When the Courthouse doors cracked opened just before midday, a throng of fifty people had gathered around. Sten eyed the people in the crowd. He was not prepared to stay in Silverton overnight if the court could not hear him today.

The crier who stepped out onto the front steps announced his instructions with the bored, flat tone of a speech delivered many, many times. "Everyone who is here to discuss taxation issues line up on my left side." The long, drooping liripipe end of his official hat swung as he pointed with his whole arm. "Everyone who is here to settle a dispute with your neighbor, line up on my right side. Everyone else, please stay in the middle and I will hear you out once I get the other two groups inside."

Sten assumed he fit into the dispute group. He was happy to see there were only a few others who joined him on that side.

The crier stepped down along Sten's line and handed out wooden cards with numbers painted on them. Sten got Six. "You will be heard in the order of these numbers. Do not lose your number, or you will lose your place in line."

Sten nodded in appreciation of the efficiency. Maybe this wouldn't be so bad after all.

The crier led Sten's group inside, through an entry hall, and into the large central chamber of the building. Although he had just seen how big the building was from the outside, the white stone columns that lined the chamber made the room seem even taller inside. The space was illuminated by narrow floor to ceiling windows between the columns. Sten didn't recall seeing any windows on the exterior of the building. The room had benches in the back and chairs up front, and was dominated by a throne behind a massive desk up on a platform at the front. They were led up the center aisle of the white tiled floor and told to sit in the chairs and await their turn.

Sten marveled at the amount of stone and heavy wood beams in the building. He had gotten used to everything in Saint Rochel being made of bamboo, palm wood, woven frond panels, and thatched roofs. It was nowhere near as hot or as humid here behind the coastal mountains. He was glad for the distracting thoughts.

A different crier came in through a side door and announced, "All present rise and bow to His High Lordship, Jesery Clune, presiding!"

A man wearing a tall, round, purple velvet pillar of a hat and a matching set of full long robes walked in and stepped up behind the desk. He waved his hand as he sat down. "You can sit. I'm glad to see there are only a few of you today. I won't have all day, as I have a supper engagement with the Governor. When I call your number, step forward and state your name and the nature of your dispute, then wait." He pointed to a table with men and papers off to one side. "The scribes will make a record. I will then ask you questions. You are only to answer the questions I ask you. I will not tolerate anyone launching into a long diatribe about how they're right. When you're done answering my questions, I will give you my judgment of your case. The adversaries in the dispute will then shake hands in front of me, agreeing to abide by my judgment. You will then go over to the scribes and place your mark on the record. Anyone who later breaks the accord we make today will answer to me as a criminal. All right, let's get started. Who has Number One?"

Two men got up and presented their dispute over sheep that had wondered from one man's land onto another after a fence was not repaired as one man had promised.

So it was also with the next four disputes. Two men got up, stated their case, answered the High Lord's questions, and he handed down decisions. Sometimes the men were happy with their results, but usually one was happier than the other. Overall, Sten thought the judge's decisions were fair. He was even-handed, even if he generally didn't seem too concerned about the details.

While watching him decide case after case, Sten tried to learn the High Lord's clean-shaven features, the way he set his jaw, or the way he twitched his brow, in hopes of being able to read the man's face when it came time to make his own appeal.

Even with the High Lord marching through the cases, the process took time. Sten began to tire of the smells of the men he was seated with. He was very thankful Silverton did not have Saint Rochel's humidity. He noted the sunlight coming into the room at lower and lower angles.

"Number Six!"

Sten got up and stood before the judge. He tried to organize his presentation, but could not help remembering the weight of the irons on his arms and legs the last time he had stood in a spot like this. He felt sweat break out across his back regardless of the dry air. "My name is Sten Holdsmith, from the village of Saint Rochel by the Sea."

"Mr. Holdsmith, where is your opponent?"

"My dispute is not that kind, Your Lordship. I am here today to inform you of a much larger conflict that is about to break out between the people of Saint Rochel and the Merrow of Celidan, the village just offshore."

"Do you have any stake in this dispute, other than just being a concerned citizen?"

"No, Sir."

"Has someone broken the treaty your two villages have?"

"It is being broken as we speak. A fisherman shot a merman who was trying to defend his fishing grounds."

"What has your constable done about this?"

"He says the fishermen and the Merrow need to work out their differences, and he is willing to wait and see. I'm here to report that we are about to see a war break out."

"The merman who was shot, did he live?"

"Yes, sir. His name is Komoa."

"Then why are you here, and not him?"

"Trust has completely broken down between the two villages. The Merrow think the humans will take any fishing grounds they can grab, and the humans think the Merrow are a bunch of sneak thieves. Since the humans have steel weapons, including guns, and the Merrow do not, the humans can take whatever they want. It has come down to spears versus rifles. The Merrow assume there can be no justice from humans."

"How do you know that?"

"I have friends among the Merrow who told me. I came here to prove them wrong."

"Did something specific happen to drive this distrust?"

"I don't know, Your Lordship. I've only been there a year, and I don't know of any event."

"What kind of justice are you seeking?"

"Enforcement of the treaty boundaries."

"How will that restore peace?"

"I don't know, Your Lordship. I just hope to limit the conflicts and hope things can return to normal."

"Your plan seems only half baked."

"Surely there is history of the Crown intervening to settle disputes like this. Was the Crown not involved writing the original treaty a hundred years ago?"

"I ask the questions here. You come dangerously close to making a demand of this office. I did not say I would do nothing. I will consider what you have said. I thank you for bringing this to my attention."

There was a long silence as the High Lord peered down at Sten. Sten knew that was the most he would get. "Yes, Your Lordship."

"Number Seven!"

4

S TEN FOCUSED ON BEATING THE IRON SHEET METAL into a uniform dome and did not notice much of anything beyond the noisy, careful job in front of him. He had known it would take a lot of up-close pounding, and he had stuffed cotton in his ears. Which is why he was surprised when Jacio waved his hand in front of him. He pulled the cotton out and was further surprised by the sound of the tolling town bell. "Is that an alarm?"

"No, the alarm is a really fast ringing," the boy explained. "This is the calling-in bell. Something must be happening in the square."

Sten looked around the shop at the various jobs on work benches. "This can wait. Let's go have a look."

As they stepped off the wooden planks of the wharf, they joined a growing crowd of folks walking up the gravel main road. Sten noticed a lot of water on the ground, leading down onto the beach alongside the wharf. It had not even drizzled that morning. He spotted cart tracks in the sand too.

Jacio met his gaze with a shrug.

Just as he was about to turn back up the road, Sten noticed several wedge-shaped impressions in the wet sand. He knew that shape. That was the heel mark of a Merrow fluke.

About fifty people, most of the men in town and a few of the women, gathered in the large open square in the middle of town. Parked in the center was a grand black four-horse coach, surrounded by six mounted soldiers. The soldiers' brass fittings shone in the midday sun, while the grey horses were all covered in sweaty salt. Sten recalled his trip on Flash three days before. They must have been running all morning.

People were milling about, some craning their necks to see over the high sides of the coach at the occupants. Constable Arum Blaine was standing up on a sideboard talking to someone inside.

Blaine turned to the crowd. "Good people of Saint Rochel. I am honored to introduce you to High Lord Jesery Clune, who has come all the way from Silverton to visit us."

Clune, wearing the same tall hat he had worn in court stood up and waved to the crowd.

Sten tried unsuccessfully to restrain his dubious frown.

"Please join me in welcoming our honored guest."

The assembled townspeople applauded appropriately.

"High Lord Clune has also invited Jeljing, the Shaman Leader of our sister village of Celidan, to join him here today."

A tall, thin Merrow in an obviously regal mantle and headdress stood up beside Clune. The crowd took in a collective shocked breath. Sten rolled his eyes in embarrassment. He also noted that while most everyone's attention was on the coach, several Indru men were actually watching the reactions of the Alcan men nearby.

"The High Lord and the Shaman will be conducting an inquest about the recent violence between the two villages. They will be in the Atlantean Lodge, and they will be calling witnesses throughout the afternoon. Please keep yourselves available, as any one of you may be called to testify."

"Well, well, well," Sten muttered to himself.

Jacio gave him a curious look. He had not told the boy the nature of his trip to Silverton.

Sten suddenly felt like someone was watching him, and he glanced around. He and Jacio were in the back of the crowd, having arrived last. He didn't see anyone looking at him, but he couldn't shake the feeling. He did spot a wedge-shaped wet spot on the ground. He looked further and found several of them, all around the outside of the square. He looked back at the coach and saw there were maybe four people inside. No doubt at least one would be a Merrow soldier escorting their leader, probably more than one. There were no Merrow guarding him outside the coach, at least that Sten could see.

Arum concluded his speech. "Thank you for your cooperation." The High Lord and the Merrow Shaman sat down, Arum jumped off the sideboard, and the coach pulled away.

Sten bent down, picked up a pebble, and threw it through the space above the nearest wet spot. The stone flew straight and hit the wall of the building behind.

"What are you doing?" Jacio had caught him.

He smiled crookedly. "Just bored. Let's go."

As they walked away from the square, Sten spotted several more of the mysterious shapes. The townspeople had been surprised when they first saw the Merrow Shaman, so clearly they had not seen any Merrow soldiers escort the coach into town. Yet there were these wet heel prints all along the path from the beach to the square.

By the time they got back to the wharf, there were no more to be found.

"Did you have anything to do with the High Lord coming here?"

"Jacio, I am often confused by life in general, but if there is one thing I can be sure of, it's that I carry no weight to move important people to do anything they weren't going to do anyway."

"I'm guessing ... you did go to see the High Lord in Silverton, about the shooting? I know you were pretty upset about it."

"I assure you, my words had no impact."

"Are you glad he came?"

"I'll be glad if he can help us regain peace."

For the second time that day, Jacio interrupted Sten's cotton-deafened working reverie with a wave of his hand in Sten's face. He pulled the wads out of his ears and waited, but no bell was ringing. "What's going on?"

Jacio stepped to the window that faced down the dock into town. "You gotta come see this."

Sten peered out and was very disappointed at what he saw. Half a dozen men were up on ladders with ropes repainting the weathered wood banner sign that was mounted across the main entrance of the wharf. It had once greeted fishermen returning from their labors with "Welcome Home". Now the new paint announced, "Fin Go Home".

Sten took a deep breath and sighed. "Things must have gone badly at the inquest. I'll go find out what happened."

Before Jacio could ask to come along, Sten was out of his gloves and apron and walking toward town.

He only had to go as far as the painters. "What's this all about?" Sten asked them.

One of the men holding a ladder steady asked Sten, "You heard about the trial?"

"I know the High Lord from Silverton was here to find out what's going on."

"Well, they tried Roff Collum for shooting the fin who chucked a spear at him. Sentenced him to three lashes."

Sten held back the flinch he felt coming on at the mention of lashes.

The man up on the ladder chimed in. "You know how many lashes they gave that damn fin for attacking Roff? Fucking zero, that's how many."

"How did that go down?" Sten asked innocently.

"Some shit about defending his turf. The High Lord said Roff he shouldn't have let himself get caught up in mob rule."

"I see." Sten considered speaking with Roff, since those lashes were going to be largely Sten's fault. "When are they going to punish Roff?"

"Already did it. Right after the trial. Roff took it like a man. Showed them damn fin how it's done."

"Oh. Well, I'm glad he kept his dignity." Sten noticed the four Alcan men were all happy to chime in griping about the trial, but the one Indru man had held his tongue. "Is that the end of it?"

"Hell no," the man up the ladder spat. "The High Lord said he'd be back if there's another scuffle, and he'll really start handing out the lashes."

"Really? So he said we're supposed to get along better. Did he tell us how we're supposed to do that?"

"Nope. He said just work it out."

The man next to Sten commented, "Fat lot of help he was. It was kind of insulting, like he was treating us like kids. When my kids fight I tell them to work it out amongst themselves, and if they can't, then I'll beat the lot of them. The fisherman did not take kindly to being treated like that."

"Are the High Lord and the Shaman still here, or did they leave yet?"

"They're leaving this afternoon. Which is why we're here giving the old fish a proper send off."

"Right." Sten looked up at the repainted sign and his heart sank. "Makes sense. Thanks for filling me in."

As he walked back to his shop, disappointment slid into despair. He asked the High Lord to come up with a plan to either enforce or change the treaty, a solution they could move forward with, but he had not. He just slapped them down, as the angry painters said, like disobedient children. He went to the capitol looking for a solution, but only succeeded in worsening tensions between the villages.

The next day, the sky was overcast and a cool wind blew off the sea. The weather perfectly reflected Sten's mood. He gave Jacio the afternoon off and let the hearth cool down. He took a chair out to the end of his wharf, out where in happier times he had hung iron and copper wind chimes. Now he sat, wrapped up in his wool coat, staring out at the grey sky and the dark sea, listening to the sad tinkling sounds, nursing a very large bottle of beer.

An enormous sea gull landed next to him and regarded him curiously.

"Find your own. This one's mine."

The bird raised its head back as if insulted, crapped, then flew off.

Chielle's sweet voice called up from the water below. "You don't look very happy for a man who succeeded after hard work."

The sight of her made him smile despite his mood. "Hello. How long have you been there?"

"A little while. I like watching you. I hope you don't mind. Did you really ride all the way to the Capitol to convince your authorities to come hear our case?"

"Nothing gets past you. Nobody up here knows it was me."

"Aren't you pleased with how things worked out? I'm very proud of you."

"It didn't work. All the High Lord did was punish the man who fired his rifle, and now the humans hate your kind more than ever."

"Wasn't justice served?"

"Chielle, it's like I said the other night. It's not about justice, it's about finding a way back to peace. I hoped the crown would have a solution, but they don't, and now I've made things worse."

"About the other night, I owe you an apology for treating you so poorly. I know you have a good heart, and I should have trusted you. I am sorry I yelled at you."

"I forgive you the outburst. I understand how upset you were. You know, I normally would not have the nerve to go to the capitol and seek an audience with the High Lord, and make demands that he intervene. I mean, what gall! You and your outspoken high standards inspired me. "

She shrugged. "My big mouth has gotten me in to a lot of trouble. Most of my village sees me as a troublemaker. My parents wish I was more like my brother and sister, hardworking and accepting of the way things are. Although my brother has been driven by anger to drastic measures lately. That's really so not like him. Being outspoken definitely has its disadvantages. It's why I can't seem to hold onto any men in my life."

Sten took a moment for that revelation to sink in. "Really? I rather like a woman who knows what she wants. It's less guesswork for me. "

She smiled broadly, in fact as broadly as only a mermaid can. The light from her expression warmed him like a roaring fire.

"May I invite you up? I'll stoke the hearth and make you something warm to drink." He held up his bottle. "This is not holding my interest."

"Thank you," she said demurely, and vanished beneath the surface.

He got up and walked to the ramp top to greet her. She was halfway up when he got there. He was still utterly fascinated watching her writhing steps. When she got to the wharf, he pointed down at the newly painted banner. "They did that after the High Lord and your Shaman held court."

She pursed her lips and blinked. "Oh, dear."

As soon as she entered his shack, he draped a blanket around her shoulders. "You must be cold getting out of the warm water into wind like this."

She just smiled back at him and pulled the blanket around herself.

He opened the grate on the hearth and threw in a couple of logs, then reset the grate and turned the bellows wheel. She held her hands up to the warmth as the glow brightened.

He filled and set a kettle on the grate. While he busied himself finding and chopping a block of cocoa, he noticed she had moved to the seaward facing window.

"As many times as I have swum past this wharf, I've never stopped to really listen to your wind chimes. They make beautiful sounds."

"I find them soothing."

"Sound is really important to us underwater. We use it to detect danger, to locate where we are, to speak. I guess that's why we picked up your language so easily. One thing I've found that's different is how you push your words out of your mouth with air, and we keep the air in and push the sound with whistles and hums."

"Whistles and hums?"

"What's a good example? Oh, my family name, Mmava."

The way she pronounced it made him stop and stare. "How did you do that?"

She giggled with a whistling sound that came from somewhere inside her head and not out of her mouth.

"And that too!"

"We're built differently. I've got lungs and gills and spaces up behind my nose where I can move air. Humming and whistles and hard clicking sounds travel well through water. Whales talk to each other with these sounds over miles of distance."

He stepped over to her. "Can you show me?"

She looked up straight at him to show him how she was moving her mouth and throat. He was completely distracted looking her in the eyes. Those amazing eyes, the color of white sand under blue green surf. He had to blink to break the spell.

"Are you all right?"

"Yes, I'm fine. Show me how you say it."

She hummed an M sound, starting with a higher note and then dropping to a lower note, then it softened into an A sound even though she did not open her lips. This then rolled into a V sound which went low again and then ended in a soft A.

"I'm going to have to open my mouth to get some of those sounds out."

"That's fine." She pointed at her forehead. "Like I said, I can move air around in here all day long."

He gave it his best try, concentrating as well as he could in his still very distracted state. "*mmmMMMaVVVa.*"

"Very good! Did you feel how the sound rattles your bones?"

"I did."

"That's what makes the sound move through water. If you feel the vibration, then the water picks that up and carries it."

"Aren't you teaching me one of the great mermaid secrets, your enchanting siren voice?"

"My what?"

"You know. Aren't mermaids supposed to be able to enchant men with their singing and lure them to crash their ships into rocks?"

"Why in the depths and waves would we want to do that?"

"I don't know. It's a legend. Are there any other mermaid secrets you want to share with me? Any magical abilities?" He considered asking her directly about how Merrow seemed to walk into town yesterday invisible, but thought better of putting her on the spot. Better to let her share what she wanted to.

"No, not that I know of," she said with a smile.

"Are you saying you don't have magic in your voice?"

"My voice is considered rather weak. It's too high to get down to some of the lower tones that really communicate heartfelt emotion, especially in song."

"May I ask you to sing me something? I don't want to embarrass you. I just want to hear how your amazing underwater voice sounds in a song."

"I'd be happy to. This is a lullaby pretty much every Merrow child learns." In spite of the occasional impossible combination of sounds, the song was instantly soothing and made Sten want to sway to its rhythm. She clapped her hands softly to keep the beat, while her voice soared up and down scales. She stopped and smiled at him.

He was breathless. "My goodness." He had to blink back a tear. "That was … that was beautiful. Thank you. I think I'm starting to understand how important sound is to you. Do you have musical instruments?"

She looked a little puzzled. "We have bells that we shake to keep rhythm."

"Oh. I guess since human voices are so limited by comparison, we've built all sorts of things that vibrate strings, or cut air to whistle, or bang on them to make hollow sounds. Wait, I've got a penny whistle over here somewhere." He stepped into his room in the back and returned with it. He held it up for her to see.

She looked with some doubt at the brass tube with holes down its length. "This makes music?'

He stood up proudly and played her a rapid trilling jig of a tune.

Her eyes went wider than usual and her mouth curled into a highly amused grin. "That's so much fun. There are so many notes. You couldn't dance to that, could you?"

"Actually, there are dances for songs like that, with lots of quick little bouncing steps. I'm not a very good dancer, so I'm a lousy example." He stepped back, took off his coat and threw it over a chair. The hearth had driven the chill out of the shack. He saw her take note of his wool jacket. "I know, it's too heavy for this climate. I use it 'cause it repels water. It's a left over from when I lived where it gets really cold."

He stood looking at his feet for a minute trying to remember the steps before attempting a jig. He stomped and bounced as best he could. "You see, lots of little steps."

"That looks like fun. You couldn't do that underwater. Underwater we have dances where you stay in place, like your stepping dance, but you move against the water back and forth. She handed him her blanket, unhunched her tail and stood up on her fluke. She clapped her hands and sang a part of her song again, while flexing and swaying to the beat.

"I see," he said nodding. "I get it."

They were interrupted by the kettle whistling.

"Your pot sings?"

He pulled it off the grate and poured two mugs. It's got a whistle in the spout, like my penny whistle. When the water boils ..."

"It makes steam which blows the whistle. I know about steam from the lava vent up the coast. What are you making?"

"You've probably never had this, but I'm hoping you'll like it. It's called cocoa."

"Is it from the coconut tree?"

"No, it's made from a bean, I think. I actually don't know how it's made. I know it's a complicated process involving drying and roasting and grinding and mixing. Anyway, to humans it's a little piece of heaven."

"Sten, are you all right? You seem kind of, I don't know, nervous."

"Oh, am I talking too much? I don't entertain much. I guess I'm out of practice. This is new for you. Oh, it's really hot, so blow across the surface to cool it down so it doesn't burn your mouth." He demonstrated and she followed. "Then sip just a little until it cools."

She tried some and blinked furiously. After a little frown, she gamely tried again. "You're right. I've never had anything like this. The hot takes some getting used to. I like the warmth it brings. The taste itself is kind of invigorating too. It's sweet and bitter at the same time, kind of confusing."

"Do you like it?"

She took another bigger sip. "Yes. It's not unpleasant. It's actually rather good. It's just really different. You like it a lot, don't you?"

Sten smiled. "Yes. It's great for a cold day. Not that we actually have cold days here."

The wind outside kicked up and whistled through the panel gaps of the shack.

"More blustery than cold."

The wind chimes at the end of the wharf clanged in protest.

"We use bells underwater. I bet wind chimes would work there too. Those hollow pipes you've hung out there should make the same sounds in water."

"Isn't sound a lot louder underwater? When I've been head under, everything sounds muffled but at the same time louder. If you clanged on chimes underwater the way those are banging away in the wind, wouldn't that make a terrible racket?"

"Yes, of course, if you struck them hard. It would certainly scare away all the fish. You could play them softly and it would be musical, like up here."

"You can take those and try it out."

She hesitated and frowned. "Wait a minute. Played loudly, they would scare away the fish." Her eyes widened and she nodded. "The fish."

Sten frowned too until he also figured it out. "Oh, the fish! In Harper's Meadow!"

"Yes! We can herd the fish out of the meadow when the boats come, they'll catch nothing and leave, then we'll let the fish come back home."

"Brilliant! The fishermen won't know it's you. They'll think the fish have moved on. At some point they will just stop coming. This could be the solution we've been hoping for. Chielle, you've got to go test this. I'll take down the chimes."

She set her mug down and caught his hands in hers. He was taken by how soft they were, especially the webbing between her fingers. She squeezed his and looked up into his face. "Thank you."

"For what? You figured it out."

"For being there for me. For believing in me. For fighting for what's important to me."

His heart was pounding, but he managed to keep his composure. "You're welcome."

She slipped her hands around his shoulders and hugged him.

He hugged her back, pressing her thin taut body against his. Through her tunic the skin on her back was harder than he expected. He felt her take a deep breath when he wrapped his arms around her waist. As he pulled her tight, his hand bumped into the top of her dorsal fin.

For just a moment he worried she might feel the skin on his back when she hugged him.

As they separated, she lifted her head and rubbed her cheek against his. She tilted her head and looked like she was about to wink at him. "You'd look a lot more like Merrow without the scruffy beard."

He smirked back at her. "Let's go get those chimes."

5

S TEN CHOSE HIS PATH THROUGH the open-air farmers market as much to avoid crowds as to find what he needed. He was pleased to find no one waiting at the melon and squash vendor.

"Good morning, Mr. Holdsmith," the dark skinned, round faced woman behind the crates greeted him with a smile.

He noted the rigid vest she wore over her dress and recalled how Indru women inland wrapped their bodices softly. Funny how he noticed that now and had never thought anything of it before. "Good morning to you too, Mrs. Ibba. These big white ones are beautiful. Are they new?"

"Yessir. They're honeydew. They're bright green inside and taste like summer sunshine. With summer coming to a close, they've been soaking up the sun all season."

"You always know how to talk me into new things. Do you have any hard gourds yet? I always look forward to making soup from them in the fall."

"No, not yet. Give 'em a few more weeks. How many of the honeydew can I get for you?"

"Oh, all right, I'll try your sunshine melon. Just one, please."

"Is that Sten Holdsmith I see trying something new?"

The sweet, lyrical woman's voice just a few feet away surprised him, and not just with its suddenness. The impeccably dressed blonde woman stepped up right next to him. "Mrs. Ibba, you have got the touch. I could never talk Sten into trying anything new."

Sten stared grinning at her for a long moment. Vanda Rymerand. He really did not know what to make of her reappearance after so long. She smelled of flowers. She had always smelled of flowers. What was she doing joking around with him? He went along with her jest. "My dear Vanda, that's not how I remember it."

She widened her eyes in mock astonishment. "You cad!"

"How are you? What are you doing here? I mean, are you just visiting? You look beautiful as always."

"Oh, do you really think so?" She stepped back and looked down at her crisp yellow dress. The pleated skirts and corseted waist made full advantage of her womanly charms. "I never know if yellow works for me."

"Of course it does. It's the same color as your hair."

She reached up and pulled a long curl from her pinned up mass of hair and held it against a lapel which framed her uplifted bosom. "Oh, I guess it is." She looked up at him, twisting the lock in her manicured fingers as a tiny grin pulled at the corner of her mouth.

He did his best to ignore the obvious flirtation. "How have you been? I haven't seen you in, what, seven or eight months? When you moved away, I heard only rumors. Something about a cattle rancher down in Pikesville. Are you just visiting?"

She looked down, the smile faded, and she sighed a tiny, but obvious sigh. "No, I have moved back to our Saint Rochel."

"I'm sorry."

She took a deep breath and perked up. "I'm not. I'm back amongst friends and life is looking good again. After all, I've only been back in town a couple of days, and I bumped into you."

"I'm no prize."

She gently touched his arm as he cradled the melon. "I disagree."

He looked straight into her beautiful brown eyes, but he was really searching his own feelings for her. He expected to feel the old fire rekindle. He was surprised to feel nothing. "Vanda, what are you playing at? You left me saying you wanted to see the world."

"I have come to regret that decision. Let's say the world wasn't everything I had hoped for."

How many times after she left had he dreamed of a moment like this? That she would come back to him out of the blue was beyond hope. Yet here she was. "It took me a long time to get over you. I spent months asking myself what I had done wrong. Eventually I saw that I had done nothing wrong. We had a wonderful time together, many wonderful times over four months that I will always treasure."

"You're talking about good times like they're all in the past."

"You have to know you left a lot of hurt behind. I know you meant no harm, you had to get out and spread your wings. Still, it hurt a lot, and I had to get over that."

She looked genuinely sad. "Aren't you glad to see me?"

"Yes, I am very happy to see you back and well. I'm sorry your adventure didn't work out."

He could see the light in her eyes turning colder with each word. She looked around to see if anyone was noticing. Sten was also glad to see they were alone in that part of the marketplace.

"Look, I do not want to hurt you. I loved you far too much to want any harm to come to you. I know this is not what you wanted to hear, but I don't want to lead you on."

She blinked a couple of times, and he braced himself for either anger or a stiff brave face. She surprised him by demonstrating the strength of character he had always admired in her. She cocked her head, squinted slightly, and grinned at him like they had shared some secret joke. "That's fair." She let the word hang for a moment. "Are we still friends?"

"I'd be heartbroken all over again if we couldn't be friends."

"Buy your friend a drink sometime, just to keep company?"

"Count on it. Welcome back to town."

She walked away, and he turned back to the stand. "How much for the melon?"

Mrs. Ibba had turned her back on their conversation and was doing a lousy job of looking otherwise busy. "Oh, yes. Ten pence."

He paid her, slipped the melon into his burlap sack along with his other groceries, and walked home. He was so distracted by his thoughts that he had to trust his feet to know the way.

Had he just made a huge mistake? He was crushed, filled with self-doubt for weeks after Vanda had broken it off with him. Yet he never held it against her. Looking back now, he wondered why not. Had she so enchanted him?

When he looked into her eyes now, he didn't feel that enchantment anymore. He saw a friend in need, but he felt no urge to fill that need. Had he grown cold and bitter?

No, he wasn't bitter. He still had plenty of love in his heart. He had, in fact, been feeling more and more love in his life.

For just an instant, when he looked into Vanda's brown eyes, when he had expected to feel that old familiar fire, he had seen instead Chielle's blue-green eyes. Those eyes quicken his heart.

He stopped walking and turned that over a few times. There was no doubt Chielle flirted with him. She had from the day they met, and he had been happy to let her. At first, he suspected her of flirting to cover an ulterior motive of meeting a blacksmith. Then he came to see it was just part of her gregarious nature. Now this had grown into something more. He just turned down the most beautiful woman in Saint Rochel, and he couldn't wait for the next chance to see his outspoken, adventurous, flirtatious, caring, fascinating ...

"I'll be damned," he quietly admitted. His lips stretched into a face filling smile.

Gonnakaa Mmava caught a whiff of something and opened her mouth wide as her daughter swam passed her into the living room. "Chielle? Can you come back here for a moment?"

She pulled to a stop with her flippers and twisted around back through the doorway. "Yes, Mother?"

She sniffed again. "Why do you smell like something is burning?"

"I was watching a fire up on the beach. I guess the soot clings to everything."

"Do you like watching fire?"

"Yes, it's fascinating. I love how it looks alive, the way it dances and changes. The heat feels good too. I catch myself just staring at it. Have you ever been fascinated by fire?"

"Oh yes. When I was young, I had a human friend and she would build fires on the beach for us to sit around at night. I used to come away just stinking of the soot."

"I never knew you had a human friend. What was her name?"

"Patry" She looked away wistfully. "Her name was Patry. Have I never told you about her?"

"Not that I recall. How old were you? Whatever became of your friendship? Now you've got my curiosity up."

"I was about sixteen. We used to sit around the fire and talk about boys. Grandma didn't mind, but Grandpa was against it. "No mingling with the landwalkers," he would say. I had to bathe twice to get the smell off of me before I could come to mealtime."

"Were you friends for a long time?"

"A couple of years. Which is a long time when you're a teenager."

"I had no idea kids from both villages would spend time together. I have never seen that in my time. All of my childhood friends were Merrow, and I'm sure none of them had any human friends either."

"Young people are always more accepting. That is, until their parents teach them to hate. You're right about how things have changed. Mine was the last generation to enjoy that kind of freedom."

"Have you stayed in touch with her?"

"Oh no. We had a falling out. A necklace of hers disappeared, and her father accused me of stealing it. There was a lot of name calling, and I couldn't go to my parents for help because my father didn't want me up there anyway. I could never convince Patry of my innocence. Her folks forbade us from seeing each other again."

Chielle hugged her mother. "Oh Mama, I'm so sorry for you."

"That's why I'm always telling you to be careful with humans. Every time the slightest little thing goes wrong, they always accuse us. It's like they blame all the world's ills on us, even though we stay away from them as much as we can."

"I am careful, Mama. I tried to stop Thymon and his friends from confronting the fishermen, but they were determined. I knew it would only make things worse."

"Well, thankfully those tubes you found are working very well to herd the fish. In another few weeks the fishermen will assume the fish have migrated, and we can have the meadows back to ourselves. You just keep being my clever girl and we'll do fine."

"Will you ever stop calling me that?"

"What, just because you're 23 does not mean you get to stop being my little girl. Sooreet is 26 and I still call her my ..."

"Little Clamshell, I know. At least I escaped being named after some cute animal."

"Oh, before you go, I suggest you bathe before supper. You don't want to raise suspicions around the table."

"Yes, Mama."

Sten had just lowered a bucket on a rope down off the wharf to pull up some sea water when he saw a distortion in the surface of the water offshore. He wouldn't have noticed it but for the late afternoon sun's shining off the water. The rippling was moving fast, and it was coming his way. He thought it might be a Merrow, maybe even Chielle, but Merrow left almost no wake, and as this approached, he could see it was bigger than a person. It stopped just off the wharf, and up popped Chielle's smiling face.

"Hello there!" she called up.

"Ahoy! What have you got there? It looks big, but I can't make it out."

"That's because it's still in the water. May I come up?"

"Of course. I'll come around." He brought up the bucket and set it down by his shack as he hustled over to the landing ramp.

Chielle was hunched up at the edge of the landing platform pulling something out of the water hand over hand.

"Can I help with that?" As he approached, he had to stop and look twice at what he was seeing. As she threw down a load, it looked like a fishing net, but the next part she was pulling out of the water was invisible. "What in the world? Am I seeing this right?"

She turned and grinned playfully. "Yep. It's not something we Merrow share very often, but it's what I'm working on today, and I thought you'd appreciate it."

He bent down and was almost afraid to touch it. "Wait, it's visible out of the water, but it vanishes when it's wet?"

"Uh huh. Works every time, even on fast, skittish fish. It's also really tough to weave while it's invisible underwater. I thought I might take advantage of your nice big dry dock here and get done a lot quicker."

"What's it made of?"

She pursed her broad lips and cocked her head at him. "That secret I'll keep. Hey, you shaved.

"I do once in a while."

"It looks good. I won't presume you did that for me, but thank you."

She pulled up the last armload and dropped it on the dock. "There."

"If we bring this up topside, we can talk while we both work."

She looked dubiously at the pile of net and then up the ramp.

"Oh, don't worry about that." He squatted down and reached his arms around the bulk of the net and pressed to stand up carrying most of it.

He caught Chielle looking wide eyed at what he had done.

"You coming?" he invited, and started stomping up the ramp, a couple of long ends dragging behind him.

"After you," she said with quiet awe.

He dropped it on the part of the wharf that faced away from his shack toward the ocean. "Whew. That's my exercise for the day. Can I help you sort it out?"

"Oh no, that's fine. Thank you for bringing it up. Sorry it weighs so much. I hadn't thought about getting it up here when I decided to bring it."

He stood up and stretched his arms over his head. "My pleasure. You know, this vanishing rope you've got just reinforces how little I know of your life undersea. I've thought about what it must be like, but I realize I'm just guessing."

"What would you like to know?"

"Your village, for example. How big is it? Where is it? What is life like there?"

"There are about three hundred of us, about the same size as Saint Rochel." She turned and pointed out up the coast. "Celidan is straight out from the northernmost edge of Saint Rochel, about a mile offshore, at the top of a canyon that drops away steeply. The village itself is about thirty cubits down, deep enough that topside weather doesn't affect us, yet shallow enough for sunlight to reach the coral."

"You said 'cubits.' Is that a measure?"

"I think that's the right word of yours for it. It's the length from your elbow to your fingertips." She chuckled at the comparison. "You know, it's pretty funny how you humans measure everything in feet, even height, as if you were going to walk everywhere."

"I guess that's because we don't think about up and down as much as we do length and width. We lead pretty flat lives that way. You said sunlight had to reach the coral."

"Yes, our homes are made of living coral. We cultivate the coral to grow into hollow shapes that we use for shelter. Our homes are generational, since they take a long time to grow. I live with eleven of my family, from great grandparents down to nieces and nephews, in a fifteen-room home that has been growing with my family for five generations."

"That's a big house." He looked at his two-room shack. "I had no idea you live in a mansion."

"It doesn't feel very big when you fill it up with all my family."

He grabbed an end of the net and started to pull it out flat. She did the same.

"I'm trying to picture this in my mind. That far down and inside your home, doesn't it get kind of dark?"

"We have sunstones."

"I don't know what that is."

"Oh, right, you just use fire for light. We have stones that soak up sunlight and then they shine for what you call an hour or so. We cycle them during the day up to rafts at the surface so we always have bright ones in the house. When the last stone fades after sunset, it's time for sleep. Our last meal is always just before sunset. That's also why we measure time in 'sunstones,' if you ever hear me use that term."

A rumbling sound grew louder as something approached coming out the wharf. Chielle looked around the house to see.

"That's Jacio pulling the wagon. I sent him into town to get more firewood."

She smiled and waved at him. Then back to Sten she asked, "Is he related to you?"

"No, he's just a kid from the village who wanted to learn the trade. He's really quite good at figuring out how things go together."

"Do you tell him that?"

"I give him more responsibility as time goes by, so he knows I have faith in him."

Jacio pulled the wagon up to the shack and came around to the front. "Hello Chielle."

"Hi Jacio. Sten was just telling me what a fine blacksmith you are turning into."

The boy raised surprised eyebrows at Sten. "That's great to hear."

Sten smiled but did not take the bait. "You can head home after you unload the wood. I won't be starting anything new this late."

"Thanks."

Sten noticed Jacio left with more bounce in his step after Chielle's comment than when he arrived from dragging the loaded wagon. Clever of her.

"Speaking of jobs, what does a workday look like in a Merrow village?"

"Everyone pitches in on household and village tasks. There is the sense that we all need to help to get everything done. We have more specialties than occupations. Mine is obviously weaving rope and fabric. I'm usually done by mid-afternoon, which is why I can come visit later in the day."

They got the net untangled and she sat down to start work on the unfinished end.

"I have a pet octopus named Nru who follows me around the house looking for treats."

"This all sounds really ordinary, like just normal life, only underwater."

"Yes. Were you expecting something else?"

"Well, I guess so. There are all these myths and legends about mermaids having magical powers, that you can change the weather, or heal magically."

"You asked me about my enchanted singing voice. No, those are all just stories. Most of them are told out of fear and misunderstanding. Only Rorra can perform miracles."

"Rorra is your sea god?"

"Rorra is the sea. She has great wisdom and patience, and she watches out for everything she touches. We say Rorra abides and provides. She created everything we have today. I think my favorite story is how she created the Merrow so we could breathe air or water, since you can't laugh underwater."

"Right, since you don't blow air out when you speak down there. What about the myth that mermaids can turn invisible?"

He watched her reaction carefully and did catch the faintest twitch of surprise. "Invisible? I've never heard that one. I know some humans don't trust us because, when we dive, they can't see where we've gone."

"You're saying it's just another crazy human myth?"

"Yes."

"But you have figured out how to make that net disappear."

"It doesn't disappear. It turns clear when it's wet. There's a big difference."

"All right. Let me grab something I'm working on. I'll be right back." He stepped into the shack and retrieved the taps and pipes he had started threading. He also picked up the bucket of sea water he had fetched.

"Now can I ask you a question?" she asked.

"Sure."

"Who is Atlan?"

"Atlan is the father of humankind. We believe a long time ago, there was a great cataclysm, a time of frozen barrens and fiery volcanoes, a time of great testing. Out of that trial, one man emerged as the ultimate survivor, with all the finest qualities you can have. He was brave, strong, smart, and resourceful."

While he talked, Sten twisted a tap down around the end of a pipe, forcing shiny slivers of metal to curl out around the tool. The filings clung to the pipe, and every few minutes he shook the end clean in the bucket of water. He caught Chielle watching this process.

"Atlan and his family led mankind out of the darkness. His children and their children's children eventually bred with all the other surviving families, so that all humans have Atlan as our one common ancestor.

"Each human now has a fragment of his superior abilities. Therefore, each person has it within himself to be better, stronger, smarter, and braver than you'd think."

"My brother Thymon questioned why you wanted to help us. You've only been here a year. This isn't really your fight. Does your faith in Atlan compel you to help people? If it does, then the people of Saint Rochel seem to have forgotten that."

He hadn't expected her to see through him like that. He smiled and shook his head to cover. "Atlan did teach us to be humble and to use our gifts to help others. Personally, I have a hard time not sticking my nose in trying to help even when it's not, as you said, my fight. It's gotten me in some pretty serious trouble at times."

She stopped weaving and looked at him earnestly. "Wanting to help isn't a bad thing, if help is really needed. What did Atlan teach about patience?"

Again, he had to think about his answer. "Not much. He taught more about destiny, and living up to it. Because so many people perished in that original time of trial, we believe each of our lives is a gift. Each drop of water that hits you as you stand in a river was destined at the beginning of time for that collision. Each person has a role to play and a place to be. Since we are the ones who survived, it is our obligation to be good enough to deserve that place. We can rise to be deserving because each of us has a piece of perfection inside."

Chielle blinked a few times. "Wow. That's so ... different. The whole view of how you fit into the world is so ..."

"Rugged individual?"

"Lonely."

They were interrupted by a conversation in the shack. Sten set his pipe down. "I'd better go see who that is."

Jacio was chatting with Corm Neeley, a master mason with blotchy pale skin and thinning grey hair.

"Corm, how are you?" Sten greeted him with a hand shake.

"Mr. Neeley is here for the clamps," Jacio supplied.

"Very well, they're right in here." As Sten stepped into his workshop, he noticed Corm had not followed him. When he returned, Corm had stepped around the shack and was standing with his fists on his hips and a scowl on his face, looking down the wharf clearly at Chielle.

"What in the hell is a mermaid doing on your dock?"

"She's a friend of mine, Corm. Have you never met a mermaid face to face?"

Corm looked shocked at the prospect. "Hell no, and I'm not going to today. It's an outrage, I tell you. Having a thieving fin at a blacksmith shop. Naked savage."

"Now hold on a minute." Sten dropped his friendly tone and stepped up to the old man. "She is my guest. You are my customer. That does not give you the right to insult her."

"What in hell has gotten into you, son? Don't you know what you're dealing with?"

"Yes, I do — a bigoted, closed-minded old man who can take his business elsewhere if he's going to be so rude."

Corm looked at the clamps in Sten's hands, and then up into Sten's eyes.

Sten did not waiver.

He looked again at the clamps, and then at Chielle. "You know you're the only blacksmith in town who can do this good a job. I need those clamps."

"Then pay for them and go. Or apologize to my guest and you can stay as long as you like. Maybe stick around and learn something, like how the mermaids are our neighbors and not our enemies."

He twisted his lips into a sneer, pulled out a purse and handed it to Sten.

Sten handed him the clamps. "Ever worked with coral limestone?"

Corm looked surprised at the mention. "Sure. It's wonderful stuff."

"If you ever want any, just remember who can get it for you." Sten pointed his thumb over the side of the wharf.

The old man recoiled as if he had bitten a lemon. "No thank you." He turned and left, grumbling the whole way.

Sten tossed the purse to Jacio and walked back to Chielle. "I am so sorry you had to hear that."

"It's not your fault. It certainly isn't the first time I've been called names by people who haven't even met me. Thank you for standing up for me. You could have lost a customer."

"No, he knows my work, and I know how much he wants it. These people are just not interested in learning more about you. Their minds are made up, even though they have no information. You saw him. He didn't even want to meet you. If that treaty did not keep our peoples separated, then the humans would see they have nothing to fear and nothing to hate."

"We have the treaty to preserve our Merrow way of life."

"I'm starting to think the humans a hundred years ago convinced the Merrow to sign that treaty because they knew it would be a way to keep your people from ever having the things we have. Sure, it has preserved your way of life, the way of life your ancestors had thousands of years ago."

"Oh, now you hold on. You cannot assume your ideas of justice or progress apply to my people. Our minds, our brains are different. We've talked about how I always think in three directions, that up and down are just as important to me as side to side. More than that, we don't think we personally own anything. No matter how easy or difficult life may be, it is always the ocean that provides, and there is always enough. No one owns anything, because everything belongs to everyone. No matter how angry we get when the humans fish in our waters, we can't really say those waters are ours. That's why every time the humans take a little more, the Merrow let them.

"Our religions even point out the difference. You believe in this divine right to excel. I believe in patience and letting the sea provide."

"Then why did your people take up arms?'

"We've run out of waters to give up. If Parker's Meadow falls to the fishermen, my village won't have enough food to stay here. We will have to abandon our homes and move somewhere with no humans."

Sten noticed that Jacio was standing by the corner of the shop, listening. He looked shocked.

Sten looked back and forth between the two of them. "We, we are not going to let that happen. I haven't seen your village, and I'll be damned if I'll let a handful of greedy fishermen drive you out of it before I ever get to see it."

"See my village? No human has ever seen Celidan."

"Because of the treaty?"

"No, because it's impossible for you to breathe at that depth."

6

S TEPPING IN FROM THE CHILL MORNING FOG, Sten was assaulted by the pungent smells of leather, dye, and polish as he entered the cobbler's shop. "Good morning, Bom!"

Bom Stickney looked up from his workbench and cracked open a smile that lifted his enormous red moustache to reveal equally large horse-like teeth. "Sten Holdsmith. You haven't burned a whole in that leather apron, have you? That's the heaviest leather I've got."

"No, no, the apron's fine. Better than fine, it's a marvel. No, today I've got another challenge for you. A couple of them, actually,"

At this the cobbler stood up to his full six-and-a-half-foot height and joined Sten at the front table.

Sten put a pair of low boots on the table, then pulled out a large roll of paper. He spread it out to show two large wedge-shaped outlines. He smoothed out the sheet and placed the boots on the drawings.

"You gonna go stomp in the snow?"

"Ocean. I figure this long flap should push back water like a seal flipper."

"The mermaids are gonna come after you, invading their domain."

"Can you do it? Replace the soles with leather fins?"

"Sure. It's weird, but hardly difficult. You said you had a couple of challenges."

Sten grinned, reached into his satchel and pulled out another scroll. "You're gonna love this."

He rolled it out to reveal an oddly shaped but clearly carefully drawn outline.

Bom took a guess. "This big flap pulls up and these holes match up for stitches. And these big holes are for what, laces? Looks like a boot for a stump." He turned a dubious eye on Sten as he loomed down. "Somebody lose a foot?"

"Yes, a friend of mine in Silverton. The boot he's got is crap, so I designed him a new one. What do you think?"

"Should work, if you got his shape and size right. I'd close up these big gaps on the sides."

"He needs those. He's pretty deformed."

Bom frowned at the drawing. "I'll say."

"I need this one made out of softer leather. It's got to flex. The flippers should be good and stiff. Will you need more than a couple of days?"

"I'm not real busy right now. I can have it all for you by the day after tomorrow."

"Great."

The door opened and Arum Blaine stepped in. "Good morning, Bom, Sten. Just making my morning rounds."

Sten walked around in front of the table, blocking the constable's view of the drawings. "Arum, I wanted to ask you something. We've talked about the Celidan treaty. You told me it's illegal to trade with the merfolk."

"That's right. Both villages have laws against trade."

"What does our law carry as a punishment?"

"I think it's a day in the public stocks. Why? Are you planning on selling them more weapons? They've already got steel spear points. You wouldn't happen to know how they got those?"

"No. I did not make those spear points. I believe they forged those themselves out of desperation in an underwater lava vent."

"Damn," interjected Bom. "Isn't that awfully dangerous?"

"Yes. They were desperate. If they could get their weapons from me, they wouldn't go to such extremes."

"What do you want to trade?" Arum asked.

"Just basic fixtures. Maybe tools. Things to make their lives easier."

Arum made no effort to hide the doubt in his voice. "What are they going to give you in exchange?"

"Hand crafts, pearls, coral limestone, seal pelts."

Bom perked up. "Seal hide is really nice to work with."

Sten turned back to Arum. "See?"

The constable remained unconvinced. "You're a fool. The reason I've never had to pillory anyone for a trade violation is no one on my watch has been stupid enough to trade with the merfolk. I'll tell you what. If I find you've been trading with them, I will turn a blind eye, and not prosecute you. When you find you've been cheated, and you will get cheated, don't come crying to me to settle a dispute. Consider yourself advised."

"Fair enough," Sten agreed.

"You gentlemen have a ..." he paused for emphasis, "... peaceful day."

"You too," Bom said with a wave at the constable's exiting figure. He turned to Sten. "Hence the flippers."

"Indeed. Hey, I've got a question for you. When I was in Silverton seeing my friend with the bad foot, I noticed the Indru women there don't corset up their breasts the way they do here. Do you ever make any of the over-the-blouse ... whatever you call the vest that holds everything up."

Bom laughed. "It's called a 'bodice' when it's worn over a blouse. And yes, I've made a few leather ones."

"Is that a style the Alcan brought to this region?"

"That's right. The natives here in the tropics have much less structured clothes. Their women wrap up their breasts the same way they wrap up their outer dresses. Not much tailoring there. The corsets and bodices our women wear have to be tailored to each woman's shape and size. Why are you so suddenly so interested in women's clothes? Or do you just love titties?"

"It just seems odd that Indru women adopted the more restrictive Alcan style here at the coast where it's hot and humid, and where you'd think it would be more comfortable to go with their traditional looser outfits. Back inland, where it's not as sticky, they kept their native clothes. Any idea how that happened?"

"I grew up in this town, and it's always been that way. If there was a change, it happened a long time ago."

Chielle's heart was pounding with a confusing rush of worry and anticipation as she floated up under Sten's landing. She gripped the edge of the platform and looked up the ramp. The gentle slap of waves under the wooden floats measured her tense breathing. She glanced back at the setting sun, and then up at the shack. Surely Jacio would have gone home by now. Sten would be alone. Her heart pounded even harder.

Courage. This has to be done. Courage.

She hopped up on the deck and made the long climb up the ramp. Maybe this will turn out well. Why did this ramp have to be so steep? Oh, right, low tide.

The half dozen steps from the wharf edge to the door never looked so far. Now or never, she thought as she walked. All or nothing. She knocked.

Sten opened the door and a rush of warm smoke-scented air spilled over her. He was silhouetted in the orange glow from the roaring hearth. She suddenly felt cold and outside.

"Chielle. What a happy surprise. Please come in. Isn't it kind of late for you to be out?"

She stepped in and smiled at how much she liked being here. Her smile faded as she turned to face him. "There is something I need to talk to you about."

"Sounds serious. Shall we sit over here on the bench?" He invited her with a wave of his hand. "Can I get you something? Maybe some cocoa?"

"No, thank you. I will sit. Please stop being so nice. I've got a confession to make, and I just need you to hear me out."

He joined her on the wooden bench. "All right, I'm all ears."

She took a deep breath and let it out slowly. "That first day that I rescued you from the net? I was not just casually swimming by. I had been watching you for a while."

"Good thing. I will never regret you being there."

"For days. I knew you were a blacksmith. I acted surprised to learn your trade. I had been waiting for a chance to talk with you — because you're a blacksmith."

"I understand."

"When you offered to teach me how to work metal, I thanked Rorra for my amazing luck." She looked away. "Then I abused your trust a second time."

"You taught your men how to make those spear points."

"Yes," she sighed. "I didn't know they were going to make weapons. I thought, I thought, I don't know what I thought. Of course they were going to make weapons."

She looked up and met his gaze. "I am so sorry. I lied to you, and I betrayed your trust."

He shrugged his eyebrows and pursed his lips. "The good news is, you're not a very good liar. I suspected all this pretty much from the beginning. My only regret is that you felt you needed to lie in the first place. It certainly makes sense. You probably grew up hearing it all the time. 'Never trust a human.'"

"That's true. I'm still ashamed, especially now that I've gotten to know you and found what a kind and thoughtful person you are." She caught herself before she started gushing.

"That says a lot for you. You feel guilty for acting the way you were taught."

Her heart pounded again, this time with a glimmer of hope. She lowered her head and looked up at him. "Can you forgive me?"

He turned to face her fully. "Yes, Chielle, I forgive you."

She sighed so big her shoulders dropped. "Thank you."

"Were you worried I'd say no and throw you out?"

"I didn't know what to think. The thought of losing you was tearing me apart." She caught her breath when she heard the words that had spilled out.

Sten smiled the most charming, bemused grin she had ever seen. "Losing me?"

Her heart just about jumped out of her chest. Now or never. All or nothing. Even with all of her courage gripped tightly, all she could manage was a quiet but sincere, "Yes."

She didn't see when he moved so close, but suddenly his face was right up to hers. He was breathing just as hard as she was. She was pretty sure the pounding vibration she was sensing was his heart matching hers. He leaned in and puckered up, so she did the same.

At first contact she found the mix of soft lips and muscular pressure fascinating, but this was swept away by a sudden flood of giddy joy that completely surprised her. She held his face in her hands and he wrapped his strong arms around her body, pulling her up against his chest. She let his love wash over her and she dove in.

When at last he broke the kiss, she rubbed her cheek against his in a stroking motion. She was very happy he had shaved again today.

He seemed confused.

"That's how we kiss." She pointed down the side of her face. "Remember the pressure nerves."

"Oh, right. You're really sensitive there."

"Very."

"Which is why you don't like beards."

She stroked his bare cheek with her webbed fingers. "Yep." She wrapped her arms up under his and around his back, pulled him tight, and buried her face in his neck. "You make me so happy."

She thought she felt him stiffen under her hug. Was she moving too fast? Then he squeezed her back.

She reveled in the connection, warmed by feeling his heart beating next to hers. She nuzzled his neck and was pleased his sweat tasted like sea water.

He stroked the back of her head with his hand, caressing the fringe edges of her gill flaps. Even though his hands were rough, it was the gentlest thing she could remember.

She loosened her hug and looked up into his eyes again. His breathing quickened right with hers and they fell into a mouth kissing, cheek rubbing, head clutching frenzy. He once pushed his lips too hard and opened her mouth, only to encounter her full row of pointed, razor sharp teeth. He pulled back in surprise.

She shrugged, puckered up her full lips, and gave him a reassuring smooch.

He launched back into kissing her and her excitement overwhelmed her. The smell of his body, the texture of his loose shirt, the taste of his breath, the hair on his head, his strong hands grasping her body, fumbling with her dorsal fin, it was all intoxicating.

She was so lost in the moment she did not notice her body was gyrating, her tail was lashing, and she started to rub her breasts against him. He looked down and she saw what she was doing.

"You're getting pretty excited," he commented with a chuckle.

"How embarrassing. I'm sorry. My instincts took over." She wrapped her arms around her chest. "I'm just mortified."

"Your instincts?"

"Courtship dance, underwater. Everything is always in motion in water. We don't just embrace, we swim around each other, brushing our bodies together. You must think I have no self-control."

"Hey, abandon to the moment isn't a bad thing. I'm kind of flattered that you trust me with such an intimate ritual."

"I really did not mean to do that."

"Would you stop apologizing? You are who you are. I'm still learning all this. Believe me, I've got habits and instincts that I'll be apologizing for as well." He caressed her cheek and held it in his hand. "Besides, when I look into those astonishing eyes of yours, I'll forgive you anything."

"I promise not to take advantage of that. Your trust is so important to me."

"You've got it." He leaned in and touched his forehead to hers. "Hey, it's way past sundown. How are you going to find your way home?"

"I'll use the moon and echoes." She was sad he had moved so quickly to her departure. He really did think she was moving too fast. She joked to cover her doubts. "You're not trying to get rid of me, are you?"

"No, of course not. I've got a lot to do tomorrow, so I need to get to sleep soon. I also didn't know if you could navigate in the dark, or if your family would worry about you. Or does your family know where you are?"

"They will worry if I'm out too late. No, I have not told them about you. I told my brother about you and the metal working, but frankly, I didn't know what else to say."

"Have I really been that vague? Chielle, you stir feelings in me that I have not felt in a long, long time. I don't know how safe it would be to go tell your family that you're seeing me romantically, but please do not doubt that I am very fond of you."

Fond. Now there's a word to ponder. "May I come see you again tomorrow?"

"Um, not tomorrow. I'm going to be tied up all day. The day after next would be great. Can you make it day after tomorrow?"

"Yes, of course."

He stood up and stepped to the hearth. "Can I get you anything before you go?"

"No, thank you." She got up and straightened her erda. "You're right, it's late, and I should be going."

He intercepted her at the door. He wrapped his big arms around her and drew her up close. "I'm really happy you came tonight." The way he smiled at her nearly dissolved her apprehensions. The warm kiss he gave her finally removed her doubt.

She grinned up at him. "Day after tomorrow."

"Good night, Chielle."

"Good night, Sten."

She turned at the wharf edge and smiled back at him in his glowing doorway. She waved and thanked Rorra he was such a patient man. She nearly ruined it. As she leapt off into the black sea, she thought she must slow down, take it easy, let things flow naturally. Rorra would want it that way. Sten was worth the wait.

7

S TEN'S STOMACH NOISILY REMINDED HIM that he had been running errands since dawn without eating breakfast. He set down the large bundle of bamboo in front of The Pied Cock and went in for a bite. "Mister Caron!" he called to the bartender. "Have you got any of those pickled eggs behind the bar? You got any of those pickled eggs behind the bar?"

Paulbert Caron came out of the kitchen wiping his hands on a towel. He had his long, straight black hair pulled into a ponytail. Sten thought it made him look a lot different, cleaner somehow, exposing his high dark brown forehead. "I most certainly do. You don't usually breakfast with us in town, Sten. You up to anything interesting?"

Sten appreciated that Caron had to keep up with all the local news since his pub was the central exchange for gossip among men. He did not appreciate how much Caron seemed to enjoy sticking his nose into everybody's business. "Not really. I've just got a lot of work today and wanted to get an early start. Besides, I really like these eggs."

The bartender fished two out of the barrel and put them on a plate.

"Better make it three," Sten requested. "What have you got to drink?"

Caron smiled. "You mean, that goes with pickled eggs and won't get you drunk at ten in the morning?"

"That would be good."

"You're actually in luck. Some kids came by yesterday with a fruit cart and I got some pineapples. Let me bust one up for you."

Sten picked up the first egg and started to take a bite. "Damn, Paul, eggs and juice? I'm gonna have to come into town for breakfast more often."

When Caron went into the back, Sten looked around and spotted a couple of old sail makers having a rather heated discussion at a table toward the back of the pub. One of them caught Sten looking and called out to him. Sten thought he remembered his name was Finkle.

"Who do you think did it?"

"Did what?" Sten called back without getting up from the bar.

"Called in the crown and got poor Roff lashed like a dog."

"How do you know anybody summoned the High Lord? A gunfight is pretty big news. You don't think word travelled on its own?"

"Too fast," Finkle insisted. "Somebody went over Arum Blaine's head."

"And behind all our backs," his tablemate chimed in.

"Would it make any difference if the merfolk punished the young mermen who attacked the fleet for starting the fight? What if their authorities didn't like resorting to violence either?"

"Damn right they should be punished! About bloody time they acted with some honor. Still, Roff was just defending himself."

"I doubt they punished anybody," the other man grumbled.

Sten bit back and sighed quietly to himself. He had considered coming clean once things had settled down. His justice seeking hadn't improved things at all. This was going to be a long, hard road.

Sten and Jacio sat on the end of the wharf, watching the sun sink into the west, surrounded by the fruits of their day's labors.

Drilled out bamboo poles, tapped pipe fittings, a crank-powered bellows, and a beaten metal bell fitted with a window were all stacked in a line.

"Sten," he began cautiously, "I know you said this project was to satisfy your curiosity. I've known you for almost a year, and I can say you have a pretty strong curiosity."

Sten smiled at his apprentice's careful choice of words. "Thank you."

"That said, even after working on this all day to make sure it works, this is a really dangerous thing you're planning. I have to wonder if you would take this kind of risk just out of curiosity."

"Why else?" he baited.

Jacio took a breath and smirked at him. "You're not going to make this easy for me, so I'll just come right out and say it. Are you falling in love with Chielle?"

"You know I could just say that's none of your business. On the other hand, if I die trying this dive, then I guess it will be your business. I'll level with you. I think so, but I'm still wondering myself. I love being around her. She's so full of wonder and hope and love for the world. She flirts with me shamelessly. I find myself daydreaming about her."

"Does it matter that she's ... not human?"

"Ah, now, my young friend, your curiosity is showing. I keep wondering that myself. I mean, seriously, that can't be overlooked. You're right, though. It doesn't seem to matter when I think about her and joy overtakes me."

"They say love is blind. I wouldn't know. I've never been seriously in love."

Sten punched him in the shoulder. "You'll get there in due time. I don't think love is blinding me to her differences. I would never have taken the time to get to know her if I hadn't been attracted. I actually think love is opening my eyes to see the wonderful person behind the alien form."

Sten stepped out of Bom Stickney's cobbler shop holding the swim flipper boots in a burlap sack. He glanced around the town streets brimming with folks finishing up their afternoon errands, going through his mental list, wondering if he had forgotten anything for his grand adventure. He was distracted enough he didn't see Corm Neeley standing in his path with his arms folded over his chest.

"Well, if it isn't the traitor in our midst," the stone cutter accused.

Sten looked up and saw him for the first time. "Oh, good afternoon to you too, Corm."

He started to walk around the man, but Corm stepped in his way.

"What is it?" he asked as patiently as he could. "Don't tell me you're picking a fight right here in the middle of the street. Shouldn't we leave that kind of carrying on to the teenagers?"

"I don't think it's childish to stand up for what's right," he began loudly enough to draw attention. "You're cozying up with the mermaids while we're trying to carve out a living. Those thieving fins have even found a way to steal the fish out from under our boats."

Sten stood up before him and set his shoulders. "The Merrow are not our enemies. They work hard to get by just like us. Nobody has to steal or cheat or attack anybody."

"Listen to yourself. The 'Merrow.' Who the hell calls them that? That's what they call themselves. You don't give a damn about us! You're too busy making friends with them."

"You know what? I am trying to make friends with them. They have a lot to offer. You want them to stop stealing your scrap iron? Try treating them with a little respect. They were here first."

By now a crowd of over a dozen men had gathered around at a safe distance. Barging through them and stepping right up was Selric Boole. "I'll bet my nets it was you who called the High Lord to come whip poor Roff for defending himself."

Sten looked down straight into his beady eyes. "I have no sway with the law."

"Somebody called him," the wide-shouldered captain spat. "Somebody who cares more for fish than men."

"You're just hate mongering," Sten dismissed him.

Corm chimed in, "Good ol' Roff took it like a man. Didn't cry out once."

Sten turned to him pointedly. "That's right. He did take it like a man, because he knew what he did was wrong. I spoke with Roff the night he shot that merman. He was completely guilt-stricken. He knew he had to pay, and he did, and now it's done. He's clean, and so is his conscience."

"What a load of shit!" Boole insisted.

"Look, Boole, you talk a lot about what it means to be a man. Do you think Atlan would approve of us subjugating a simple, natural-loving people?"

Boole stiffened up at the mention of their ideal.

Sten turned to the crowd. "Seriously, Atlan would expect us to do better, to be wiser."

"Now you've crossed the line" Boole growled through gritted teeth as he swung on Sten.

Sten barely veered out of the way, but there were more punches coming. Boole landed a solid hit in Sten's stomach, but Sten was ready for it. He jabbed back with an elbow across the bridge of Boole's nose. That only slowed him down for a second before he launched back with both fists flying. Sten responded in kind, toe to toe swinging savagely. Sten was surprised how little a punch in the face hurt. So he hit Boole harder. Still the short sailor kept swinging. Sten lost track of where the punches were coming from or where they were landing. He just stiffened his body under the onslaught and fired back as many as he could land.

Boole wasn't trying to defend himself either, as both men relied on their sheer toughness and concentrated on full tilted attack.

Sten lost track of time. Maybe it had only been a few seconds, it could have been many minutes. He hurt all over, but he still had strength in his arms, so he kept on punching. He did notice the crowd wasn't stepping in to break up the fight. They were cheering. He wondered if any of them were rooting for him.

He had expected Boole to be strong, but the man's ferocity was unending. Sten wasn't sure he would be able to make much difference against so much pent up anger.

Sten knocked him back and Boole charged right back at him. Sten ducked down and flipped him up. His momentum carried him right over and into a stack of barrels. One of them shattered and Boole came up covered in molasses. His enormous beard hung like a muddy bib, which made him even more furious.

Sten tried to warn him, but his lips were swollen and bleeding too much to speak clearly. "I swore to myself I'd never lay into a man like this again. Don't make me hurt you."

Boole ignored him and stumbled back to his feet.

Even though Sten regretted it, he needed to end this with some real damage. He took a second and gathered all the strength he had left. Boole landed a couple more punches in the meantime, but that didn't faze him. The shorter man finally left him an opening and he hauled back and struck him with all his might right in the face. He felt something crack, and it felt good, until he wondered if it had been Boole's face or his own hand he broke.

Boole went down in a halo spray of brown sticky droplets. Sten looked at his hand and it was covered in blood, his own from loss of skin and Boole's too. He was aghast to see both his hands were chewed up like this. At least neither of them felt broken.

He swayed and had to steady his step. He tried to look around the crowd but couldn't focus. He couldn't really form much thought either. He noticed his whole face felt huge and stiff.

He did make out Arum Blaine pushing his way through the crowd and grabbing him by the shoulders. He tried to say something to the constable, but it wouldn't come out. The only other thing he noticed through the blur was his hands were suddenly held together with shackles. He smiled as he recognized them as his own handiwork.

The next few minutes made little sense or impression. When he finally found focus again, he was inside a jail cell. Boole was in the next cell with his face covered in bandages. Sten's entire body ached deeply like he was broken inside. He didn't see any coughed-up blood, at least not yet. On the other hand, he didn't feel like doing anything more than curling up on the cot and trying to ignore the pain enough to sleep.

The last time she floated up to Sten's dock, Chielle had worried she wouldn't have the courage to tell him how she felt about him. This time she was overrun with caution not to scare him off. Act casual, she kept telling herself. Tell a joke to get him talking. Let him do the talking, even though he doesn't say much about his feelings. She stopped herself before she wound herself up too tightly. He did invite her back. He made her wait a day, but he did say come back tonight. She kept telling herself this all the way up the ramp.

Jacio was closing up the shack when she got to the wharf. "Hi, Jacio. Is Sten around?"

"Oh hi, Chielle. No, he didn't show up all day."

"Did he say where he was going to be?"

"No. Nice dress."

She smiled that he noticed the modest long white gown she wore. "Thank you. Might that mean he's hurt or in some kind of trouble?"

"No, not really. Sometimes he takes off for a day or two without telling me where he's going. I won't worry unless he's still missing tomorrow."

She was very confused how this could be all right. "Is this his only home? I mean, does he have somewhere else he could be staying?"

"No. This is it."

"Yet you're not worried?"

"No. Not yet. You shouldn't worry either. Hey, can I ask you a personal question?" He came over to her and lowered his voice.

They were a hundred yards from the nearest person, so she could see how uncomfortable he was. "I may not answer, but you can ask."

"I know this is none of my business, but you and Sten are getting pretty close, right?"

"Yes."

"Well, have you two talked about, well ...?"

"What?" Now her interest was piqued.

"How he's going to break it to the townspeople."

That wasn't what she thought he was going to say. "No. I know they're not ready to accept me."

"No, I'm sorry, this is too rude," he said with a wave of his hand. "I shouldn't have brought it up."

"No, wait. You're obviously concerned about something. Can you tell me?"

"Sten thinks they need his skills too much to stop doing business with him for befriending you and your people. I'm not so sure that's true. The townspeople are pretty riled up these days. I'm just afraid Sten is going to get himself into some real trouble."

"You think I am endangering him?"

"No, no, see that's why I shouldn't have brought it up. I like you Chielle, I really do. I never thought I would say that, but these last few weeks have really turned my head around." He rubbed his dark face to collect his thoughts. "These people, they're still stuck in their hate. I don't know what to do about it. I do not think it's your fault or anything. Sten gets these causes in his head and there's no stopping him."

Her heart felt heavy. "It sounds like it would be a good idea if I didn't come around as much, just to avoid the chance of putting Sten in harm's way."

"I'm sorry, Chielle. I don't know what else to say."

"That's all right, Jacio. I'm glad you told me. I only hear about what's going on in Saint Rochel from Sten, and he's been acting like he can handle the townsfolk just fine. If that's not true, then I'll do my part. Thank you for telling me."

"Sure. I've got to go home now." He turned to go. "I'll see you later, right?"

"Of course," she called after him. "Good bye." She watched him walk away.

Walking away. Not an option she had ever considered. She felt like someone had stepped on her heart.

8

T ODAY WOULD BE A DAY OF REST, Sten decided. He managed to stagger home after Arum released him and Boole. Boole seemed to have finally lost the fighting spirit and went on this way peacefully. Not too many people stared at Sten as he made his way through the streets and down to the wharf. He must have looked a sight. He felt crushed inside and nothing worked without effort. That was enough work for today.

He got home mid-morning and gave Jacio the day off. He deserved it too. Poor Jacio was horrified when he saw Sten. The boy got him out of his blood-soaked shirt and into a clean one. Good lad.

He dragged a chair and his second set of windchimes down the ramp to the landing. He hung the chimes in the water with a rope he could pull between sips of wine and naps.

He owed Chielle an apology for not being there the night before as he had promised. He hoped she would hear the chimes. He had no other way to reach her. It would be lovely to see her. He started to smile at the thought of her smile, until his face spasmed.

The morning clouds burned off, a gentle warm breeze caressed him, and the sun felt good. This would do just fine, he thought as he drifted off again.

He was awoken by the sound of his wind chimes being laid down on the landing deck. He blinked his eyes open to see a merman sitting on his hunched-up tail looking down at Sten. "Are you Sten Holdsmith?" the visitor asked.

Sten lifted himself up from his slouch and sat straight. His body spasmed at the movement. "Yes, and who are you?"

"I'm Thymon Mmava, Chielle's brother. What happened to you?"

"I had a disagreement with someone."

"I'll say. Chielle said you were kind, not violent."

"Did she? I didn't start it." He paused and chuckled weakly. "I finished it." Then he considered who he was talking to. "I apologize for my appearance. I would have liked to make a better impression on her family."

"Well, I'm the only one in her family who knows about you. I heard your chimes and I assumed they were to call my sister, so I thought I'd come meet you myself."

Sten tried to stand up and his legs did not want to move. He forced himself up, walked over to Thymon and held his hand out in welcome. "Please let me try this again. Welcome to my home."

The merman sat up straight and shook it while continuing to size him up. Sten took a good look at him too, with his square jaw and his muscular shoulders standing out from his long black tunic. Sten had only ever seen Chielle wear light colors.

"May I offer you something to drink? I have some excellent red wine here. I can get you a glass."

"Thank you for the hospitality, but I have never tried wine. I've heard that it makes humans act like fools."

"It can if you drink too much, or if you're angry when you start drinking. It relaxes us, and makes it easier for us to show how we feel. If you're mad or feeling mean, then it comes out more. If you're feeling happy, then that comes out more too. We also drink it because wine will never make you sick the way tainted water will."

"It's purified water?"

"No, it's mostly grape juice. But the alcohol in it kills any sickness."

Thymon did not look convinced. "We don't drink liquids underwater."

"I understand. Chielle said it felt odd to drink for pleasure."

"You fed my sister wine?" he spat, not trying to hide his angered concern.

"No, no. I've never given her wine. I gave her a warm, sweet drink called cocoa on a cold night. Cocoa doesn't change your mood at all like wine."

"Do you have different drinks for different weather?"

"Yes, and different situations. Sitting here being social on a hot day would call for wine or maybe beer."

"All right, I will accept your offer of this wine. Let no one say I don't know how to be a good guest."

Sten was taken by Thymon's manners. Chielle had said they lived in a tight social order. He hadn't thought about it in terms of manners. "Shall I get you a glass?"

Thymon looked at how Sten was not moving freely and then glanced up the ramp to his shack. "No, this will be fine." Sten was glad his guest had figured out how much trouble a glass would have been. Thymon took the wine skin and examined the mouth.

"Just sip from the opening."

He did so and blinked his enormous merman eyes several times. "It is sour and sweet at the same time. It makes me salivate." He took another sip. "I can see why you would find this refreshing if you were parched." He handed the skin back.

"Welcome to the fine human art of wine."

"It is an art to make this?"

"Yes, the grapes are squeezed and then juice is fermented for just the right length of time to make the alcohol. Then it's put in bottles and aged for months or even years."

"Fermented? You mean rotten?"

"It's a controlled rotting. I think there is yeast involved. People figured out how to make it ages ago."

"When things rot in the sea, the water carries everything away."

"Oh, so you wouldn't be able to capture the alcohol. That's unfortunate." Sten took a sip.

"You know I did not come here to talk about making wine."

"I understand. You wanted to meet this human your sister is spending so much time with."

"May I ask what your intentions are with Chielle?"

Manners? Mostly. Direct? Absolutely. "I will not lie to you, Thymon. I am falling in love with her. She makes me happy like I have not been happy in years. I want to protect her and care for her. She has shown me just how wrong the folks in Saint Rochel are about the Merrow. That was what my disagreement was about that left me looking like this."

"You fought for my sister?"

Sten weighed that. "Yes."

Thymon regarded him for a long moment. "Let me have some more of that wine."

Sten handed him the skin. Of all the reactions her protective older brother could have had, Sten was happy with that one.

The merman took a big drink and handed it back. "Do you have family here?"

So this was going to be *that* conversation. "No. I used to have a younger sister, but she's gone."

"Oh, so you know how I feel towards Chielle?"

"Yes, I was a protective older brother too. Only I ... well, she passed away." Sten took a big drink too.

"I'm sorry."

"It was a long time ago. To answer your question, no, I don't have any other family."

"There is a boy who helps you with your work. Is he related to you?"

"No, he just works for me. That's funny, Chielle asked the same question. I guess family members work together a lot in your village."

"Yes, everyone works together."

"Chielle explained that. I think that's great. Can I ask you a question?"

"Of course."

"Were you part of the group that attacked the fishing boats in Parker's Meadow?"

"Yes, I was their leader."

He didn't sound proud. He just stated the fact. Sten knew he had to tread lightly here. "Our judge punished the man who shot your comrade. The fishermen weren't supposed to be there according to the treaty. But the man was punished for using too much force. Your men threw spears that could have killed someone. Did your village judges have anything to say about that?"

Thymon rolled off his tail and straightened it out. A large rounded stone was bound to the base of his tail just above the fluke fins.

"Doesn't that make it really hard to swim?"

"That's why it's done. I and my fellows are nearly housebound. We can't do our jobs, and we are ridiculed whenever we are seen. It took me tiresome sunstones to get here today." Thymon took the wine skin back and took another drink.

Sten worked this through in his head. 'Sunstones' were hours, he remembered. It took a little while with the wine. "Being a part of the working village is really important to you. Being shackled like that cuts you out, right?"

"Yes."

"Humans value their freedom more than anything, so we hold our criminals captive for long periods. I can see where this is just as bad for you." He held out his hand for Thymon to give him the wine.

When the merman handed it over, he blinked and shook his head. "Oh, now I'm feeling this relaxation you spoke of. I know this feeling. We get this way to be social too."

"Really? What do you drink?"

"It's not a drink." Thymon fingered through the pockets of the sash belt he wore over one shoulder. "Ah, here it is. I couldn't remember if I had one with me." He held up between two webbed fingers a thin pointed object about as long as a finger, with stripes of black and orange down its length. "It's a quill."

"From what?" Sten asked as he squinted to see it better.

"It's from a fish with fins all striped like this. These spines are along its back. They are filled with a venom that keeps predators away."

"Do the predators know to stay away from the stripes?"

"That's a good general rule in the ocean, that striped or brightly colored things are usually poisonous."

"What do you do with this quill? Surely you don't poison yourself with it."

"Why, yes. The poison only harms other fish. We're not fish. We're mammals like whales and you. The venom only makes us high, like your wine."

Sten suddenly realized Chielle's straight-laced older brother was in fact like any other bored, thrill seeking young man. "Let me guess, you get high on this venom with your friends, as opposed to when you are courting a mermaid."

"That's true. Would you like to try it?"

Sten very nearly blurted out no, but checked himself. Here was his lady love's older brother offering to share his own personal stash. Thymon had been game enough to drink his wine despite having heard bad things about it. Mammals, he said, like whales and humans. How bad could it be? Think of the trust it could build with her family. "Sure. How do you do it?"

"It has a point. You just prick your skin and a drop goes in."

"That's all it takes?"

"Yes. It takes a few minutes to take effect, a lot like your wine." He handed Sten the quill.

Sten looked at the quill, looked at Thymon, then looked back at the quill. He didn't have much choice now. His heart started pounding faster. He was tough. Of course, he thought he was tough enough to take Boole head on and look what that got him. "Is my forearm a good place?"

"Yes."

He unbuttoned his cuff and pushed up his loose white shirt sleeve. He scratched his skin with the point, but nothing seemed to come out. He was actually relieved. "I think I did it wrong."

Thymon stepped over and took it from him. "It's more of a puncture," he said as he poked it straight into his arm. "There."

Sten looked on, trying his hardest to hide his terror and regret at going along with this. "Ow, it's burning." He rubbed the spot, but that did not make it feel any better. "Is it supposed to burn?"

Thymon frowned. "No. It doesn't feel like anything more than a prick."

"Hey, it's getting worse. It's spreading too. Man, it's getting really painful. I think I'm having a bad reaction. What can I take to stop this? Is there an antidote?"

"Not that I know of. I'm sorry, Sten. I don't know what to do."

Sten grabbed his arm at the elbow with his other hand and squeezed to slow the blood flow. I need to find something to keep this in my arm. Here, squeeze my arm like I have it here."

Thymon did as he was told. Sten undid his belt and wrapped it around his arm and pulled it tight."

"I am so sorry. I had no idea this would hurt you."

"I know, it's not your fault. I should've been more careful too. Oh, man! This is really hurting." He was suddenly lightheaded and nauseous. "Oh no." He ran to the edge of the deck and vomited into the sea. Dizziness overtook him and he rolled onto his back, looking up at the sky. He couldn't concentrate to keep the tension on his belt, and he let it slip. He went limp and everything blurred to a fog.

He saw Chielle fly up out of the water and start screaming at her brother in their underwater language of squeals and rattling clicks. The last thing Sten thought before he blacked out was how good their language was at conveying anger.

"How could you be so stupid?! He doesn't have a blubber layer like us!" Chielle wanted to throttle her brother but was more focused on what to do for poor Sten. "Ugh! The both of you stink of wine. Let me guess, you two were drinking and decided to go the next step higher. Reckless, idiot men! Why is he so bruised? Were you two fighting?"

"No, he got in a fight yesterday with someone in town. He was fighting in your defense."

She shook her head. "More male stupidity." She whipped her knife out of its shoulder belt. "Here, hold still." She slashed the ropes that held the weight on Thymon's tail. "Go get Mama."

"What? I'll be branded if I'm seen without the tetherweight."

"Risk it. We need Mama here now. Drunk or not, you're fast enough, so get going."

"What do I tell her?"

She bit back and made a hard decision. "Tell her the truth. The time for secrets is over."

He paused meaningfully. "Really?"

"Yes, we have to tell her so she can decide what's best."

"All right." He leapt into the sea and was gone.

Chielle felt Sten's forehead and it was hotter than it should be. She hunched up her tail and grabbed him under the armpits. The last time she grabbed him like this, he was underwater and she could move him effortlessly. Now she was saving him again, but he was a whole lot harder to move on land. She pushed as hard as she could and managed to lift his torso up and drag his legs behind him. She had to get him to his shack and into bed with blankets. She pushed again and gained another few feet. Thankfully it was high tide with the landing platform up and the ramp was not steep. Half a dozen more heaving pulls and she had him to the top.

Jacio was walking out the wharf. "Jacio, thank goodness! I need your help getting Sten inside."

He ran up but hesitated when he saw his boss unconscious. "What happened?"

"He got drunk and fell. He may have accidentally poisoned himself too. I've got help coming. Can you help me get him into bed?"

"Sure." He grabbed one shoulder and Chielle grabbed the other and between them they dragged him into the shack and up into bed.

Chielle turned to thank him, but Jacio ran out and up the wharf without saying a word. She wondered what he was doing, but couldn't take time to go after him. She pulled the blankets up around Sten and tucked them around him. She checked his breathing and found it steady. He was still way too hot. She laid her head on his chest and prayed. "Rorra, please watch over this good man. Please bring him back to health so I can tell him what a fool he is and how much I love him."

9

"**W**ELL, NOW I SEE WHY you come home smelling of smoke."
Chielle was startled by her mother's voice. Gonnakaa
Mmava walked into the shack's bedroom waving her hand in front
of her face. Thymon followed meekly behind her.

"Mama I'm so glad you're here."

"This is quite the secret you've kept."

Chielle got up from Sten's bedside and let her mother step up
to examine him. "I'm sorry Mama, I didn't want to tell you until I
knew for sure if ..."

"If you really love him? Do you know now?"

"Yes, I do."

Her mother looked at her and sighed. "You've carved out a
hard life for yourself."

"I know, Mama."

Gonnakaa looked over his unconscious form. "He's so beat up."

"He got into a fight. Defending me."

"Really? It looks like he fought the whole village." She picked
up his arm and prodded the sting.

Seeing her mother out of water and next to Sten, she was taken with how petite and old she looked, despite how beautiful she was in her long yellow erda. This struck her as odd, since her mom was such a source of strength in her life.

"Humans usually don't pass out from Lionfish venom. The sting hurts them a lot. He must be allergic. I have a mud that will help with the venom. He's going to have to recover from the shock on his own. I hope he's strong."

"He's very strong," Chielle said a little too quickly.

"Thymon, give me my bag," she directed. "This mud should be mixed up with hot water and smeared all over his arm."

Chielle walked from the bedroom into the shop front half of the shack. She grabbed the tea pot off the grill and stepped over to the rainwater barrel. She caught her mother watching her through the door as she filled it and set it back on the hearth. She turned the bellows crank and brought the coals up to glowing.

Her mother didn't say anything. Her knowing look said it all.

"Yes, I know my way around this shop."

"Does he live here alone?"

"Yes."

"Do you know if he has always lived alone?"

Thymon spoke up. "He told me he used to have a sister, but he didn't say how long ago that was."

"What's your point, Mama?"

"Humans often don't stay with their families. They like to strike out on their own. If he has been living alone for a long time, then maybe that's because he likes living alone."

"Mama, I'm not planning on settling down with him. Yes, I love him, but we're only dating."

"I'm just looking out for my girl. How long have you been dating him?"

Chielle had to think about that one. "Coming up on four weeks."

Gonnakaa turned to Thymon who was standing idly by. "That goes back before you and your crew started making iron spears. Let me guess. Sten showed her how to craft iron, she showed you, and you went and armed yourselves." She rolled her eyes. "My enterprising children." She turned to her son. "Oh, but at your trial you didn't say anything about Chielle."

"She didn't know I was going to make weapons. In fact, she was really upset with us when we showed her. That's why I did not mention her."

Their mother turned back to Chielle. "I hope you realize if it comes out that Sten here was the source of the knowledge that led to those weapons, the Shaman will probably forbid you from seeing him again."

"That's not fair. He showed me so I could make tools. I showed Thymon so he could make tools."

"I didn't say it was fair. I said it was likely."

Lying flat on his back, Sten began to snore.

"Mother of Riptides," Chielle blurted. "What is that sound? Has he stopped breathing?"

Gonnakaa touched his jaw and shifted his head. "It's called snoring. Their tongue falls back when they sleep on their backs. It's not dangerous, just loud."

The kettle began to whistle and Chielle pulled it off the grill. She grabbed a bowl and came back into the bedroom. Her mother scooped out a handful of the mud from its jar and Chielle dribbled in hot water. Gonnakaa mixed it in and applied a handful across the length of Sten's injured forearm. "The heat breaks it down," she explained, "while the mud draws it out."

Thymon said, "We've got company."

Chielle had been so focused on what her mother was doing, she hadn't heard anyone approaching. She started to walk to the front, and met Jacio in the doorway.

He looked from her to her brother and to her mother, suspicion and dread growing by the second. "Chielle, what's going on?"

She shifted to English. "Jacio, it's fine, this is my brother and my mom. I called them here to help Sten with his injuries."

A dark-skinned woman with gray streaks in her pinned-up, long black hair stepped up behind Jacio and said, "My son came and got me for the same purpose."

Chielle heard her mother let out a tight chirp of shocked surprise. The woman spotted Gonnakaa and she too looked shocked.

"Do you two know each other?"

They both ignored Chielle and neither of them said anything for a very tense moment. "Gonnakka, it's been a very long time."

"Patry, it certainly has."

Chielle lit up when she recognized the name. "Oh, Mama, you told me this story. You two used to be best friends when you were teenagers. Now you're Mrs. Bilboa, Jacio's mother. How delightful."

Chielle noticed neither of them were smiling, In fact, neither of them had moved. Watching the two of them stare each other down, Chielle feared they would stop helping Sten. She was about to say something when Patry turned to Chielle.

"My son tells me you and our blacksmith are having an affair."

"Yes. Sten is very dear to me, which is why I sent for my mother to come help."

"He's important to us too," she commented coolly as she stepped over to his bed. Chielle noticed a rustling sound from under the woman's full, black skirt as she walked. "Oh gracious. I heard about the fight. He's worse than I thought." Without looking up to make eye contact, she asked Gonnakaa, "What's wrong with his arm?"

"He was also stung by a lionfish. He had a bad reaction and passed out. The hot mud will break down the venom and keep it from spreading and doing any more damage."

Patry unlaced his shirt and examined his torso which was almost entirely covered in red and purple bruises. "He hasn't seen a doctor. These wounds haven't been treated."

"No," Jacio confirmed. "He came straight here from jail. I changed his shirt this morning when he got back. It was covered in blood."

"Jail?" Chielle asked.

"He and Captain Boole were arrested for public fighting and held overnight."

Patry felt his body and face with her weathered hands. "He's got two broken ribs, but I think all the rest of his bones are intact. Did any of you see if he was vomiting blood?"

"He threw up some food after the fish poison," Thymon said. "But no blood."

Patry shook her head down at Sten. "You are one tough customer. I want to bandage these cracked ribs so they can heal straight and not puncture anything in the meantime."

Gonnakaa, who had been quietly standing by, spoke up. "If he's in shock from the venom, shouldn't we keep him warm?"

"I don't think warm will be a problem." She grabbed the bottom edge of her corset through her white blouse and straightened it gruffly. "It's just another hot, humid day in our tropical paradise. Some of us don't get to run around in our swim suits. I think he'll be plenty warm."

It pained Chielle to watch her mother force herself to not react to the slight. "Can we do anything about the swelling on his face?"

Patry met Chielle's gaze. "If you have some way to apply cold. Cold will take down the swelling."

"Will cold meat work?"

"Sure."

Chielle caught her brother's attention. "Thymon? Get us some fish? A couple of fat perch should do."

He perked up at the chance to do something. "No problem," he said as he slipped out the door.

Chielle found a large empty cloth sack. "Will this fabric work for bandages for his ribs?"

"Yes, that will do fine."

Chielle took out her shell knife and started cutting the sack into strips. The fibers were dry and stiff and hard to cut. She spotted a steel dagger on a workbench and picked it up. She brushed her fingertip across the curved blade and was impressed with its edge. It sliced through the canvas with ease.

Patry lowered her voice and half turned to Gonnakaa. "Is Thymon your son?"

Chielle caught her mother crack a half smile. "Yes, he's my eldest. I have a middle daughter too, Sooreet." She waited for a reaction but got none.

Patry started to lift Sten up into a sitting position and take off his shirt.

"Is Jacio your only child?"

"No. His older brother Horel is grown and moved away."

"Two sons. I bet their father is proud."

Chielle thought she caught Patry flash the tiniest smile, but then it faded. She brought the strips over and stopped cold when she saw his back was covered in long vertical jagged scars. "Oh, Rorra!"

The two older women followed her horrified gaze and looked around at his back. "Oh my, he's been flogged," Patry concluded.

"This is ten, twelve, fifteen lashes. Well, he's been a bad boy. You only get fifteen lashes if you burn somebody's house down, or kill someone. He came to Saint Rochel about a year ago. I don't think I have ever heard where he came from."

Gonnakaa looked up at Chielle. "Does that mean you haven't seen him with his clothes off?"

"Mother!"

"Has he ever mentioned having a criminal past?"

"No, I had no idea. He never let on at all. I guess that means they don't hurt him."

"Scars sometimes don't have any feeling," explained the human. "I'll have to ask Constable Blaine what he knows."

"Or we can just ask Sten when he wakes up," countered Chielle. "Jacio, has he ever talked to you about his past?"

"Only that he apprenticed to be a blacksmith in a town on the far coast."

"It sounds like he came here to make a fresh start," Chielle asserted. "We should give him a chance to tell us the whole story."

Patry and Gonnakaa traded a knowing look. Even though she understood they were patronizing her, Chielle was happy to see the two sharing a motherly moment.

"Fair enough, sweetheart," her mom assured. "We'll let him speak for himself."

"Thank you." Chielle noticed she still held the bandages in her hands. "Do we just wrap his whole chest?"

Patry stepped aside and instructed Gonnakaa, "Here, take his arms and hold him up." She then started wrapping the strips around him, instructing Chielle, "Just keep wrapping them overlapping, snug and smooth."

Gonnakaa commented, "You've done this before."

"My husband is a farrier. He is forever getting stepped on or kicked by horses. I've learned a lot about patching up men."

Chielle caught her mother's eye and saw a flash of daring. "Who did you marry? Would I know him?"

Patry stepped back and let Chielle take over the wrapping. She sighed quietly and turned at last to Gonnakaa. "Yes, you would. I married Wilton."

"I remember Wilton! How wonderful for you."

"And you?"

Her mother tilted her head and smiled. "You're going to laugh. I married Chambor."

"No. You hated Chambor."

"I know, I did. And then, I didn't. People grow up and see things differently."

Patry's smile faltered and she looked away. "Sometimes."

"Look, Patry, I see you are trying really hard to stay mad at me. I don't expect us to go back to being best friends after thirty years just because we ended up in the same room. I just don't see why you have to still carry hatred for me."

Patry turned and looked her in the eye. "You never even apologized."

Chielle could see her mother had played this conversation in her head by how she stayed calm and collected in what was painful just to watch. "How can I apologize for something I did not do? Everyone was so quick to accuse me of stealing that necklace. I knew it was precious to you. I would never want to take something important away from my best friend. You were more important to me than any piece of treasure."

"You could have said so. You didn't even come to me to explain."

"I couldn't, our parents separated us before we could even discuss it."

"You're going to blame this on our parents?"

"I'm not blaming anybody. You may have been heartbroken to think your best friend had chosen a trinket over our friendship. Well, I was heartbroken to see how quickly you believed people who didn't even know me. I can still hear them. 'Of course she stole it. She is after all a mermaid.' I was your friend first, regardless of our species."

Patry looked away. "I don't know, Gonnakaa. That's a lot of water under the bridge. I don't think I can just re-cast you in a different light after all these years of distrust."

"You said I never apologized. I am sorry. I am sorry anything drove us apart. I am sorry we have grown so far apart for so long. We can't go back. We're grown up with children of our own. I am sorry thinking of me still makes you angry. I wish your memories of me made you happy instead."

Patry thought quietly for a long moment. "You're saying what we lost was more valuable than that stupid necklace."

"Oh, absolutely."

She looked up at her old friend and took a deep breath. "That's a big step for me. I'm going to have to think about this."

"Thank you for trying."

Chielle wished the woman had looked more hopeful, instead of confused and sad.

"I will try. I'll stay in touch through your daughter." She turned and left with Jacio following.

10

S TEN STARTED STIRRING AROUND NOON, and Chielle decided she would just wait until he awoke on his own. She wasn't sure how sick he would be, and she figured more sleep was better. His arm was looking much better. She had applied, washed, and reapplied her mother's mud a half a dozen times through the night, and finally removed it for good. His face was also vastly improved. The cold fish filets had pulled the swelling down, even while they had made her hungry. His fever also subsided during the night. All that was left was for him to sleep it off.

Jacio had come at dawn and finished up what work he could without pounding on any metal. Then he ran an errand for supplies, and went home for the day.

She puttered and tidied around the shop while she waited. The sound of the wave swells rushing around the pilings below the wharf was very soothing to her. It really was the best of both worlds. The smell of the hearth she had come to cherish together with the sound of her beloved ocean.

The only thing that would make it more complete would be if Sten would wake up and join her. She considered singing to him or cuddling in next to him to rouse him, but then decided patience would bring its own reward.

When he finally opened his eyes, she was glad to be the first thing he saw. She sat down on the bed next to him and smiled. "Hello there, sleepyhead."

He blinked at her and started to frown, but then smiled. "Hi." He looked around. "How did I get here? Why do I smell fish?"

"Do you remember my brother poisoning you?"

"Oh. Right."

"That was yesterday. You passed out, I dragged you up here, then Thymon and Jacio got my mother and Jacio's mother who treated the poison and bandaged you up from your fight. You've got two broken ribs under those wrappings."

He looked around the room, clearly visualizing the activity she described.

"Yes, it was pretty crowded in here. We patched you up, and I stayed to keep treating your arm and your face. Oh, the fish smell is from the cold compresses to bring down the swelling. You actually look like yourself again today."

He felt his face. "Wow, you really rallied the troops for me. Thank you. Wait a minute. Fish? You put fish on my face?"

"Cold cut filets. It worked too."

He shrugged. "Thank you. Hold on. Your mother. Your mother was here? So she knows ..."

"Everything."

"She let you stay?"

"She wasn't going to drag me away, if that's what you mean."

He digested this for a moment, then realized, "You stayed here taking care of me all night."

She rolled her big glassy eyes. "Yes, I did."

"Sorry, I'm a bit slow taking this all in." He sat up and felt his ribs. "Great job with the bandages."

She reached around and stuffed a pillow behind him to lean on. "Jacio's mom showed me how."

Sten frowned like he was trying to remember something. "Hold on. Jacio said his mother thought very poorly of Merrow, that she had raised him to distrust your people. Yet she came and helped?"

"Well, she came to help you." She tilted her head and squinted. "But that can't be right. Mrs. Bilboa turns out to be my mother's best friend from when they were young."

"Really? That must have been quite the reunion."

"Actually, it was really tense. They had a big falling out and haven't seen each other in decades."

"Wow." He took her hands in his and looked her in the eyes. "Thank you so much."

She slipped her arms around his shoulders and leaned in to hug him. "I wasn't going to leave you in the state you were in."

He squeezed her back. "I remember seeing you shoot up out of the water and start yelling at your brother, and that was the last thing I recall. I guess you heard the chimes after all?"

"No, I didn't hear any chimes. I think the chimes were up on the deck when I arrived."

"How did you know to come?"

"Rorra told me you were in trouble."

He frowned and tilted his head. "How does that work? Don't get me wrong; I'm really glad she told you. I just don't understand how."

"Sound isn't just sound underwater. We've talked about how sounds are muffled yet louder at the same time. Well, for us Merrow, all that vibration creates a sense of place and motion. It's more than just noise. I'm not describing it very well. Along with telling what's around you and what's making noise, you can feel what the ocean is doing. You get an intuition into what's happening all around you, not just within earshot. Sometimes you have to listen for a quiet moment to hear it, and other times it comes at you like a bell. I don't know how else to tell you. Rorra told me you were in trouble."

"That's amazing. How marvelous that you are so in tune with the whole ocean. I'm frankly jealous. We humans don't commune with our god at that literal level."

"No? How do you pray to Atlan?"

"We don't pray to Atlan. We hold Atlan as our ideal. We pray to God. Mostly we pray to God for the strength to be more like Atlan. God doesn't actually answer us. It's a different kind of prayer. In any event, thank Rorra you came."

"I wouldn't have had to if Thymon had thought about what he was doing. He knows you don't have a blubber layer like us."

"Is that why your skin is so firm?"

"Yes, it's our armor against cold, and poisons."

"In his defense, I shared my wine, and he wanted to share his favorite intoxication."

"I understand, and I'm glad you two had your buddy moment. I'm still mad at him."

"All right. I'm not. By the way, I am sorry I wasn't here, let's see, that would be night before last. I told you to meet me here and I wasn't able to make it."

"Yes, you were in jail for public fighting. Jacio didn't know where you were either. I wasn't sure what to think."

Sten looked at her carefully. "I'm sorry if you thought I was standing you up. I was looking forward to seeing you."

She considered his apology and what it meant. "I'm actually glad to hear you say that. I thought maybe I had been moving too fast. I'm still embarrassed about the courtship dance thing."

He caressed her face. "Don't be. I thought it was great. That whole evening was magical."

She looked him in the eyes, those tender if slightly undersized brown eyes, and saw only love. She let herself sink deep into his gaze, deep enough to get lost.

He parted his lips and took in a breath. She waited on his words. "I'm really hungry."

She blinked. "Excuse me?"

"I just realized I am famished. I guess that's a good sign after being poisoned."

She recovered her composure. "Sure, sounds right. I actually wondered if you would be, and I asked Jacio what I should have on hand. He showed me how to make porridge. I'm still amazed at how you rely on fire to do so much. He explained that you grow these grains which you can't chew, but you boil them till they finally soften. Why don't you just grow plants you can eat? I admit it was fun watching it boil down. It just seemed so different than how I would have prepared the grain." She got up and walked to the front room. "Let me get you some."

"Did you say boiled down? Did you take it off the fire?"

"Oh yes. This was a couple of sunstones; I mean hours ago. If I had left it on the grill it would have burned up."

"I'm glad Jacio pointed that out," he called to her.

"Oh no, he left a long time before I started," she called back. She returned and handed him a bowl full and a spoon.

He looked at it and tilted the bowl around. The porridge did not move. The spoon stuck in it did not move. He smiled up at her, then carved out a spoonful and tried it.

She awaited his approval, but it was slow coming. "Good flavor," he said as he chewed deliberately. "Comes out tasting nuttier when it's this dense. This will be filling." He took another bite. "Thank you for making this for me."

"You're welcome."

"I look forward to showing you more of how to cook with fire."

Sitting on the edge of the bed, she reached over and took his hands in hers. "Sten, there's something I need to ask you about. I want you to know I trust you and believe in you."

"All right, this sounds serious."

"We've talked about trust. I promised to always tell you the truth. Now I need you to do the same for me, knowing I will believe you and not judge."

Sten half-smiled knowingly and nodded. "You saw my lash scars when you bandaged me up."

"Mrs. Bilboa counted fifteen and said that would mean arson or murder. I told her not to jump to any conclusions, that we needed to hear it from you first."

"Thank you for that. I don't usually get such an open-minded audience. All right. Let me tell you the whole story. It's not pretty. I have been afraid it would drive you away. I didn't want to keep it a secret, but I couldn't find the right time, or the nerve. Better to be honest.

"Three years ago, I lived with my teenaged sister on the far eastern side of the continent, up in the mountains where it's cold most of the time." He took a breath. "My sister was murdered by a man in our village. He was known to be insane. People just stayed away from him. But he got hold of Sesha and, well, he did terrible things to her before he finally killed her. Only thing is, no one could prove it was him. Everybody knew it was him, but our lawman and judge couldn't make the charge stick. It drove me over the edge.

"When our parents died four years earlier, I stepped up and took care of her. She was my whole life. I lost my mind." He paused and looked away.

"Did you kill the man?"

He looked at her and sighed. "Yes. With an axe. I didn't even try to hide what I'd done. They brought me in. The judge didn't give me the noose because he agreed the guy probably did it and deserved to die. Instead he gave me the most lashes allowed by law. Fifteen. I almost died, but I didn't.

"After that punishment, I thought the townspeople would think I had paid for the crime. But everyone saw me as capable of cold-blooded murder. I had to leave. I spent the next two years wandering all across the land until I found Saint Rochel. It was far enough away that my reputation wouldn't catch up with me."

"I've seen you get angry. You don't seem like someone who loses control and kills."

"I swore I would never strike a man first again. I know what I can do with these hands. I didn't want to hit Boole in the street, but he came at me and I had to fight back. Another act of violence I'm not proud of."

"Does your constable know about your lashes? Mrs. Bilboa said she would ask him about it."

"Shit, really? No. I guess I better explain myself to him then. I'm sorry this came out as some big secret. I really wasn't trying to hide it from you. My coming here was supposed to be a fresh start, a clean break from the past. I don't think of myself as dangerous."

"I don't think of you as dangerous either. You do have a strong urge to save people, even if they don't need it. I wondered why you took up our side so quickly. I see how not being able to save your sister left you feeling. I am so sorry to hear about your loss. I can't imagine what that was like. No, Sten I don't see you as a threat. I see you as a good man who has had to deal with a lot."

"I am very relieved to hear you say that. I want to be completely honest with you."

She squeezed his hands. "That's important. Tell your constable, and no one else needs to know."

He turned his hands over and squeezed hers back. "Thank you."

Patry Bilboa was just leaving the Garden Market Apothecary when the door opened and in walked Vanda Rymerand. Patry was first taken with the light-skinned woman's elaborately pleated bright yellow linen dress, and didn't recognize her right away.

"Mrs. Bilboa, what a lovely surprise!"

"Vanda? Little Vanda, all grown up. My goodness, look at you. What a vision of loveliness you've become."

"Why thank you. You're looking beautiful yourself."

"How is it that I haven't bumped into you in years? This town just isn't that big."

"I left town for a while, but I'm back now."

"Isn't that nice. Welcome back. Are you married?"

"No, ma'am. Almost, a couple of times, but still single."

"That doesn't speak well for the young men around here, what with you wearing bright colors and necklines like that one, and still no suitors."

"I'll take that as a compliment, thank you."

"Well it is grand to see you again. I'm always reminded of how old I'm getting when I see someone I knew as a child, like yourself, suddenly all grown up. Please tell your mother Hello for me. Goodness, it's been an eternity since I saw Selna, at least fifteen years."

"I'm sorry to be the one to tell you, but my mother passed away about a year ago."

"Oh, I am sad to hear that. Was she ill for long?"

"No, she caught a fever years ago that weakened her heart. It suddenly gave out with no warning. Thankfully, she did not suffer."

"I am so glad to hear that. She was such a dear friend for so many years."

"She did mention you from time to time."

"Here I thought it was my lucky day to see all my old friends from when I was young. Selna and Gonnakaa and I were inseparable, you know."

Vanda frowned and grimaced for no reason, but then covered with a smile. "It's good that you have those happy memories."

11

S ITTING ON THE SHOP BENCHES, Chielle watched Sten finish the bowl of porridge she had made one carved-out spoonful at a time.

"I made it wrong, didn't I?"

"What?"

"It's not supposed to be that dense, is it?"

"Well, not really. It's a subtle timing thing. Cooking with fire requires standing there watching it a lot. You did great, given how little instruction you had. Like I said, I'll be happy to show you more about our crazy use of fire for everything."

She rolled her eyes mischievously. "Oh, I found this on the workbench when we cut up a bag to make your bandages." She pulled the steel dagger out of her shoulder sash where she had tucked it alongside her shell knife. "It is so sharp, and it keeps its edge really well. Is it your work?"

"Yes, that's a really fine steel blade, probably one of the best I've ever made."

"It's curved just like my shell knife."

"Do you think anyone in Celidan would give you a hard time about where you got it?"

"What, on me?"

"It looks good in your sheath, there. You can have it."

"Are you sure? Oh, by the swells, thank you. It's beautiful. That's too generous." She smiled at it and slipped it into her sash. "Right, and speaking of gifts, Jacio also brought you something this morning from town." She turned and retrieved a sack. "He said the constable gave it to him, that he found it after your fight. Jacio told me I was not to look, that it was surprise you wanted to show me. I was sorely tempted to peek, but I held off," she said as she handed him the bag.

"Oh, that's right, I almost forgot. This is why I went into town that day." He set the bowl down and opened the bag. "I had our shoemaker build these so I can swim with you. I don't know if they'll work, or if they'll just weigh me down, but ..."

"They're ..." she cut him off, beaming at the flippers, "they're wonderful. This is the best present ever."

"Really? I thought they were kind of clumsy."

"Are you kidding? What could be better than having you in the water swimming at my side?"

He smiled up at her. "I was hoping you'd like the idea."

"I love it, but we're going to have to wait until you've healed. Mrs. Bilboa said she felt two broken ribs, and all those bruises. Your body is four different shades of purple under those bandages."

"Yes, but these bandages are holding everything in place," he said, patting them. "I feel fine. I'm rested, I'm in no real pain. I say, let's give 'em a try."

"You mean take the bandages into the ocean?"

"Don't Merrow ever bandage injuries while in the water?"

She remembered poor Serool's burned hand. "Yes, that's true."

"Well then, what are we waiting for?" With that he grabbed the flippers, stood up and headed out the door.

She caught up with him halfway down the ramp. He paused as he struggled to get his shirt off while the bandages held his body stiff. She stepped up and helped him, only to be surprised at how long the tails of his shirt were. "Your shirt goes all the way down into your pants?"

"Yes," he said frowning at her. "You didn't know that? The pants are way too rough for my crotch and the shirt is much easier to wash."

"Your shirt is a lot like my erda. You just wear pants on over it."

He looked her up and down. "Yes, I guess that's true." He walked down onto the landing and sat down on the edge. She watched with some amusement as he unlaced his boots, took them off, replaced them with the flippers, and laced them up. She was not used to seeing his hands doing the kind of work she usually did.

She slid into the water without a splash and turned to help him in. He lowered his legs in and she took his hands so he could ease down without jolting his body.

"Hey, it's a lot easier to tread water."

"Good." She was concerned with how much he moved his arms around to stay upright. "Please take it easy." He was so clearly not suited to open water.

He leaned over and started swimming, alternating his feet up and down along with his arms, as if he was crawling. He was faster than without the flippers. About as fast as a newborn Merrow, Chielle thought. He pulled up and smiled at how far he had gone. "That works for me!"

His joy at being in the water touched her unexpectedly. She felt her heart flutter and she couldn't help but grin at him. She swam over next to him, took his hand, and began a slow, undulating tail kick, leading him by example. Dipping shoulders, then hips, then fluke, they pushed smoothly through the water. He was having a hard time getting his shoulders to start the wave motion, since he had to keep his face out of the water most of the time. Even with this plowing of the surface, she was pleased to show him how it was really done.

They pulled up for him to catch his breath. He turned around and saw they were several hundred cubits from his wharf. "Holy smokes! Look at how far we came! I had no idea."

She shrugged and smiled at him. "Shall we swim back?" She took his hand and led him again.

He figured out how to breathe in on the upswing so he could push harder with the flippers. By the time they were halfway back to the wharf he had a pretty efficient stroke. She was again surprised at how happy she was swimming alongside him. It felt natural despite his unnatural effort. She reveled in the feeling the rest of the way back.

"It's easier once you get the hang of it," she encouraged.

"I'll say. I never imagined swimming could be so much fun."

She sidled up to him. "You can't imagine how happy it makes me to hear you say that."

He nodded. "I can imagine."

She started to hug him but realized he had to keep moving his arms to stay upright. She leaned in and gave him a quick kiss. Then she instinctively kicked passed him, brushing her body across his.

She pulled up and was just as surprised as he was. Instead of the quizzical look she expected from him, he perked up and grinned widely with understanding. She grinned coyly and did it again, being careful not to bump his bandaged torso too hard as she brushed by. He surprised her by caressing her tail with his hands as she swam by.

She turned to make another pass and saw him attempting to swim passed her. She stayed still and made an easy target of herself. Between his bandages and his pants, his brushing wasn't as sensual as she had hoped, but it was still pretty exciting.

She turned quickly and caught up to him from below, teasing her body the whole length of his. When she came up face to face with him, he wrapped his arms around her and pulled her into a deep passionate kiss. They sank below the surface, but he didn't seem to mind as they tangled legs and fins and arms and lips.

After a moment, he had to break free and kick back up for air. "Sorry."

"Don't be." She stroked his cheek. "You want to get dry?"

He looked her in the eyes, grinned foolishly wide, and nodded.

As he pushed off toward the landing, she circled him, letting her instincts take over. She slid her breasts across him in coiled curves and he fondled whatever part he could squeeze as she swept past. She felt a wave of joyous tension rise all through her body, up through her tail, rippling up her spine, and ending in a wide, shuddering gasp of water through her open gills. A love song of long wavering notes spilled out of her without her even thinking about it. She caught Sten gawking at her underwater with a look of utter fascination. When she danced the side to side writhing dance that went with the song, he stopped swimming, floating there captivated.

She grabbed him by both hands and pulled him along in a spiraling dance. Body against body they spun rolls through the water. She was so caught up in the moment, she had to remember to let him go every few seconds so he could bob back up for a breath. Each time, he held his hands back out for her to spin him around some more. All the while she sang long and sweet, straight from the heart.

When they got to the landing, Sten struggled to lift himself in obvious pain. She gave him a push up and found her hands firmly on his buttocks. He turned around surprised. She hopped up, scooting her own bottom onto the deck. He pulled off his flipper boots while she stood up and straightened her dress. He got up and wrapped his strong arms around her, holding her waist firmly against him. He rubbed his face against hers in the sweetest Merrow kiss. She felt like she would melt in his arms, and suddenly she was in his arms, up off the deck, cradled like a baby, her tail draping down. "Sten, your ribs, you're going to kill yourself."

"Nah, you're light enough" he dismissed as he walked up the ramp.

She wrapped her arms around his shoulders to help hang on. They were solid under her touch. She couldn't help but kiss the muscles that bulged on the base of his neck as he held her aloft. She giggled as he spun her around trying to navigate through the doorway with her long tail sticking out. She coiled it up to help. She wasn't thinking about where he was taking her until she saw the bed. Ah, of course.

"Can I lay you on your fin?"

"Yes, it just folds aside."

He laid her down and he winced as he bent over.

"Sten, we should wait. Your pain is telling you to stop."

He climbed in next to her and grinned. "Yes, but lots of other things are telling me to go." He kissed her face with his lips and his cheeks, starting with her forehead, down the front of her gill fringes, under her chin, and onto her neck. She stretched out her tail and wagged it over the foot of the bed. His kissing journey moved southward and onto her dress. He tenderly scooped up a breast in his hand and kissed it. He didn't seem very sure of what to do with it.

"Let me guess. It's different than you're used to?"

"I'm sorry. It's so firm, it doesn't hardly yield under my touch."

"That's the blubber layer we talked about. I assure you, they are every bit as sensitive as breasts should be."

"Good," he said as he tried unsuccessfully to slide her tunic off her shoulder. "Oh, it's two layers."

"It's actually three. Here let me," she said as she sat up. "These wrap around and hold everything in place," she explained as she unwound the criss-crossed bands of cloth from around her torso and hips, leaving only a simple, loose, translucent light green sheath dress. "There," she said invitingly.

"There indeed," he said as he slipped his hand up under the hem and caressed her hip, waist and ribs. He pulled her close with his other hand and kissed her firmly on the mouth.

Not satisfied to just let him make love to her, she clutched at the base of his neck with one hand while sliding the other around his waist below the bandages. His skin was soft and pliable, yet through it she could feel hard flexing muscles. That, and how every bit of him was covered in hair made him fascinating to touch.

He pulled her dress up and lowered his head to take a breast in his mouth. As he licked her tiny hard nipple, she ran her webbed fingers through the hair on his head. All these sensations were so new and so strange and yet so right and wonderful.

She reached up and pulled the dress off completely. He stared wide eyed, then saw that she had caught him. "Chielle, you are more beautiful than I could imagine." He ran his hand around the edge of her smooth white tummy where it met the silver gray of her back while his eyes drunk her in.

"Thank you."

He found the vents at the bottom of her ribcage and paused uncertainly.

"They're drains for water from my lungs."

"Really?" He went back to massaging her tummy.

"Let's have a look at you," she said reaching for his belt. She had no difficulty figuring out how the buckle worked, or the buttons below it. On the other hand, when she slid her hands around his hips and pushed the trousers down, she was not prepared for what popped out. Now it was she who was caught staring.

"*Pkwee!*" she let slip.

"What?"

She caught herself and raised a hand to her mouth. "Sorry. Little surprised there."

"Surely you've seen one of these before."

"Well, yes. But I'm not sure ..."

"Humans aren't built that different than whales and dolphins, are we?"

"I am not a whale." She let that hang for impact. "I am a mammal, but I also have gills like a shark. I also don't have ... that shape."

He looked down at her genital vent, which of course showed nothing.

"Merrow men are much wider, and nowhere near that long."

"Really? Well, do you want to try this or not?"

"Of course I want to try it."

"What was that sound you made? Was that a swear word?"

"Well, yes."

He smiled broadly. "Which one?"

"Here I am naked talking about sex, so I guess it's only appropriate. I think your word for it is fornicate."

He burst out laughing and went on for a moment. "No, it's not. Our word is 'fuck'. And 'fuck' is the perfect choice of words. Pakwee," he tried.

"Not quite. The *'pkw'* is all one sound. Oh, you can't do that, can you?"

"Pakwu ... nope. Dang. I was hoping to be able to swear in Merrow."

"I think your word 'fuck' works just fine."

"Shall we?"

She grabbed his pants and pulled his legs free. "Depths and waves, you are completely covered in hair."

"Yep, that's me. Lay back and let me see what I can do."

"All right," she said with more than a little doubt in her voice.

He draped himself across her and kissed her cheeks and chin. She rubbed faces and kissed him back, as they worked themselves up. Their hands moved down, clutching and stroking, exploring each other with touch.

One of his hands slid across her tummy and she held her breath. He found her lips and stroked her until he got his fingers inside. She was happy to find she was quite aroused and wet for him. That could only help. His touch was tender and cautious despite the roughness of his fingertips. "Doesn't seem all that different to me." He probed around while watching her reaction.

"Find it yet?"

"What?"

"Whatever you're looking for."

"I'm looking for the sensitive spot to get you ready."

"Sten, foreplay for me is that dance we did in the water. Believe me, I am as aroused as I can be."

"Oh. Really? Great."

She looked down, trying to hide her alarm under humor, and asked, "Are you ready?"

He looked down too. "Oh yes." He straddled her hips and lowered himself against her. He used his hand to guide himself inside. He seemed pretty satisfied until he started to push.

"That's all I've got," she said.

He took hold of himself with his hand again and tried to reposition, seeking another angle.

She grimaced apologetically as he kept trying and finding no way to get deeper. "You feel good inside me, nice and warm," she tried. "Maybe I can find a better angle. Here, you lie back and I'll get on top."

As they traded places, he chuckled, "We're like a couple of teenagers trying to figure it out for the first time."

"It'll be even more fun if we can figure it out." She spread his legs and bent her tail up under her on the bed so she could lower herself down over him. She balanced herself by holding onto his hips with her pelvic fins. He seemed a bit alarmed at the configuration. He probably just wasn't used to having the woman on top.

She rotated her hips and got him inside her without any problem. Again, though, as she twisted and bent to find a way to take in more of him, she just ran out of space. "This is so annoying."

"Is this working for you at all? I mean are you feeling anything?"

"As you can feel for yourself, you are right up against my cervix, which feels great, but you're barely touching the walls of my vagina and that's where all the feeling is."

"Really?"

"Would you stop saying, 'really' every time you learn something new about me?"

"All right, sorry."

"No. I'm sorry. I didn't mean to snap at you."

"This is pretty frustrating." He got a glint in his eye. He grabbed her under the ribs with his fingertips. "Are you ticklish?"

She squirmed off him laughing. "Why, yes I am." She grabbed him by the backs of the knees, hoping they were as sensitive as they looked. "How about you?"

He jumped and howled with laughter. "Yes, yes, I am too." He looked her in the eye. "Chielle, I love you so much. You're a weaver and I'm a blacksmith. We're makers. If anyone can figure out how to do this, it's going to be us."

"If it can be done."

"Oh now, wait a minute. You said the side walls are where you're sensitive."

"Yes, but you're the wrong shape."

"Ah, maybe not." He guided her onto her back and moved down to face her crotch.

"What are you up to?"

"Watch and see," he said before licking her outer lips. He opened her up with his fingers and started licking the inside edge.

"That's nice," she said with a curious nod.

He pulled her open a bit farther and stuck his tongue much deeper.

"Oh, but what about your teeth?"

He looked up with his mouth open, showing his small, blunt teeth. "What about them?"

"Oh," she said, greatly relieved. "Merrow don't use our mouths for sex, because of our sharp teeth."

"There, you see, our different anatomies are going to be good for something after all." He returned to his licking and at last he found the right place.

"Oh, there," she gasped. "That's a good spot."

"All along this edge here?" He stroked her with his finger.

"Yes, but it's much better with your tongue."

"Like this?" he asked rhetorically as he dove in.

What started as an exciting tickling sensation rapidly grew into muscular waves of heat that rolled up her body and down her tail. She found herself gasping for air and clutching the covers. The feeling piled higher and higher and she wasn't sure how or where it would end. "Slow down, too much too fast."

He obliged, but even licking more gently, the waves kept coming. Her tail started quivering and jerking uncontrollably. She caught him looking back at her tail's antics. Her pelvic fins started slapping the bed next to him. He licked deeper and faster and held onto her hips tighter so she wouldn't flip out of the bed. She heaved impossibly guttural groans.

Finally she reached a breaking point and she felt her entire abdomen seize up in pulsating spasms. She gripped his shoulders with her pelvic fins and her tail wrapped over the bottom of the bed and seized the edge. She let out a deafening squeal of pure delight. The first spasm carried all her might, then each one came calmer than the last. After a few moments of complete mindless ecstasy, the waves subsided to a warm glow that flowed through her whole body.

She noticed that she was lying on the bed motionless and limp like a dead body except for her shallow panting breath. She looked up at Sten, who was sitting by her side looking very proud of himself.

She pushed herself up on her elbows. "I have never, in my life, ever, oh come here," she said as she draped her arms around his shoulders and held him. "That was wonderful. I don't know what to say. Thank you. I wish I could do the same for you."

"Ah, but you have those amazing teeth of yours."

She let go and looked him in the eye. "True, but you have that length."

"What do you mean?"

"Merrow men are built short and wide. Merrow women can't pleasure them with our mouths because they're too short to get past our teeth. It's the same problem our men have trying to do what you just did."

"You're saying I'd get past your teeth?"

"Yes, Sten, I'm not going to bite you. I'll hold my lips over my teeth. I've got all kinds of room back in my gill manifolds. You don't look convinced."

"Let's just say I'm cautiously optimistic."

"You said yourself, let's use our differences to make this work."

Chielle lifted her head from his spent penis and Sten immediately pulled her up under her arms and covered her face with kisses. She was so surprised by his reaction she didn't know what to make of it. He held her by whatever he could reach, her head, her shoulders, her waist, as he squeezed her and kissed her a dozen, two dozen times all over her head and neck. He rolled over on top of her and held her tight, burying his face in the crook of her neck.

She laughed at his enthusiasm and wrapped her arms around him. He had made it clear during her pleasuring him how much he enjoyed it. Even with his visceral eagerness, she was surprised at his outpouring of emotion now. He repeated, "I love you, I love you, I love you," into her neck as he held her.

She took a breath and sighed pure joy, "I love you too."

After a moment, she realized he had laid his head on her shoulder and wasn't moving. She pulled back and saw his eyes were shut. He had fallen asleep. "Rest, my darling. You have had quite a day."

She found herself opening her mouth and gills and pulling big breaths trying to figure out the odd taste he had left. It wasn't entirely unpleasant, but she couldn't decide if she liked it or not. No, she didn't like it. He had certainly enjoyed it. She decided she could live with this taste if this was how they were going to make love. Still, she couldn't stop trying to air out her passages.

She gently slid out from under him and twisted off the bed. She went into the front room and found the water bucket and a length of rope. She tied the rope to the handle as she walked out to the edge of the deck. The sun had gone down, and she wasn't concerned about being seen nude in the dark on the vacant wharf. She lowered the bucket and filled it with sea water. Tilting her head back and opening her mouth and gills completely, she lifted the pail up and poured the water in and through and out, flushing everything clean. She tasted again, and was pleased with the result.

When she came back to bed, Sten was awake. "Everything all right?"

"Oh yes," she said climbing in beside him. "Nature calls."

"Hey, is your skin going to dry out sleeping above water?'

"A little rough skin will be worth sleeping in your arms," she said snuggling in.

"Is there anything we can do about that?"

"We use cocoa butter to protect our skin when we are going to be out of the water for long periods."

"I'll get some and keep it on hand for you."

"That would be very sweet of you."

He wrapped his big hairy arms around her and held her snug. "It's the least I can do for my favorite house guest of all time."

12

S TEN FELT HIS BODY GENTLY SWAYING AND ROCKING. It felt good, very natural, like he was being cradled. He felt the sun warming him, and realized he was floating on his back in the ocean. He opened his eyes and confirmed where he was. He had no clue how he got there, but somehow he didn't really care. He wondered what part of the sea he was in. With nothing visible on the horizon, he turned over and swam down into the water. He had forgotten to take a breath, but that didn't matter either, as he was breathing fine underwater. Inexplicably, this did not alarm him. Again, it all felt perfectly normal. Yet he realized this was not normal for him. On a hunch, he glanced back and saw his long, graceful Merrow tail sticking out from his tunic where his legs should have been. Or should they? The tail felt so right.

He marveled at how clear the water was, and how his eyes could focus. He looked at his hands, his webbed hands, and could see every texture. He liked how the back of his hairless hand and arm was gray while the inside was white. He returned to his dive and was amazed at how easily he slid through the water, and how fast he could go with only the slightest effort.

He swam down and the village came into view. His village? Round coral houses were nestled in canyons that surrounded a town center with open markets and an amphitheater gathering place. Merrow swam from building to building, going about their business. He looked up and checked how the village was still close enough to the surface to get plenty of light. He swam down onto a "street" and looked in a window or two to see the sunstones illuminating the interiors. No one noticed him. He felt right at home, even though he knew he didn't belong here.

He avoided making contact with anyone because he was sure he would be found out if he tried to speak their language. He swam into the market to see the shops. To his surprise, they weren't selling goods, but rather taking orders to make things. He saw no money of any kind change hands. He was also pleasantly surprised that he could understand what they were saying. Everyone was friendly with one another and seemed content. He was taken with how peaceful and happy the village seemed to be, and how being there made him feel the same way.

He caught a shadow move out of the corner of his eye up on the surface. He looked up but couldn't see anything. No one around him seemed to notice it. He was going to dismiss it as a passing cloud, but thought maybe he should make sure. He swam up, and again was pleased with how quickly he covered the distance.

He opened his eyes and was a little shocked to find himself dry and in bed. In bed with Chielle, who was still sound asleep. He caught his breath and smiled at his wondrous dream. He played it back in his head, highly amused at how his mind had translated her words into this vision of life beneath the waves. Had she really given him such detail? He loved how the dream had let him see it as a Merrow, the same way Chielle would see it.

Chielle. He turned and lovingly studied her face, the curves of her big eyelids, her darling tiny nose, her wide lips over her pointy little chin. How he had come to love looking at this face, so alien yet so beautiful. He traced the lines of her gill fringes with his eyes, how her ears fit into the rows of gills that folded so neatly together to lay flat, dark in the back and light in the front like the rest of her.

He saw for the first time a scar across one of her gills. It didn't look like a major injury, yet it had not healed right. He started to touch it but stopped himself. He was enjoying watching her sleep too much to disturb her.

How had he come to love her so much? Just the thought of her made his heart ache with joy, even with her right here in front of him. She had become part of him. He had been in love before, but it had never felt so encompassing. Maybe her being so different made him notice more. Or maybe he loved her more than he had ever loved anyone.

He felt the bandages around his chest were tighter than the day before. They seemed to have shrunk when they dried around him over night. They were uncomfortable enough to distract him from his musings. He considered rewrapping them, but decided getting them wet today would loosen them up enough.

The blanket had fallen off her shoulder as she lied on her side facing him. His eyes followed the grey to white dividing line from her neck, over her shoulder, down the length of her arm, and onto her delicate webbed hand. It was all he could do not to follow his eyes with his hands. Oh, how he loved to touch her. The firmness of her skin, and how she felt cool at first touch but then warm once he held her, it wasn't just fascinating, it was intoxicating. It was like her skin was showing what he had learned of her, strange at first, but warm and loving once he was close.

He wondered what she saw in him. This headstrong young woman from another world, why would she find him attractive? She seemed as amused by his body hair as he was taken with her aquatic skin. Beyond their surface differences, though, they had somehow connected very deeply. He didn't know why she loved him, but he was sure glad she did.

A chilling thought crept up on him. Had he forced himself on her too soon? She had seemed every bit as interested in having sex with him. Yet, with his people's history of taking whatever they wanted from the Merrow, he had to wonder if he had taken her to satisfy his own curiosity. He was sure that wasn't true, but he couldn't shake the suspicion.

He heard footfalls approaching up the wharf that he recognized as Jacio's, and realized it was at least an hour after dawn. He would have stayed in bed and bathed in her glow all morning. He slipped out of bed, the twisting of which sent a twinge through his torso, trying to move slowly and not wake her. More blanket fell away, and, when he stood up, he looked back over her naked form. His manhood responded valiantly. He gently pulled the blanket up over her and grabbed a pair of pants. He retrieved her dress from where it had been tossed, and laid it across the foot of the bed for her to find.

He greeted Jacio from the bedroom door, which he closed behind himself. "Good morning," he said quietly. "We have company, who is still sleeping."

Jacio looked at the shirt in Sten's hand and smiled crookedly. His eyes danced around the room, clearly considering all this implied. "I'm certainly glad to see you up and feeling better."

Sten smiled at his careful choice of words. "Thank you for saying so. That was quite the couple of days there, wasn't it? So today I want to move ahead with our diving adventure."

"The one with the hundred feet of bamboo tubing?"

"Indeed." He held his hand over the grate and found the fire had gone cold. He noticed the boy carried a sack. "What have you got there?"

"Bom Stickney gave me this yesterday to bring out to you," he said handing it over. "He said it was for a friend of yours in Silverton."

Sten took the boot out and looked it over. "Yes, this is perfect." He looked back at Jacio. "It's not going to Silverton. It's for Chielle."

The door opened and she stepped in, blanket wrapped around her tunic against the morning air. She smiled coyly at Sten and said, "Good morning. You've got something for me? Good morning, Jacio."

"Good morning, ma'am," he said with a nod.

Sten held up the molded leather. "It's a boot for your fluke. I've noticed the base of your tail gets pretty beat up when you walk around on these wooden planks. We wear shoes to protect our feet from rough surfaces." He handed it to her. "Why not you too?"

She turned it over and undid the laces. "That is the sweetest thing. Thank you. Let me try it on." She pulled up a chair, sat down and coiled up her tail so her fluke was in her lap. "You are so clever. The laces work great," she said as she cinched them up. "It fits." She stood up and took a couple of steps. "This is marvelous.

The leather grips the wood, and I don't feel a thing." She stepped over and hugged Sten. "Thank you. My first shoe."

"You're welcome."

She held up a finger and handed Sten the blanket. "Now, if you will excuse me, I have to take a dip."

Jacio stepped aside and let her leave.

After they heard her splash, Jacio said, "I'm sorry I almost walked in on you."

"Not your fault. You couldn't have known. I couldn't have known. We'll just have to get used to having a lady guest around." Sten spotted the pot of porridge still on the grate. He picked it up and found the already hard cereal now a solid, glued mass. "Do we have anything to eat, besides porridge?"

"You've got a bag of rice and a bag of beans in the lower cupboard. Oh, and there's a pot of lard. I think you finished the jarred fruit you got last week."

Sten grabbed a blunt ended metal file and started prying the porridge mass free. "That's the problem with living in the tropics, food spoils so fast you can only keep on hand what you can eat today."

"Have you not always lived in the heat?"

"Oh no. I grew up in the mountains on the other side of the continent. In winter we could pack food in ice and it would last for weeks. You could put together a collection of different kinds of food and make really wonderful meals." He got the edge up and was pleased to see he could peel the dried mass out of the pot. "How lucky is that? There you go," he declared as he pulled it out with his fingers. "I thought that might take all day." He threw it in the ash bin and held the empty pot up for Jacio to see. "Victory. Can you get the fire started? Chielle and I haven't eaten since yesterday afternoon. I'm starving, and I can only imagine she is too."

"Not for long," she announced at the door holding up a gleaming silver fish so long she had to use both hands. It had a large knife piercing just behind its gills and it was not moving.

"What a beauty, Chielle. Give us just a few minutes to get the fire going and we'll turn him into a feast."

She raised an eyebrow at the fish. "He already is."

"Ah, you're my guest here, so let me cook for you."

She shrugged and nodded. "All right. Where shall I put this?"

He took it from her. "I've got this. You just have a seat. Put your ... tail up and relax. You've worked long enough around here with me laid up."

"By the way, someone docked The *Back Forty* at your landing platform."

"Oh good. I arranged that with Norn Tureck. We'll use that later." He scraped out the rest of the pot with a spoon and filled it with rice and water. Jacio had the fire going, so Sten put the pot with its lid on the grate.

"Is that another plant you have to boil to eat?"

"Yes, dear," he said without looking up from what he was doing. He caught Jacio and Chielle exchanging a grin. "What are you two up to?"

Chielle, turned the grin on Sten. "Thank you for making me breakfast."

"You're welcome." He grabbed a thin knife and the fish and headed outside. He gutted it, beheaded it, and tossed the offal into the sea. When he stepped back in, Chielle looked at the fish as he walked by and he caught a flash of disappointment. "It'll be great," he assured her.

He melted a dollop of lard in a skillet while he split the fish down the middle. Chielle leaned forward to watch what he was doing as he placed the fish halves into the bubbling lard skin-side down. He checked on the rice, and watched her watching the fish. "Have you ever had cooked fish before?"

"No."

He put a lid on the skillet and moved it to the side of the grate away from the main heat. Then he went into the bedroom and retrieved a bottle of brown liquid.

Jacio recognized it. "Is that the fruit stuff that Mrs. Mitchne sells in town?"

"Yes, she calls it her Everything Sauce. Have you had it?"

"It's really good."

"Do you know what it's made from?" Chielle asked.

"She won't tell anyone, cause it's her secret, but I can taste pineapple, molasses, and some kind of nut or bean. Here, take a sniff."

He handed her the open bottle and she tried it. "Just smelling it makes my mouth water. She put her finger over the top and tilted it. She looked dubiously at her wet finger before tasting it. "Sweet and salty at the same time. It's tasty."

"I'm glad you like it, because the whole meal is going to taste of it." He checked the rice again and it wasn't yet done. "Do you have anywhere you need to be today?"

"Not really. Are we going somewhere with the boat?" she tried again.

"Yes, we are. I just don't know how long it will take."

"I always have plenty to do back home, but I don't have to be back by any particular time. Where are we going?"

"You'll see." He saw her shoot a glance at Jacio, and he held his hands up that he wasn't going to spoil Sten's surprise.

Sten checked the rice again and it was done. As was the fish. "Jacio, three plates please if you will." He doled out the rice, then scooped the fish flesh off the skins and over the rice, then liberally splashed on the sauce. "Here you are."

"The fish doesn't look like fish anymore. It smells different, too." She tried a forkful and nodded. "It tastes like it smells, which is not bad."

Jacio interjected around his own full mouth, "Fanciest breakfast I've had in a long time."

Their conversation stopped as all three dug in. All through the meal, Chielle kept shifting between dubious looks at the food and loving smiles at Sten.

When they had finished, Sten resumed his hustling pace. "Let's get this going," he said to Jacio.

"Going ... wherever," she commented to herself.

He grinned. "You'll see."

Sten headed first to the heaviest of the many items stacked up at the end of the wharf, the crank bellows. He started to lift it by himself, but his broken ribs were not having any of it. "Jacio, I'm going to need your help with this." So began the rather tedious job of carrying the equipment down the ramp and onto the boat.

Chielle stood by appraising what she saw. Sten watched her piecing the parts together in her mind. She seemed to be struggling with it, but she did not say anything. They carried the bellows, the beaten bell helmet with the sealed glass window, the twenty lengths of bamboo pipe, several coils of rope, and lastly his swim fins. Chielle helped carry some of the pipes and ropes. At one point, Sten saw her test fitting one of the rubber ball joints onto the end of one of the bamboo pipes. Again, she did not ask any questions.

When they got it all loaded, she turned to him and said, "Clearly you have your heart set on doing this, so I'm not going to try to talk you out of it. Of course I hope this works. If it fails, I will be right next to you ready to bring you to the surface. Have you tested it?"

"Individual parts, but not all together," he admitted.

She blinked and sighed. "I'll stay close by."

In that moment, he loved her more than ever. He hugged her and held her for a moment, whispering in her ear, "Thank you."

She seemed to be wrestling with something. "I've been thinking, and this is probably a good time." She reached into a pocket fold in her knife shoulder sash and pulled out a bracelet of strung shells. Before he could say anything, she grabbed up his arm and wrapped it around his wrist. Before she tied it, she looked him in the eyes. "You know that I love you?"

"Of course, and I love you."

"I want my people to see you are with me. It will show them you should be accepted."

"Why do I think this means more?"

Her gaze faltered. "You're right, it does."

He wanted to make this easier for her. "Yes, I will wear your bracelet and show the world I am with you."

She brightened, blinked, and looked relieved. "Thank you."

While she tied off the strings, he reached up with his free hand and propped up her chin. "You make me feel like an awkward teenager too."

They fell into laughter and each other's arms.

When they set sail, she directed them to the spot above her village. "Celidan is about ten of these pipe lengths straight down. With twenty, you should have some side to side mobility."

"That's what I was hoping for."

"Take down the sail. We're too deep to set the anchor, and you're above my home anyway. With the sail up, the wind will blow the boat away, with you attached, before you see anything."

Sten put on his fins and climbed overboard. Jacio handed him pieces of pipe and ball joints, and Sten stuck them together. Chielle hopped in and helped. The pipeline floated as it grew. Last out was the bell. Chielle and Sten held it upright with air inside to keep it buoyant while Jacio held the rope that was attached to its top. Once it was attached to the pipeline, Jacio handed Sten two solid metal weights, which Sten hung on either side of the bell. He yelled up to Jacio, "Start pumping!" before he ducked up under the bell as it started to sink.

Sten was pleased to see the level of the water inside the bell pushed down by the air pressure coming in through the hose fitting at the top. The air pressed down under the edge and created streams of bubbles that floated upward. It took him a moment to figure out how to hold onto the side handles and keep himself upright, with his body in the water up to his ribs. The bell just fit over his upper body with no real room to move his arms inside. He looked out the window and saw Chielle watching him with a very worried look on her face. "It's working great!" he yelled, in hopes that she could hear.

She nodded and vocalized without opening her mouth. What came through the walls of the bell sounded like, "Good."

Very clever of her.

As he descended, he realized how cramped the inside of the bell was. It only held a few breaths of air and his breathing was loud inside the metal enclosure. He never thought of himself as afraid of enclosed small spaces, but this was certainly putting that fear to the test. When he checked the fit on the surface, he had thought of it as an umbrella. Here underwater, it was his whole world. He tried to focus on how big everything was outside through the window.

Then he felt the water level starting to rise inside the bell. He yelled to Chielle, "Tell Jacio to pump faster."

She nodded and took off to the surface.

A moment later the air pressure increased and once more pushed the water down to the edge. The air pressure inside the helmet was making it difficult to breathe, and his ears felt like they were being crushed. He reached up with one hand and held his nose and blew to adjust the painful pressure inside his head. He was pleased to find that helped a lot.

He caught a glimpse up at the jointed pipeline, and saw small air bubbles streaming from around each rubber ball fitting. He wondered how long he had before Jacio became exhausted.

By then he saw the bottom coming up. He peered out the window as shapes came into view. Chielle reappeared and he gave her a thumbs-up sign.

At first, he wasn't sure what he was seeing. The bottom was made up of large round hills, one of which he was about to settle onto. Chielle motioned for him to swim to one side, which he did easily with the flippers. He landed on flat sand next to the hill, and suddenly realized the hill was a house, a round, cultivated coral house. It was just as she had described. He was also amazed it was just like the ones in his dream.

Two Merrow, a man and a child, swam around the house to face them. Chielle started talking to them. Although he could not understand them, it was clear they were upset, and she was reassuring them. There was a lot of pointing at the surface, and Sten couldn't tell if they were going to let him stay on their property.

The pressure in his ears was hurting again, so he held his nose and blew and could focus again.

Chielle turned to him and started to say something but paused. She screwed up her face as she figured out how to make English words inside her head underwater. Sten listened hard to figure out the words in the sounds. "They will let you stay, but they fear you will die in their yard."

"Thank them. I'm going to walk around," he yelled back. Walking was more swimming in long, slow leaps. The flippers let him maneuver and land without tripping.

The houses were organically curved, multichambered coral caves with all the expected reef creatures living on the outside. As he walked between two, he saw window portals. Some of them glowed from within. He turned to Chielle, and found her right next to him. "May I see a sunstone?"

She motioned for him to follow her over to a window.

"I don't want to intrude by looking into someone's home."

She held up a hand, then darted around the other side of the house. A moment later she swam out of the nearby window holding a rock about the size of a human head, oblong and smooth, glowing with a brilliant yellow light. He reached out from under the edge of the bell and touched it. It was cold. "That's amazing."

She took it back to the window and three Merrow were crowding there watching him. He waved from under the edge.

"Which way is the center of town?"

She frowned and shook her head.

"A marketplace?"

She grimaced in thought but then shook no again.

"A church?"

She brightened and nodded. She took hold of the rope on top of the bell and lifted him up over the houses. Now that he understood what he was looking at, he could see the houses lined an array of canyons. Again he was taken with how accurate his dream had been.

She lowered him down in front of a curved hollow in a hillside. This was the amphitheater from his dream. She alighted him in the bench seats that had been cut into the rock. He looked down to the center and was awe struck with what he saw. The circular "stage" shimmered like a mirror, and in it he thought he could see a reflection of not just the sea above, but of more ocean than he should be able to see at that angle. He didn't understand what he was seeing, but it was so beautiful he just stood and stared. He was sure he had not seen this reflection when Chielle lowered him. It must be a trick of the angles and the light. It looked more like a window than a reflection, a window out to the whole of the ocean.

"It's beautiful!" He tore his eyes away and asked Chielle, "What is it?"

"We call it the Eye of Rorra."

"It's like I can see the whole of the sea. Do you worship Rorra here?"

"Yes, every day if we can. It reminds us of her presence."

He looked again and let himself be absorbed, transfixed, transported by the view that seemed to open up wider and deeper the longer he stared. It was as if the entire ocean, countless miles of it, was suddenly all right in front of him to see.

Chielle was saying something but he wasn't listening. Then she knocked on the bell and that woke him from his reverie. "We have to go!" He looked up and saw three large Merrow men swimming straight at them. Chielle swam up to meet them. All three wore the same red robes. Two of them stopped to talk to her but the third swam around her and came up to Sten. He stared into the window and looked around as if looking for something other than Sten. "It's just me, Sten Holdsmith, the blacksmith from Saint Rochel." The man seemed entirely unimpressed.

Sten looked passed him and saw Chielle was in quite a heated exchange, with the two men pointing and yelling. It looked like they were about to arrest her when she darted away and swooped down to Sten. She said something curt to the near guard, grabbed the rope on top of the bell, and started up.

Sten unhooked the side weights and let them drop while he kicked with his flippers to speed the ascent. As the pressure lessened, the air started bubbling up out of the bell, since Jacio was still pumping hard enough for the deep. Sten's ears felt like they were going to blow out so he grabbed his nose and sucked in until he felt the pressure subside. It only took a few seconds to reach the surface. Chielle was clearly not wasting any time.

Sten ducked out of the bell and grabbed it by the rope. He turned around, found the boat many yards away, and called to Jacio. "We're over here! Can you pull me in by the rope?"

"Chielle, your temple was fantastic! I've never seen anything so beautiful."

She kept nervously ducking her head under the surface.

"Do you think they're coming for us?"

"I don't know. I'm afraid I may have gotten us into some real trouble showing you the temple. Those were our shaman's templar guards. They have the power to enforce our laws anyway they see fit. They answer only to the shaman."

"Did you know showing a human your sacred ground was illegal?"

"No. The temple is open to everyone. That's why there are no walls around it. It was the reason Celidan was built here. I can't imagine there is a law forbidding access."

"There doesn't have to be a law," Sten supplied. "Distrust of humans would be plenty for the guards to move to protect the site. The good people of Saint Rochel would certainly take up arms if they saw a Merrow walk into the sanctuary of the Atlantean temple. They probably saw my very stepping on that ground as a desecration." He looked around as they neared the boat. "Doesn't look like they followed. Let's just hope they're happy with shooing us away."

"How was it?" Jacio called out as they approached. He was covered in sweat.

Jacio and Chielle both needed to help Sten up the rope ladder onto the boat. His ribs were really hurting, but he was much too excited to let it slow him down. "It was everything I hoped it would be. Their town is beautiful, in the most peaceful, natural way. We may have trespassed a bit, so we need to pack up and get out of here just as fast as we can. Thank you for cranking out that air. I can see it was a chore, but the bell worked perfectly."

The three of them loaded the bell and pipes onto the boat and headed out.

As Sten steered up to dock, three Merrow men climbed onto the landing platform to greet them. "Damn, they followed us after all."

"No," Chielle corrected. "These aren't the guards. These guys are smiling."

"Hello," Sten ventured. "Who are you?"

"I am Aalto, and these are my brothers Pinngot and Raggeck. We are the Blauoon Family Builders. We are fifth generation stone masons."

Sten left the tying up to Jacio and he climbed off the boat to face them. "I am Sten Holdsmith, Saint Rochel's town blacksmith."

"Oh, we know who you are, Mister Holdsmith. We heard about your visit to Celidan today, and we wanted to congratulate you on your adventure in person."

Chielle stepped up alongside Sten. "Blauoon. Yes, I've heard of you. I don't mean to be suspicious, but there must be something more pressing than congratulations for you to risk censure to come here."

"You are right, Miss Mmava. It is in fact the risk you speak of that brought us here. We had hoped that your visit was a sign that our two villages were now dealing more openly."

Sten smiled and shook his head. "If only that were true. I'm sorry to say, gentlemen, that my visit was not official or sanctioned by either village. It was just me risking a peak at your beautiful town."

The three brothers traded disappointed glances. "Does that mean we are not yet able to trade for steel tools from you?"

Sten took a long deep breath, as deep as he could with the bandages confining his chest. "You're stone masons. I imagine you could use tempered hammers and chisels?"

"Oh, most certainly."

"I'll tell you what. Sometimes you have to just make the changes you want to see in the world. It takes several steps to work up tool quality steel, so it's going to take a day or so to do it right. What do you have to trade?"

"Pearls. We just finished a job for a jeweler who gifted us with bags of pearls."

Sten heard Jacio on the boat involuntarily cough. Sten had to restrain his own reaction. "That should do nicely. Three sets of hammers and chisels. Can you come back the day after tomorrow, say in the afternoon?"

This time the three exchanged broad surprised smiles. "Yes, sir."

Sten held out his hand and shook with each of them. "It's a deal. Safe journeys, gentlemen."

"Good day to you, sir."

When they had left, Sten turned to Chielle who regarded him with one raised eyebrow. "You just can't get into enough trouble today, can you?"

"So it would seem."

By the time they got the diving equipment off the boat and up the ramp onto the wharf, the heat of the afternoon was upon them. Chielle cooled off with an occasional dip in the ocean, while Sten and Jacio consumed quite a bit of his rainwater supply.

Once they were done, they relaxed in the relative cool of the shack, lounging on chairs and benches. "Sorry that took so long. I had hoped to be done before the heat arrived. That's something I don't think I will ever get used to about living in the tropics. Every afternoon you lose two or three hours because it's just too hot and humid to do anything."

"I must say, we don't have that problem under the surface."

"I've been living that pattern my whole life," Jacio added. "I just plan around it and enjoy the break. Some folks eat their biggest meal of the day during the heat, since you're not going to move around much afterwards anyway."

Sten got up and started poking around in his larder. "Speaking of meals, maybe one of us should run into town and get something. I'm running low on everything."

"You're going to make me run into town at midday for groceries," Jacio said, without making it a question.

"Heads up!" Sten called as he threw a bag of coins to him.

Jacio grabbed a sun hat and headed out. "Be back soon."

Sten found a sketch he had been working on. "Speaking of going into town, I've been thinking about what life will be like once we get passed this time of conflict. I've only been here a year, but my impression is things weren't always this hostile between the two villages."

"My mother says everyone got along much better when she was a girl. Jacio's mother and my mother were best friends."

"You said they had a tense moment when they bumped into each other helping me."

"Yes, that was quite the reunion. They parted badly years ago, and they weren't sure how to handle suddenly being in the same room."

"If things used to be better just twenty years ago, then lots of people on both sides must remember those times. That means there is hope we can repair things if we just remind those folks how good it used to be."

"Everything is so different than how my mother describes it. Something must have changed. I don't know if anyone was ever really satisfied with the treaty, but at least young people worked around it."

"Young people who hadn't learned to hate yet. Chielle, I have a question for you. You'll probably have to ask your mom."

"All right. You sound like this is something that's been bothering you."

"It is. It's been gnawing at me ever since I went to Silverton. You know how all the women here in Saint Rochel wear stiff bodices and corsets?"

"Sure. Human women need to support their breasts."

"It turns out that style is Alcan in origin. Indru women traditionally hold their breasts in place with wrapped soft fabric, which they then wrap all the way around to make a dress."

"Sounds pretty."

"It is. And it's less binding in this heat and humidity. When did the Indru women here give up their traditional soft clothing and start wearing the Alcan stiff bodices and corsets?"

"I don't know. A better question is why."

"I think it had to do with being accepted by Alcan society, but I haven't figured out how that works. If this shift happened in your mother's generation, or even in her mother's generation, that might point to a change in racial attitudes, which might shine some light on why things have broken down so badly between the humans and Merrow."

Chielle thought about this for a moment. "You've got some big jumps in there, like there are big pieces missing. I will ask my mother what she knows about a change in women's clothing. Was it just the women?"

"No, the Indru men inland have traditional clothing too, again, softer and looser. They also gave that up for more Alcan styles out here on the coast."

"Do you think figuring out how things have changed will show us how to set things right again?"

"I hope so. In the meantime, if things haven't always been this bad, maybe we can change some minds by educating them, and showing them we aren't enemies. I visited your village, and at least some of your people seemed happy about that, like the mason brothers. I wonder if we should let my townspeople see you here, one at a time, to see Merrow are not a threat."

"They already know I'm here. Your stone mason was very angry to see me here. Your fishermen beat you up for sympathizing with the Merrow. I don't think Saint Rochel is ready to accept me."

"You're probably right."

"What have you got there?"

Sten looked at the drawing and sighed. "Just me being a dreamer. Jumping to conclusions." He handed her the paper.

"It's a chair with oversized wheels."

"You turn the wheels by pushing on the tops of them."

"This would be a way for me to get around on land. In the village?"

"That was my thought. Pretty silly, now that I think about it."

"No, not silly. Just a few years ahead of time. It's lovely to think we will see a day when I can roll around town and be welcomed as normal. Maybe I'd wear a dress to cover my tail. Your people seem most distressed by bare Merrow tails. It's a great idea, Sten. Just a bit soon, I'm afraid."

Jacio ran back down the wharf and burst in. "You gotta hide, or run, or something," he told Chielle.

"What's wrong?" Sten asked.

"There's an angry mob right behind me!"

Chielle and Sten looked out the wharfside window and saw about ten men, led by Selric Boole.

"They're going to see you leave," Jacio insisted. "They're already boiling mad. Who knows how much worse they're going to be if they see you here."

Sten and Chielle stepped to the door and stopped. When they unloaded the boat, they had piled the diving pipes up along the edge, and so the two-step path was now a six- or seven-step path. Thinking fast, Sten grabbed a bucket of sea water that he used for cooling hot metal. He held it up and asked Chielle, "Will this work? Or not?"

She regarded the bucket, looked him in the eye, took a breath, and nodded.

He poured it over her, and she disappeared. Her clothes were still visible, so she peeled them off and handed them to an astonished Jacio. They watched as her fluke made wet footprints, one after the other to the edge.

Boole and his mob pulled up in front of the door. He was hobbling on crutches and his face was covered in bandages. It was obvious how mad he was even with the mask. "What the hell is all this for, diving? You've been down to the fin village, haven't you? I knew it! You're conspiring with them against your own people!"

Sten stepped out to face them. "You don't know the first thing about them. I'm at least trying to learn. It's a big ocean. There's no reason our two villages can't get along. We need to know more about them so we can work out something more than just driving them out of their fishing grounds. Yes, I visited Celidan, and you know what I found out? They arrested the young mermen who attacked your boats in Harper's Meadow. They don't want the violence either. The only person who wants a war is you, Captain Boole. You only want those fishing grounds if you can take them by force."

A couple of Boole's men looked at their bearded captain suspiciously.

Sten pressed his point to them. "Wouldn't you rather live in peace? Do you really want more blood on your hands, especially if we find there is a better way?"

Boole heard the mutterings behind him and scowled back at them. "Don't listen to him. He's on their side. He'll say anything to stop us from defending what's ours."

Sten caught Jacio out of the corner of his eye, headed around the mob towards town. Jacio tossed Chielle's clothes over the side. He winked at the boy and Jacio took off running.

"Sten, you've become more of a hazard to the safety of this town than the value of your workmanship. We can get another blacksmith. We can't live with the man who taught the fin how to make steel weapons to use against us. Seize him, men!"

Four men surrounded Sten and held him by his arms.

"Oh, now you're my judge? Who gave you authority to arrest anyone?"

"Somebody's got to stand up for what's right. Bind him!"

The men grabbed ropes and tied his arms to his body and his feet together.

Sten was undeterred. "Look at me, Selric. I'm standing tall after defeating you in single combat. You're crippled up and need to turn your sailors into lackeys to do your dirty work for you. I'm diving to the ocean floor, trying to find a peaceful solution, looking to the future. You know why I'm not afraid of you, and why you slink out here like a thief? Because I'm right. My righteousness makes me invincible."

The men all stepped back, and Boole clenched his fists and turned bright red around his bandages.

"That's right, I'm quoting scripture. I am living the Atlantean ideal. I am seizing every moment for the betterment of all."

Boole screamed and threw down his crutches. He staggered up to Sten, attempting a string of insults that just came out as furious gibberish. "Fucking fin lover! Taunt me with Atlan! Go die with the damn fin where you belong!" He threw his arms around Sten's waist and picked him up while driving him backwards and over the edge.

Sten was surprised but not disappointed. "You're going to kill a tied-up prisoner? What a coward!" He had half hoped Boole would lose control and commit a real crime. As he went over the side, Sten saw Boole's men were shocked as well.

13

S TEN HIT THE WATER A LOT HARDER than he expected and pain lanced through his ribcage. He tried as hard as he could to hold his breath in, but the spasm was too much, and his air jetted out of his mouth. With no buoyancy, the heavy ropes dragged him down like a stone.

Chielle was waiting for him, the steel knife in hand, as he had hoped. He held still and let her cut his arms free until he could pantomime that he had no air. She grabbed him by the face, sealed her lips around his, and breathed into his mouth, filling his lungs. Her breath was sweet and hot. She then freed his legs.

He motioned for them to leave underwater. He pointed up and shook his head no, hoping that made it clear that he wanted the men to think he had drowned. She smiled and nodded, then grabbed him under the armpits and swam away. He winced as his ribs protested against the strain, but he managed to hold onto his borrowed breath.

The air she gave him did not last long, but he wanted to be far away from the pier before they surfaced. She must have felt his struggling because she looked down at him and nodded toward the surface. He shook his head no. He pointed up at the bottom of a boat sailing by. He expected her to keep swimming, but she let go of him and swam down.

In a few seconds she returned carrying a hideous creature with a coiled shell on one end and a mass of wriggling tentacles on the other. He could not imagine what she had in mind to do with it. She held it up and let it go, at which it started to dart away. She caught it and motioned to him that it floated. She pulled the tentacles to one side and showed him a gap next to the edge of the shell. She puckered up and indicated that he should stick his lips into the gap.

He thought about this as long as he could with his lungs burning. It floated, so it had air inside. She couldn't mean he was supposed to suck the air out of the shell.

She must have read his expression, because her reaction was to nod yes and push it up to his face.

He raised his eyebrows and hoped she appreciated the trust he was putting in her. The creature was reaching and grasping angrily at her hand with its tentacles. He was not usually squeamish, but this pushed him right to the edge. He grabbed the shell, blew out his remaining air, pressed his lips into the gap and sucked hard. The gap popped open and he got a lungful of the foulest smelling air he had ever inhaled. He held back the urge to cough, held on to it tightly, and felt his lungs ease. It was good air even if it did smell bad. She grabbed him under the armpits and raced off again. The poor creature tumbled from his hands and sank.

He faced her stomach when she swam with him like this. He wrapped his arms around her hips below her dorsal fin, hugging her around her tunic, wanting to make it easier for her to hold him yet not get in the way of her tail that was propelling them both. Her muscularity and athleticism were impressive and tantalizing.

She brought them to the surface as Sten saw the bottom come up shallow beneath them. He had not seen any boats for a while. He poked his head up and took a much-needed breath of fresh air.

They were at a narrow beach that was backed by a cave. He swam in and stood up in the lapping surf. He looked around and saw only ocean. "Where are we?"

She kneeled on her folded tail next to him. "Around the point to the south of your town, facing west. A rocky reef runs right in front of here," she said with a wave of her arm. "Boats can't come near this place."

"Very nice," he said absently as he looked around. "By the way, will that shelled creature be all right? It dropped once I stole its air."

"Yes, it will be fine. It makes the air naturally inside the shell. It will be floating again by tomorrow. I used to suck the air out of them for sport when I was little. I never thought I would use that trick in an emergency like today. Do you want everyone to think Captain Boole killed you?"

"Our Constable refuses to punish anyone until a crime has been committed. Boole is stirring the whole town against the Merrow. If we are ever going to move toward understanding and peace, then Boole has got to go."

"You're not going to go back?" she asked.

"Oh, I'll go back, and Boole might not be tried for murder, but he has shown everyone what a madman he is. Blaine will keep him locked up for that."

The two of them walked out of the surf and sat on the beach while they talked.

Chielle seemed troubled. "I don't understand how waiting helps things. If you go back, you can testify against him."

"Jacio ran to get Blaine. Boole's own men were horrified when he threw me over. I want to give them the chance to testify against him. If his own men turn against him, he will lose credibility with the whole town."

"But you don't know if they will."

"I'm willing to give them the chance to do the right thing." Sten laughed out loud. "Sweetheart, look at us. You, the Merrow, are wanting to take action right away, while I, the human, want to wait and let things run their course. Isn't that backwards?"

She squinted and sniffed. "Are you laughing at me?"

"No, not at all. I think it means we're rubbing off on each other." He scooted over on the sand and put his arms around her. "No, Chielle, I am not laughing at you."

She finally put her arm around his waist. "How long are you planning on staying away? You could borrow your friend Norn's boat and stay on it anchored to this reef. No one would ever see it."

"Well, I don't want to put Norn on the spot with a secret like that. Yet I can't just borrow it without asking, since that would be stealing. Besides, he'd come looking for it. This cave is pretty, but not much of a home. Maybe I'll just stay away for a day or so."

He lay back on the warm sand. "I welcome a day of quiet. Today has been probably the most exciting day of my life, and the most exhausting."

"How are your ribs feeling?"

"Bad, like everything's come lose. I'll rewrap it when I get up. Right now, I'm just going to soak up this peace." He closed his eyes for just a moment, but they stayed shut as he fell fast asleep.

Chielle made plenty of noise unpacking the net bag of jars she had brought from home, hoping the clatter would wake Sten. She finished setting up the meal and he still hadn't stirred. "Sten. Sten?" She jostled his shoulder. "Sten, wake up. We have to rewrap your broken ribs. I also brought dinner for us."

He finally roused. He blinked and rubbed his face with both hands. "Hi." He started to sit up but flinched. He rolled to one side and pushed himself up carefully. "Did you say something about dinner? Oh, wow. Look at that."

She sat back and let him take in the spread of prepared plants, fish, and other meats she had laid out on some rocks on the beach.

"This is beautiful, Chielle. Thank you for going to all this trouble. It all smells great too. I'm famished. I guess we haven't eaten all day."

"You made breakfast, I made dinner. It was something I wanted to do for us."

He got up and kneeled in front of the food. "You're going to have to tell me what each of these are, 'cause I actually don't recognize any of this except for the fish slices."

She scooted in next to him. "This is roe; it's the eggs from this really big deep-water fish. This is sea urchin. This is shark meat, which you eat with this spicy spread made from sea grass. This is abalone, which is the foot from this big flat snail like creature. It's my favorite. This is pickled kelp."

He picked up a leaf. "It's lacy, pretty." He took a bite. "It's crunchy … tasty too. Not as salty as I expected."

"Do you want to re-do your bandages first, or eat first."

"Are you kidding? You lay out this wonderful food and ask me if I want to wait?"

"You're right," she chuckled. "I'm pretty hungry too."

He picked up a slice of abalone. "Is this all raw, and it's all right for me to eat it?"

"Absolutely. Everything was harvested this afternoon. It hasn't had time to go bad."

"You know, this morning I was griping about how I can never keep food fresh for more than a day, and how I was spoiled in winter with the snow that I could stockpile all different kinds of food. Your village must pick and catch and prepare food constantly to have everything fresh, since you don't dry or cook anything. How do you keep up with that?"

"There is always plenty to do, and Rorra provides whatever we need."

He took a bite of the abalone. "That's delicious. It's chewy, but I like it. It tastes a lot like clam chowder, only richer. I can see why it's your favorite."

"What's a chowder?"

"It's a soup where you cook meat in milk with potatoes to thicken it up."

"Sounds … interesting. I'm not sure I will ever understand the thinking that goes into cooking food."

"Don't even get me started on all the stuff we steam wrapped up in banana leaves. That took me a while to appreciate when I first moved to the tropics."

She stared at him waiting for a punchline.

"Well, I love what you did preparing this. Everything is so clean and neatly sliced and stacked. I want to try all of it." He handed her a slice of abalone. "Here, dig in yourself."

She did enjoy the food, but she enjoyed watching him explore it even more. It was another way for her to share her world with him. He had proved that at best he would only be able to make short visits. This was a way for her to bring it up to him. As she explained the dishes to him in between taking bites herself, she realized what she was doing, and wondered at how she wanted to share. Of course she wanted to, she was giving her heart to him, and he to her.

After he had sampled everything and she had answered all his questions, they turned while finishing the meal to watch the sun going down in the west. It had not rained, the ocean was calm, the usual afternoon breeze was mild, and the sun was warm even as it sank. She cuddled up next to him and he put his arm around her.

"That's a beautiful sight," he said softly.

"That's Rorrapanga. The sea of love."

"Does she have different names for her different moods?"

"Yes, she does. She's a goddess. It takes a lot of names to describe a goddess."

"I think that's true of all women. That's certainly true for you."

She looked up at him without taking her head off his chest. "Do tell."

He looked into her eyes and she looked into his. He didn't look away, and she let herself get lost in his loving gaze. "Let's see. There is Chielle the Daring, Chielle the Inquisitive, Chielle the Capable, Chielle the Inspiring, and I mustn't forget Chielle the Assertive. There is also Chielle the Caring, Chielle the Generous, and Chielle the Loving. Then there is also Chielle the Exotic, Chielle the Beautiful, Chielle the Fascinating, Chielle the Sensual, and lastly, Chielle the Captivating. It's that last one, Chielle the Captivating, who can perform real miracles, like turning a blacksmith into a poet," he said with a wink.

She wrapped her arms all the way around him and rubbed against his bandages. "Oh, we need to rewrap these or you're not going to heal right."

"Ah, now? I wouldn't want to ... break the mood."

She sat up and started unbuttoning his shirt. She grinned mischievously and said, "Not at all. This way I get to put my hands all over you."

"Well, if you put it that way." He got up on his knees and pulled the shirt tail out of his trousers. He sat back down and pulled the shirt off.

She found the bandage end, pulled it out, and started unwinding it. "This is pretty nasty after two days. I'm going to want to rinse it out before we put it back on." She got down to the last couple of layers and started to expose skin that had been covered. "Oh, my," she muttered as she worked.

"What is it?"

"Colors. Purple and red mostly. Oh." She wrinkled her nose at the sight as the last layer came off. "Some of this is fist impacts, but a bunch of it looks like your ribs bled inside when they broke."

"I think it looks worse than it is," he said looking down. "There's a lot of loose blood, but I don't feel that injured. My body will soak it back up over the next couple of weeks. You're going to see some amazing colors when that happens. It changes from red to purple to green to yellow."

Chielle was not convinced. She caressed his bruised ribcage and said, "You need to slow down and take it easy for a few days."

"Your hands feel really good. Let me see," he said as he took one of her hands in both of his. He stroked the palm of her hand and felt the webbing between her fingers. "Your hands are so soft and smooth. Your webs are so strong yet so flexible."

"You like that?"

"They feel great, especially after having cotton fabric scraping against me."

She resumed gently rubbing him and her hand wandered around onto his back. She felt his scars and hesitated. "Do your scars hurt?"

"No. In fact, they're kind of dead to any sensation."

She leaned forward and put her head on his shoulder, wrapped her arms around him and held him.

He patted her on the back of the neck. "Hey, I'm all right. Thank you for the sympathy. They are a reminder of bad times, but I live with it."

She leaned back and faced him. "I will let them be a reminder of how passionate you can be."

"Passionate is better than dangerous."

"Passion is good," she said. "Maybe it makes us dangerous. It certainly moves us to do things we wouldn't otherwise." She ran her fingers through his chest hair. "Like this."

He stroked her neck and arms. "I love touching your skin."

"Is that so? 'Cause I'm starting to really appreciate all your body hair." She squeezed his chest and shoulders and then gently ran her hands over the curves. "All these hard muscles covered in soft furry curls."

His hands wandered over her tunic, gently massaging her sides and back, all the way down to her dorsal fin which was planted in the sand behind her. "Oh, damn. I wanted to get you some cocoa butter so your skin won't dry out."

"Actually, I brought some." She reached over to the net bag and pulled out a jar. In reaching over she stretched out across his lap. He took the chance to start massaging her back.

"Mmm, that's nice. It works even better with this," she said as she handed him the jar over her shoulder.

"I can't use this with your tunic still on."

"Well then do something about it."

He ran his hand up her tail, lifting the hem as he went. He slid the cloth up over her fin and up to her shoulders. She heard the jar pop open and then she felt his hands, greasy with the butter, sliding and squeezing up and down her back muscles. She moaned, relaxed over his legs and wrapped the end of her tail around his back, hugging him.

She reveled under his strong hands. He worked up and down her length, and seemed quite taken with her fin. He also spent some time massaging her hips, behind, and the top of her tail. She knew she was built differently there than he was used to, and it felt good, so she let him rub her there if he wanted to. Then she noticed a distinct bulge pressing against her side that wasn't there before in his lap. She was glad he was enjoying this too. She rolled over and swept the tunic up over her head and off. She sat up halfway, wrapped an arm around him, and started stroking and kissing his chest.

He held her up with one arm while caressing her ribs and fondling her breasts with his other. "Oh, the sand is sticking where I used the butter."

"That's all right. There's nothing back there that sand will hurt. Just don't get sand on my front and we'll be fine."

He seemed to take a minute to think about this.

She realized why. "That's right. With her legs spread, you can enter a woman from behind. I noticed you were examining my backside. Sorry, I've only got the goods up front."

"I'm fine with that," he said as he slid his hand down over her tummy.

She reached up and pulled him down to kiss his lips as he rubbed around her opening. He tasted good, like a Merrow, after eating her food. She caressed his cheek and decided two days of beard would be too scratchy for a proper kiss.

He massaged her hip bones and the muscles of the top of her tail, again exploring how she was built and giving her great pleasure at the same time. She waited for him to slide his hand into her. She surprised herself getting so aroused in the anticipation.

She kissed him with vigor and slid her tongue into his mouth, licking his stubby teeth. He surprised her by capturing her tongue with his lips and gently sucking on it. She was thrilled by the sensation just as he slid his fingers inside her. She moaned into his mouth and involuntarily tightened her grip around his back with her fluke.

He released her tongue and grinned. "I guess I won't be needing any more butter. He slid his fingers in deeper and suddenly stopped. "What's that?"

She blinked and frowned. "Let me explain." She reached down and extracted a handful of round stones. "After our attempt the other night, I thought maybe there was something I could do to help things along."

"You've been stretching yourself with stones? Chielle, have you hurt yourself?"

"No. It was a bit painful at first, but mostly it's just been sore up in my abdomen."

"You didn't have to go to such extremes."

"You said yourself, we are makers, and we can find a way to make things work."

"I kind of thought ... the solution we came up with the other night ... worked fine."

"That was a lot of fun." She lowered her head and looked up at him. "The truth is, for all your hairy, lumpy, sharp edged self, I want you inside me."

He scooped her up in his arms and hugged her to his chest. "I'm not going to argue with you."

She hugged him back, but then slipped her hand down between them. "You, sir, are overdressed." He released her and she unbuckled his belt.

He leaned back on his folded legs and raised his hips so she could slip his pants off. His manhood sprang out in all its glory as she pulled them down.

She reached around behind her and grabbed the jar of cocoa butter. She smiled up at him. "My turn." She started rubbing her hands over the muscles of his stomach and the bones of his hips. She kept eyeing his swollen member, knowing he wanted her to work on it, but she made her way around it and down onto his thighs. She reached around and squeezed the taut domes of his buttocks. His shaft was almost in her face when she squeezed, and it jumped, as if begging her to suck on it. Finally, she ran her hands up his inner thighs and caressed his sack. What a strange place to put them. Again, his member twitched. She smiled up at him and his face was aglow with anticipation.

At last, sliding and squeezing, she ran her hands around the hairy base and inched her way up to the head. It was longer than the widths of both her hands. She knew how long it was. She had sucked its entire length into her gill channels the last time. She wondered how much of this she was going to be able to get up inside her, even with the stone stretching. She swirled and squeezed up and down its length, it swelled under her touch, and his breathing deepened and quickened.

When it was as big as it was going to get, which was rather daunting, she rolled back onto her tail, pressing her pelvis up as fully as she could. She looked down and her opening was standing wide. "Your turn."

He leaned forward over her and hesitated for a second. He looked at her position, folded back at an extreme angle, and must have been alarmed at how alien she looked. He spread his knees and positioned up against her. He slid himself up and down across her opening and let the head dip in. Everything was slippery and the motion was effortless. She felt his size stretch her open and probe for depth.

She held her breath waiting for the pain of him hitting bottom. He rocked his hips with small thrusts, each one a little deeper. She hadn't even noticed, but she had wrapped her pelvic fins up around his bottom and her hands around his waist. His rocking and pushing was as much her pulling him in.

He noticed her holding her breath, "I got this," he assured her. At last he pushed and could get no further. He pulled almost all the way out, then pushed all the way in, seeming to measure how much stroke he had. "This will work." He ground out a rhythm, slowly at first.

She was taken with how gentle he was at the bottom of each stroke, clearly not wanting to hurt her. She looked up at him and he smiled back lovingly, she felt like she would melt under his touch. She looked down and guessed he was getting about halfway in. He seemed pretty happy with that. She was ecstatic. She finally felt like they were really mating.

She still wasn't feeling much for width, which was key for her pleasure. "Can I try something a little different?" She slipped her tail out from under herself and rotated her pelvis to the side. This let her bend herself more open to him.

He watched as she squirmed into position, then nodded his agreement. "Sideways," he commented. He grabbed his member to guide it, and she gasped at how his lifting pressure rode right along her inner sides where she wanted him. He rolled his hips and pushed it up into her, smiling at the fit. His width finally was hitting her sides right. She reached around and held him, though at an angle, with her pelvic fins.

He found his stroke, and she could feel the muscles of her pelvis squeezing against him inside her, caressing his length, sucking him in with each hastening thrust. Her breathing quickened as did his pumping.

His hips bumping into her rocked them both and she reveled in how the rhythm felt like surf surge.

She let go of his buttocks with her fins and let him take over with his rapid pace. He was sweating all over, and his skin glistened in the orange light of sunset. She loved how he smelled musky in his exertion, like seaweed. He breathed in short, forceful blasts through his nose, while she found herself gasping for air through her mouth and gills. She lost track of what sounds she was making, and surprised herself with a loud guttural groan. They hesitated at the sudden sound of seagulls she frightened flapping away in the dark. They laughed and got right back to it.

As he resumed his thrusting, she felt growing deep spasms roll out of her hips and down her tail. She loosened her hands around his waist, grabbed him by his powerful shoulders above her, leaned her head back, and just let him take her.

After what seemed a blissful eternity of flailing abandon, he grabbed her pelvis hard. "Look at me," he said between heaving breaths. He stared deeply into her eyes, and she let herself fall into his. Their connection was so intense it almost frightened her, until she saw he was giving himself completely to her. He gave one final deep thrust and she felt a flood of warmth rushing up inside of her. She wrapped her fins and arms and tail around him and held him tight, savoring his muscular pulsing. He held his breath and twitched his whole body against her while holding eye contact.

The waves down her tail mellowed to ripples. She took a deep, shaky breath and smiled up at him. "Told you we could make it work."

He scooped up her torso in his arms and leaned over her in a long tight embrace while she reveled in sheer joy.

Chielle opened her eyes and looked up at the clear blue sky. She was lying on her back on solid ground. The air on her face and in her lungs was freezing cold, yet her body was warm. It was also covered in clothes. She held her hands up and saw they were in sleeves and wearing gloves. Heavy, fur-lined gloves ... with fingers and no webs. She blinked and frowned and blinked again. Oh, a dream.

She turned her head and realized she was wearing a hood, that was attached to the coat with the sleeves. She thought about this for a moment and deduced that her tail was probably legs in this dream. She wasn't sure she wanted to see that, but curiosity got the better of her. She sat up, and although she had anticipated it, it was still shocking to see two legs in heavy britches, wearing bulky fur boots on her ... feet.

She looked around and saw she was sitting in the middle of a field covered in white fluffy powdered ice. Snow? She grabbed a handful and it compressed in her hand into a lump. The dream quickly went from alarming to fascinating.

She considered what it would take to stand up on her feet. She had no pelvic fins with which to balance herself. She bent the legs and tested how the knees only bent in one place. She lifted herself up with her hands and scooted her legs around and under herself. Kneeling. Now to press up. She leaned forward and steadied herself with her hands as she straightened her legs. She was very pleased to find this dream body knew how to do this, and she found herself able to straighten up into a stand. Standing, on her feet.

As soon as she thought about walking, she found she was doing it. It felt really strange, but really good at the same time. It felt like falling forward onto the next step, over and over. Her steps compressed the snow with a crunching sound, but it held her weight. She liked the rhythm and the smoothness of the motion.

She looked around to see where she was walking to. The field was actually the space between several hills. Off in the distance she saw stands of trees, all laden with snow. She hiked up a hill and looked around. She spotted a group of buildings with smoke coming out of their chimneys. A destination.

She struck out and found a pace that worked with her swinging arms, her pumping breath, and her trudging legs against the snow. Just out of curiosity she tried running, but found the force drove her feet too far into the snow and she lost all her forward speed. She couldn't really tell how far away the buildings were, with everything smoothly white. She settled into the pace she found worked.

She covered the distance in less time than she expected, and soon saw the buildings were actually a village. A village would have people. She pulled off a glove, tried not to be alarmed at her pink-skinned, webless hand, and felt her face to see if she was human there too. Her nose was too big and her eyes were too small. She had hair on her head instead of gills. It was too short to pull forward and see, but it was definitely hair. Human. That would make things a lot easier.

The buildings she first saw were just the end of a street of shops. As she approached, she saw there were houses nestled back in the trees all around the main street. She walked down one side of the street, looking in the shops. There was no one else out on the street, but there were plenty of people inside. One shop had cooking pots, another had wooden furniture, one had shelves full of bottles and jars. About halfway down the street she found the public house, with lots of people eating and talking. She knew she didn't know anyone, but she felt drawn to go in and see the people who lived here.

She pulled open the door and a wall of warm, sour-smelling air hit her. She stepped inside and immediately felt too warm. She pulled off the gloves and stuffed them in the coat pockets, then pulled down the hood and unbuttoned the coat. She was pleased to find she was wearing a heavy red cotton shirt under the coat. No one paid her any attention, which was fine with her. Most of the people were men standing or sitting around tables in groups of three and four. There were a few women, all with a man. She saw no families or children. From where she had seen the sun, it was late afternoon, and she wondered why so many men were not working. Maybe they were done with their daily work.

Being in a warm room, she realized she was chilled inside. She stepped up to the bar and caught the barkeep's attention. "Do you have anything warm to drink? Like cocoa?"

The man smiled and shook his head no. "No, lassie, I don't serve cocoa. I do have a glogg that'll warm you up."

She had no idea what a glogg was, but she figured this was a dream, so why not go where it was taking her. "Sure, I'll try a cup."

He set down a glass jar filled with a dark red fluid. It was steaming hot and smelled powerfully of spices and alcohol. The taste was even stronger than the smell. She wasn't sure how much of this she could drink. On the other hand, it was warm, both in temperature and in flavor. She swallowed and the warmth went all the way down with it. It felt good. "You're right," she told the barkeep. "Can you tell me, what is the name of this village?"

"Nathanson. You ain't never heard of Nathanson? We're famous for our maple syrup. There's even a touch of it in that glogg you're drinking."

"Really?" She took another sip. The flavor was easy to get used to, and the warmth was seductive. A few more sips and she started feeling lightheaded. She never wanted to get drunk. She objected to the whole idea of getting drunk. Yet she wanted more of this drink. It made her feel like everything was going to be all right. She felt sleepy, which made no sense, since she knew she was in a dream. Yet she couldn't hold up her head and leaned over onto the bar. It felt hard.

In fact, it was uncomfortably hard. She opened her eyes and it was dark. She heard surf, and Sten breathing. She lifted her head and could see by starlight that she had rolled over onto the rocks she had set up for their dinner. She moved back onto the sand up against Sten. She laid her hand gently on the bandages she had rewrapped around his ribs after their lovemaking. She was glad to have her tail back.

She tried to make sense of her marvelous dream. Had Sten described his life in the snow so well that she could piece it together in a dream? He had never mentioned the gloves, or the boots, or the crunch of snow, or the glogg. It had all felt so real.

She was still pretty tired, so she curled up and in no time fell back asleep.

14

S TEN WOKE UP TO THE SOUNDS OF CHIELLE picking up their dinner dishes. "Well, hello lover."

She rolled that around. "I guess we are now."

"I'd offer to help but you're done. You should have woken me up."

"Gurrirr," she dismissed with a wave of her hand.

Sten chuckled. "I love your slang. You look like you're headed off. Anywhere in particular?"

"I want to let Jacio know you're all right. And I need to check in at home. I'm sure my cousins will need help with their kids. They usually have me to count on late mornings."

"That reminds me of something I thought of last night. Not that I was doing a lot of thinking last night, but now is a much better time." He grimaced. "Actually, this is far too late, really."

She stopped and listened.

"Do you think it's possible ...? I mean is there any chance, that I could get you pregnant?"

"I did think about that, before last night, and I don't think so. Humans and Merrow have nothing in common. Does that bother you?"

"Bother me?"

"Well, not to jump ahead or anything, but does it bother you that I can't bear you children?"

"No, that doesn't matter to me. I've never thought of myself as a father."

She met his gaze. "You'd make a good father."

"I look forward to being a good surrogate uncle to your brother's and sister's kids. Our lives are going to be complicated enough without trying to raise children in two different worlds."

She didn't look convinced.

"Would you be all right not having children of your own?" he asked.

She blinked. "Yes, I'm fine with it. My mother would be disappointed at fewer grandchildren, but I have never seen myself as a mother either."

"I hope that's not one more thing for your family to hold against me."

"Hold against you? They won't be mad at you for my swimming off with a human."

"Why not? Humans have a history of taking without asking."

She frowned and looked him in the eye. "I love you, Sten Holdsmith. You did not take me in some rapine act of superiority."

He couldn't help but falter and look away.

"Do you think you forced yourself on me?"

He tried to look her in the eye, but couldn't. "There have been moments when I worried if I was falling into the same pattern."

She rolled on her tail over to him, laid her head on his shoulder and gently wrapped her arms around him. "Sten, you are one of the gentlest souls I have ever known. Yes, your people take too much, but that's not you. You earned every ripple of my affection. Please, never doubt yourself like that again."

Sten was bored, sitting alone with his thoughts in the cave, staying out of sight of any passing boats. None came by. He explored the edges of the cave to find a way to climb around onto the point of land, but found the only way would be by swimming. He was enjoying dry clothes too much for that.

He was exhausted. He put on a brave face whenever Chielle was around. She inspired him to get up and enjoy life. Their lovemaking had been glorious. Alone and quiet here, he had to admit his whole body ached, not just his ribs. He lied down, but sleep didn't come. Eventually, boredom put him back on his feet to explore the back of the cave.

He was glad he did. He found a pile of rocks that did not look natural, back under where the ceiling was low and the sand floor gave way to weathered rock. He cleared away some of the rubble only to find larger stones obviously covering up something. Bending over and lifting seized him up, and he had to shift around to find a good angle. Even then he had to hold himself as rigidly as possible to not spasm in pain while flipping them off.

At last he uncovered a stone slab, carved with pictorial symbols. A volcano in the upper right corner led to lines of people migrating away. In the bottom left corner was the sea, with Merrow jumping in. The center was more confusing. Men with horses marched off the top led by one larger, armored leader. Behind them, an enormous woman with waves for hair lifted people up from the downward migration. He could not figure out what he was seeing. Why hadn't Chielle told him about this?

"Not only do you invade our village, but now you desecrate our history."

The female voice surprised him, and he stepped out from behind the rocks.

The Merrow woman stood up on her tail in what Sten had come to recognize as a threatening posture. The spear she held in front of her with both fists made her intentions very clear. She was bigger than Chielle, but she had very similar features. Her erda was dark grey, like her expression. "Are you Chielle's sister, Sooreet?"

"Yes. And you're Sten the blacksmith. I didn't want to believe it, but here you are."

"You know, I had this conversation with your brother."

"You got him drunk. Sympathy is easy when you're drunk. You won't be so lucky with me."

"Did you come here to kill me?"

"Not yet. I will kill you if you hurt my sister."

"Why do you think I want to hurt her?"

"Chielle is young and an idealist. She has let older, self-centered men take advantage of her in the past. She still has enough wide-eyed wonder about the world to let others do it again. I won't sit still for that."

"I'm glad she's got family looking out for her. She is young, and she is curious, as you say. But I don't want to take advantage of her. I love her. I want to support her and care for her. I've lived here for a year, and I had no idea things had gotten so bad between our peoples until I started talking to Chielle. I had no idea how honorable your people are and how unfairly you're being treated."

"I'm supposed to believe you're on our side?"

"You can believe it or not. I tried to get justice for your man who was shot. I seem to have swatted the hornet's nest, and now things have come to a head. The leader of the fishermen challenged me in combat, and when I bested him, he tried to kill me. I don't know what else I could do to show you whose side I'm on."

"Why did you come to Celidan?"

"I wanted to see for myself how civilized and peaceful you are. I needed to disprove all the terrible things the humans say about you."

"Why did you go into our temple?"

"Chielle invited me. It was wonderful. I was not there to disrespect anything."

"What are you doing with the Great Tablet back there?"

"I just happened upon it. Chielle didn't mention it. I'm not sure she knows it's here. Can I ask you a question?"

"I'm holding the spear."

"I appreciate that. If I'm going to help change the humans' minds about the Merrow, then I will need all the knowledge I can get. Are you familiar with the Great Tablet? Do you know what it shows?"

"It shows how your people came here, overran the natives, and settled Saint Rochel. How you waged war against us over the fishing, and how we wrote the treaty to keep your greedy ways from corrupting our people."

"Have you ever seen it with your own eyes?"

"No, of course not. It stays protected under those rocks so our people never forget why we have the treaty."

"Is there a taboo against looking upon it?"

"No."

"I uncovered it without knowing it was something to be treasured. I will cover it back up. While it is uncovered, would you like to see it?"

"Is this a trick like when you got my stupid brother drunk?"

"No, no trick. I'll step away and you can come look for yourself."

She lowered the spear point and motioned to the side. "Move."

He stepped away and she walked around the other side. She did not say anything from behind the rocks.

"I'm not sure it tells the story of the treaty," Sten ventured. "That volcano and the leader taking the men away on horses looks like our myth of Atlan at the dawn of civilization. If I'm not mistaken, that's Rorra creating the Merrow. Why do you think these two events are shown in the same picture?"

Sooreet stepped out with a deep frown on her face.

"I think that story is a lot older than the hundred years the Alcan have been at Saint Rochel. I think it tells a story going back many thousands of years. I think it says our peoples have a common ancient history."

She held up her hand to silence him. He noticed she wore a shell sweetheart bracelet. She started to walk away. "Cover it up."

"That would explain why your people know our language so well. You've been speaking it all along, long before this bunch of humans settled Saint Rochel."

She stopped and turned to look at him. The frown had not moved.

He pressed one last time. "Chielle told me her favorite childhood story about Rorra was how she gave the Merrow the ability to breathe both water and air, because you can't laugh underwater."

She blinked several times, took a deep breath, and let it out slow. The sound of the breakers echoed through the cave. "I will be watching you."

"Would you prefer I not tell Chielle you came?"

She did not answer. She lifted her head, walked into the waves, and vanished.

He put the rocks back. The afternoon rain came and went.

He saw a shape rising in the swells and was pleased that Chielle had returned with food. It wasn't one shape, though, that emerged, but six mermen. He recognized the front three as Aalto, Pinngot, and Raggeck Blauoon, the builders who ordered tools. He also recognized the three very large mermen who followed from their red church guard tunics. This did not look good.

Sten walked down to the beach to meet them. "Aalto! What brings you to my little piece of paradise?"

"Mister Sten, I have come to apologize. I think I gave you the wrong impression yesterday about needing tools from you."

The Merrow hunched up on his tail at the water's edge with his brothers close behind. He nervously averted eye contact as he spoke. Sten watched the red guards standing straight with their tails planted in the shallows, looking on sternly.

Sten saw the right thing to do. "No need to apologize. We were just talking. I understand Merrow don't need anything from humans. I certainly did not think we were trading for anything."

Aalto and his brothers sighed a little breath of relief.

Sten spoke loudly enough for the guards to hear. "I hope someday our peoples will come to trust each other enough that you can use my tools to make a better life for yourself. In the meantime, I know you will do just fine."

"Thank you, Mister Sten. I doubt we will ever speak again. Have a pleasant life."

"You're welcome. May Rorra watch over you."

One of the guards bristled at his comment, but they then all turned back to the sea.

Sten was really glad Chielle had missed this. Sten had feared this would happen. He was even more disappointed that it was the temple guards that enforced it. That meant the disapproval was official, possibly even from the Shaman himself. This was a huge setback.

Sten was pondering this when Chielle swam up, a bag slung over her shoulder.

"Hello, Sweetheart." He stepped up and kissed her.

"Sweetheart," she pondered playfully. "I like the sound of that."

"Well, you're not going to like the sound of this. The Blauoon brothers came by, escorted by three of the red temple guards. They withdrew their order for tools."

"Oh no, that's very bad."

"Means the Shaman ordered it, right?"

"I'm afraid so."

"I brought this on myself. I did invade your town unannounced."

Chielle was distracted in thought. "I'll have to find out how far this goes."

"Now I've got both villages up in arms. For a man who set out to make peace, I seem to be stirring up a lot of anger."

"Speaking of your village, that's where I went to get you some food." She reached into her shoulder bag and handed him a sealed pot that was made of some kind of pink rock, but it was much too light to be stone.

"Is this coral?"

"Yes," she said opening it to reveal rice cooked with flecks of fish and egg. "Jacio had a funny name for it that he said he couldn't pronounce. His mother made some for him and he gave it to me to give to you."

"Kedgeree. Good lad."

"While I was there, I learned that indeed your constable has arrested Captain Boole and is holding him until your High Lord can decide his fate."

"Is the High Lord still in town?"

"It would seem so, yes."

"May I ask how you found all this out?"

She hesitated, but only for a moment. "I spoke with some friends of mine who keep an eye on things in Saint Rochel."

"I take it they are well practiced in the art of staying concealed."

"Yes," she said with a coy smile. "Yes, they are."

"Now that your red guard knows where I am, I'm vulnerable stuck here on this beach. Maybe it's time to borrow Norn's boat. Let's have breakfast, and then can I ask you to take me out there?"

"Of course."

"We'll have Jacio go tell Norn what I'm up to. Norn won't tell anyone. That way I can go into town when the time is right."

"When will that be?"

"Give it one more day. I want the villagers united in thought that Boole and his approach is the wrong way to go."

"All right. After I get you to the boat, I want to go check with my family and see what's been said since your visit. It's really rare for me to spend this much time away from my home. I'll spend the night there."

"Of course. Your mother and brother know about us." Sten chose to not complicate matters by including her sister. "Does your father?"

"I don't know if my mother would wait for me to tell him myself. She had to tell him something with me gone for three days and two nights."

"I wish I had met him before now."

"What, to show him your feelings for me are genuine?"

He looked her in the eyes and grinned. "Well, yes. I would also hope my fighting for Merrow justice would sway his opinion."

"My father is in a tough spot over that. He's old enough to remember when we all got along, but as the head of our family, he has to uphold the official doctrine of separation. He had a hard time balancing that when Thymon armed his friends and went into battle. I'm afraid he might feel he needs to be strict with me. I'm really going to have to move carefully."

"You know your folks better than anyone. I'm sure you'll work it out."

Thymon followed his sister up the anchor chain to the surface. "Back Forty?" he read on the prow.

"It's a ranching term. The owner raises cattle."

"Still doesn't make sense," he muttered to himself as they kicked up out of the water, over the low rail to scoot, behind-first, onto the deck.

"Sten? Sweetheart?" Her voice wavered. "Are you up yet?"

Thymon thought the gray, overcast sky less than a sunstone after dawn was sadly fitting for their mission.

Sten stepped up from below decks wiping his face with a towel. "Yes, I was just shaving. Thought you'd appreciate that. Oh, hi, Thymon."

She got up and hunched over to him. Even from behind, with her shoulders slumped, Thymon could see how dejected she was.

"Whoa," Sten said. "That bad?"

She just nodded.

"Your father ... banned you from seeing me. Which is why the escort."

She flung her arms around him and buried her face in his shoulder.

Sten looked up to Thymon. The usual ruddy color of the human's face blanched. "I've been living in a fool's paradise, thinking I could just do whatever I wanted and people would come around to my way of thinking."

"She argued brilliantly." Thymon got up while he spoke. "She said you were our only hope of making peace with the villagers. She even told Father about her dreams of walking in the snow."

Sten pulled her back. "What dreams?"

She looked up at him with the saddest eyes her brother had ever seen on her. "When I sleep in your arms, I dream of having legs and walking through snow in the mountains. At first it felt so strange, but then I started really enjoying it."

"You never told me about this."

"I wasn't sure what it meant, or if it meant anything. It does mean we have a special bond. It didn't convince my father, though."

"This is amazing. I've been dreaming of having a tail and swimming through your village. I thought it was just my imagination, but then when I went there, my dream was right, down to the details."

She looked at him for a long moment. "Have you ever heard of a town called Nathanson?"

His face lit up. "That's ... wow ... yes, I grew up in Nathanson. I spent many an hour stomping around in the snow, in fur boots, all bundled up. Is that what you dreamt?"

"Yes." She smiled weakly.

"Then we really do have a bond. I don't just mean you and I, but your kind and my kind. We couldn't be sharing memories in our dreams unless there was something much deeper connecting us." He flashed on the Great Tablet. "Didn't this sway your father?"

"It kind of terrified him, actually," Thymon added. "Our father has always been strongly isolationist. My going to war didn't help matters. This time he was acting on our shaman's orders, but after hearing about the dreams, he was even more convinced."

"On the Shaman's orders? Your religious leader can just order people around?"

"He isn't just our religious leader," she explained patiently, though it clearly pained her to talk about it. "He is our protector, our wisdom guide, our decision maker. He talks directly with Rorra, and everything we have flows from Rorra. His word is law, and his law has always been for our best."

"What, he's never wrong?"

"There simply is no arguing with him," Thymon stated. "If Merrow started trading with humans, and using human tools, and doing things the human way, then Merrow will become selfish, corrupt, and evil like humans. We were all raised with that message. Our people are not ready to argue with that."

Chielle wrapped her arms around his torso and put her head on his chest. Thymon's heart broke seeing her usually shining confidence faded like this.

Sten put his arms around her while he talked with Thymon. "You're saying the law that was written a hundred years ago prohibiting commerce: that was a Merrow idea as much as human?"

"Oh, yes," he explained. "Our ancestors chose that path. Did you think that was forced on us by the villagers?"

"I wasn't sure. I haven't been able to get a straight answer from anyone. It must have been to prevent another war. Can't they see how being separated is driving us into war now?"

"They don't see it that way."

"Well I know you're worried about losing the last of your fisheries. You took up spears to defend yourself. If you pull back into isolation now, the fishermen are going to take everything and force you to leave your homes. You will have to abandon Celidan."

"Believe me, I agree with you," Thymon said. "My people would rather do anything but fight again."

Sten blinked hard and gritted his teeth. "Boole and his ilk are going to think themselves justified. They got away with labeling you thieves, and now they're going to label you cowards, unworthy of those fisheries the treaty is supposed to protect for you." He took a deep breath and blew it out. "I just can't help feeling I've made things worse. I drew this all out into the open to try to bridge the gap, and now I've forced the Shaman's hand into shutting you off."

Chielle looked up at him. "You did the right thing. You did what Atlan would have done. You seized the moment; you gave it your best try. Don't beat yourself up for that."

"There has got to be some way to convince your elders to stand up for themselves. Now is exactly the wrong time to go into hiding."

She beamed at him and stroked his cheek. "That beautiful tinker's mind of yours, always looking for a solution. If anyone can think of it, it will be you."

He met her gaze and held her with his massive arms. Thymon still wasn't comfortable seeing his hairy skin around his sister's waist, even if he was only touching her tan erda. "What's to become of us? I'm not giving you up. If my people drive you away, I'll come with you. Or we can both run away together."

"Our father would come after her," Thymon interjected. "It would be ugly."

Sten looked into her eyes and the anger in him seemed to melt into sadness. It was at that moment that Thymon saw just how much Sten loved his sister. "I can't believe it. They're taking you away and there is nothing I can do about it. Your mother …"

"No. My mother knows how much you mean to me. She used to have great love for her human friends when she was young. This is now. She will not go against my father."

"I promise I will not give up the fight above the surface. I will do whatever I can to show your people that most humans welcome the Merrow as neighbors. Somehow I've got to show them, or I'll never get you back."

"And I promise I will wait for you, no matter how long. I have faith in you. For now, though, my love this is good bye."

He hugged her tightly and she hugged him back. "Pray to Rorra for a miracle. Rorra abides and provides, right?"

When she pulled away, tears were running down his smooth cheeks. She touched them. "I wish I had tears too, to show you how much I am going to miss you."

15

S TEN TIED THE *BACK FORTY* TO HIS LANDING DOCK and looked around to see that no one had noticed his arrival. The village would be bustling by now with morning errands. No point in wasting time with social niceties, he thought. He marched up the ramp and met Jacio who was coming out to the shop.

"Hey, welcome back!"

Sten did not slow down. "Thanks. I'll be back later."

Gerb the sailmaker looked genuinely shocked in his shop window as Sten marched by. "Sten, you're alive!"

"Apparently so," he said with a smile but without breaking his stride.

It was the same with most folks he passed. They either lit up when they realized the Merrow had saved him, or double-took as if they were seeing a ghost. Both reactions meant people had taken Boole's crime seriously which greatly buoyed Sten's spirits. By the time he got to the constable's office, he was sure his plan would work.

"Well, well," Blaine greeted him as he entered. "If it isn't the ghost of our long dead blacksmith."

"Good morning, Arum."

The big lawman got up from his desk and shook Sten's hand. "Welcome back. Don't tell me I'm supposed to be surprised your friends under the sea saved you, because I never had a doubt."

"Just because I was saved does not mean he didn't try to kill me."

"Oh, absolutely." He pointed his thumb over his shoulder at the jail in the back. "Captain Boole will stand trial for attempted murder, especially now that I have all the witnesses."

"You also have the High Lord to preside."

"That's true. He decided to stick around for a few days." He absently rubbed his short cropped blond hair. "I think he wants to make sure Boole's trial doesn't drive us back into war with the merfolk."

"I hope that's why he stayed. I have to talk with him about what happens next."

Arum squinted. "You sound like something has changed."

"It has, and not for the better. Do you want to come along? I hope to catch him before he gets busy with other business."

Arum glanced around, then nodded. "Sure. Nothing here that can't wait." They left and the constable locked the door behind them. "The High Lord is staying at the Saint Rochel Arms."

"That makes sense," Sten said heading in that direction. "It is our only real hotel."

"Did you really build a pipe and helmet rig to breathe underwater?"

"Yes, I did."

"You saw Celidan first hand?"

"That is true."

"I bet that was amazing. Obviously you've been spending a lot of time with that mermaid lady friend of yours."

Sten stopped walking and turned to face Arum. "Her name is Chielle. Is there something you want to get off your chest?"

"Don't take offense, and tell me to drop it if you want to, but they are so mysterious, I have to ask. What are they like in conversation?"

Sten was relieved Arum did not go where he thought he might. "In conversation? They talk just like you and me. What do you mean?"

"Well, do they speak their mind openly, or do they hide their feelings? Are they kind to their women? Do they make jokes? You know, are they really different than us?"

Sten was dismayed. "Holy Atlan in the grave, are you kidding me? Do people really not understand the Merrow are exactly like us except they live underwater? Do you really think they are so different that you can't even have a normal conversation with them? Have you never spoken with one?"

"Well, no, not casually."

"Of course they speak their minds. Of course they are kind to their women. And yes they make jokes. They hold some things more dearly than we do, like sharing and community. Their culture is geared to their life in the sea. But they love and get angry and get drunk and laugh and cry just like humans. How in the world did you come to think otherwise?"

The townspeople walking nearby heard Sten laying into Arum and slowed down to listen.

"They've been here alongside you for the whole hundred years you've been here. I happen to know that thirty years ago you used to get along with them as neighbors. Humans had Merrow as best friends." Sten noticed the crowd growing around them. He didn't try to hide his desperation. "I thought I was just up against greedy fishermen. Does everyone harbor these same suspicions? Have things gotten that bad?"

"I don't know, Sten. I haven't asked a lot of people, and people don't speak up if they don't have to. I just thought, since you've been around them so much, I should get the facts from someone who knows."

Sten looked up at the tall blond and caught his gaze squarely. "I'm glad you did. I wish I could tell this to everyone in Saint Rochel." He turned to the onlookers. "They are just folk like you and me. I knew this was bad. I've been here over a year; how could I not know it? But to think you can't even talk with them? Lord, have I got my work cut out for me. Starting with the High Lord," he said as he began walking again.

On the rest of the way to the hotel, the surprised looks at Sten's reappearance were accompanied by a spreading wave of chatter about what he had said. Sten saw that Arum noticed it too. Sten hoped this was the sound of good news.

Sten marched into the hotel straight to the front desk with Arum close behind.

"Good morning," the young Indru clerk in the jaunty pillbox hat greeted them.

"Good morning. Who can I speak with about seeing the High Lord?"

Footfalls from the stairs behind them were followed by a man's voice. "That would be me."

Sten and Arum turned around and faced Jesery Clune himself. Sten almost didn't recognize the judge without his official headgear. With his large bald spot and his unassuming street clothes, he looked positively normal.

"Your Lordship, how good to see you again."

"Constable Blaine. Mr. Holdsmith, it is so good to see you recovered from your watery grave. I usually don't hear petitions before breakfast. As I am headed to breakfast now, and you have managed to catch me, I will make an exception. Why did you want to see me?"

"I have disheartening news from Celidan. With all this conflict, the Merrow have decided to retreat from all contact with us."

"I was told the same thing through official channels."

"Oh no, really?" Arum let slip.

Sten jumped in. "If left unchecked, the fishermen are going to take advantage of that and seize the rest of the fishing grounds. The Merrow have given up all the fisheries they can afford to lose and still sustain themselves. If our fishermen harvest Harper's Meadow, the Merrow will have to abandon their village and migrate away. They were here first. We will have taken unfair advantage of their good nature and driven them from their ancestral home."

"I agree that would be a great injustice. What are you asking me to do?"

"Start by enforcing the treaty. It sets Harper's Meadow aside for the Merrow. Forbid the fishermen from going there."

"I understand the Merrow have arranged that the fishermen cannot find any fish there anymore. They seem to be enforcing the treaty themselves."

"We can only hope they continue. Then ask the Merrow Shaman to alter the treaty to allow commerce. The ban has driven a wedge to where our people think of them as brute savages that can't even communicate. We have to open up the chance for healthy contact."

Clune raised his eyebrows and sighed. "The Merrow leaders wrote that treaty to keep their people away from our influence. If they have decided to withdraw, that is their choice. It has worked for them for a hundred years. My asking for a change would just convince them how right they are to withdraw. I understand you have conversed with them extensively."

"He went to their village using a breathing device," Arum interjected.

"Indeed? Impressive. Does your coming to me now mean your efforts at building rapport have failed?"

"They saw me as an invader."

"There you have it. They would see me the same way if I asked to change the treaty." The judge regarded Sten for a moment. "Being fairly new here, it seems you don't understand how badly the Merrow want to stay separate from us. When the Alcan came to this bay, the Indru had not developed it at all. They were living in huts on the beach. When the Indru saw the Alcan take control and build this village, the Indru had to choose whether to join the new occupants or be pushed aside. When the Alcan fisherman went to war with the Merrow over fishing rights, the Indru decided to blend with Alcan Society in any way they could, so that the fight would be human versus Merrow and not Alcan versus Indru."

The Indru desk clerk choked involuntarily at hearing this.

They all looked over at him and he scurried off to his duties.

"It's not something anyone is proud of but that is how this village developed."

"Is that when the Indru adopted the Alcan style of dressing?" Sten ventured.

"Yes. Inland, the Indru continue to wear their traditional garb and pursue their traditional occupations. For the last hundred years the Indru here in Saint Rochel have dressed like Alcan to blend in."

"Weren't the Indru friendly neighbors with the Merrow before the Alcan arrived?"

"That's true, but faced with the Alcan determination to get what they want, the Indru chose to not object to the conflicts with the Merrow."

Sten sighed. "Our Atlantean right to excel."

"It has served us well. There wouldn't be a town here without it. The crown has been watching the situation unfold for several generations. When you came to Silverton, I realized things had shifted again. There does not seem to be much we can do about it right now, but it is not at all surprising that things have come this far."

Sten wanted to argue with him, but he knew when all was said and done, the High Lord was right. Even if Boole was discredited and his hatred rejected, even if the people of Saint Rochel opened their arms to the Merrow, nothing would convince the Shaman or his followers that humans could be trusted. Sten found himself just standing there in the hotel lobby staring at the red carpeted floor between himself and the judge with nothing to say. He felt like something vital had leaked out of his body onto that worn carpet and left him empty.

The judge asked Arum, "Why has Saint Rochel never replaced Mayor Grenley? He died over a year ago."

"The townsfolk just didn't think we needed one."

"If you had a leader who could speak for the whole town, he could have kept this situation under control. People don't want leadership, they need it."

He turned back to Sten. "I am sorry. I know you wanted to fix this now. I appreciate your efforts to bring these two villages together. By enticing the fishermen to overreach the law, you have probably helped avert any further open combat. Your message of peace and goodwill will likely grow here in Saint Rochel. In time, the Merrow may see that and open their borders again. These things take time, and you are doing the hard work that needs to be done. I hope you continue."

Sten saw the judge's eyes latch onto the shell bracelet on his arm. "I am also sorry for your personal loss in this matter."

Sten held up his wrist and nodded. "Thank you."

He paused and waited. "If there is nothing further, I bid you good day." He turned away toward the hotel's café.

"Thank you for your time, Sir," Arum said.

The walk back through town took forever. Though he was greeted with smiles by everyone downtown he passed, he felt utterly alone. Having Arum walking alongside him gave him no comfort.

"Are you noticing how happy everyone is to have you back and alive?"

"I guess," Sten agreed glumly. "So what?"

"So now that they have seen where Boole's hatred leads, they're more likely to listen to your message of peace with the Merrow."

Sten glanced over at Arum. Arum used the word "Merrow" for the first time. "That's true. It's a start. It's not going to convince the Merrow to open their borders."

"You know," the tall blond said confidentially, "I'm not as thick as I look. I know your real loss is your girlfriend. I guess the High Lord recognized your bracelet from her. I understand that taints everything else, but don't miss the good you've done for the town — for both towns."

They arrived in front of the jail. Sten held out his hand. "Thank you for backing me up with the High Lord. Let me know when you want me to testify against Boole."

Arum shook his hand. "I will."

By the time he got to his shack, he had thought over what Clune and Blaine had said about what good he had done. He was able to manage a smile for Jacio when the boy greeted him enthusiastically with a bowl of warm porridge.

He tried to keep himself busy and distracted. He taught Jacio how to cut fine gears out of brass to repair a mantle clock. He pounded out a hundred nails for the carpenters' cooperative. In fact, he was so productive, he finished all the orders he had in the shop with plenty of sunlight left. He let Jacio go home and then swept the soot out of all the corners of his living quarters.

None of it helped. The hole he felt in his chest grew deeper by the hour. He considered sitting out in his wharf chair and drinking, but it was such a beautiful sunny day, it just didn't feel right. Drinking the blues worked so much better in foul weather.

He did not feel social, but he did feel like being waited on, so he ended up in the Pied Cock for dinner. Paulbert Caron made an excellent shepherd's pie, just the kind of comfort food Sten needed.

"Oh thank Atlan, you are alive!" Vanda Rymerand rushed up to his table like a ship with full blue linen sails billowing in a strong, flower-scented wind. She grabbed a chair and sat down, her hand clutching his forearm.

"Hello Vanda. Please have a seat."

"I was horrified when I heard that crazy fishing captain tied you up and threw you in the sea."

"Yes, well, he's in jail now."

A gold band on her finger caught his eye. "Why are you wearing the engagement ring I gave you last year?"

She held her hand up and fluttered it. "Because I like it. You don't mind, do you?"

He wondered what game she was playing at. "We are not engaged. We never were. You could at least wear it on a different finger."

"Oh, all right." She tried to pull it off but seemed to have difficulty. "Oh bother. Here," she said sticking her hand out to him, "you try."

He touched the gravy on his plate and applied it to her finger. The ring came right off. He wiped it on his shirt and handed it back to her.

She stuck out her other hand, presenting her right ring finger.

He slid the ring on. "Thank you," he added.

A sound at the window next to him caught his attention. He looked but saw no one there. He noticed a wet spot on the outside of the window which seemed odd.

"What is it?" she asked.

"Nothing, I guess."

"As I was saying, how awful for you that you had to be saved by a Fin. It feels wrong to say it, but thank goodness that Fin was there to help."

Sten was too tired to try to find a gentle way of breaking the news to her. "Vanda, that mermaid, who saved me, is my girlfriend. She was there to save me because she had just jumped off the wharf when Boole and his goons marched out to lynch me."

Vanda blinked in several short but fast bursts as she digested his words. "Girlfriend. This was what, three maybe four weeks after you turned me down? So you were seeing her ... oh no. You threw me over for a mermaid?"

"Vanda, please keep your voice down. We agreed to stay friends. Let's act like it now."

Her face flushing red did not bode well for quiet conversation. "What? You weren't joking in the market about trying new things. Holy shit, Sten!"

"Vanda, don't impugn yourself with foul language."

"I have every right to swear." She sniffed at him. "What's that smell? Cocoa butter? Cocoa butter?! You're sleeping with her? Do you realize that's … bestiality?!"

"All right, now you've gone too far." He looked around and not surprisingly, everyone was watching. Most weren't even trying to be subtle. "Fine, yes. I love Chielle more than I have ever loved anyone, including you. She is brave and kind and selfless in ways you will never understand. By the way, how do you know they use cocoa butter to protect their skin?"

"My mother always hated Fin, and now I can see why."

"You and I were over last year when you left town. I made that clear last month when we talked. You have no reason to be jealous."

"Jealous? You think I would stoop to be jealous of a Fin?" She stood up abruptly and let her chair fall to the floor. "This isn't jealousy. This is disgust." She turned and walked straight out the door, her bustle jerking side to side as she marched.

He surveyed the collection of squinting eyes around the room. "Show's over folks." He took one last bite of his pie and decided he should leave too.

On the way back to his shop he realized he had publicly declared his love for a woman he might never see again. He certainly had driven Vanda away once and for all. Better to be alone than with a bigot like her.

He was so riled up from his fight with Vanda that despite being bone tired, sleep just wasn't an option. He tidied up around the shop, trying to calm himself, when he came across his sketch of the wheeled chair for Chielle. The drawing ripped open the hole in his heart he had been trying to ignore all day. His chest hurt worse than after Boole had broken his ribs. He felt weak in the knees and had to steady himself on the bench. She was gone. All the hopes and dreams he had let himself grow around her were shattered, the shards too small to even grasp.

He clenched his fists and gritted his teeth and let all his anger and frustration and confusion and torment boil over. He grabbed an ingot and threw it into the hearth. He spun the bellows wheel furiously and drove the embers to spewing white. Pausing only out of habit, he donned his apron before he grabbed the glowing block with tongs and seized a hammer. He brought it down on the metal bar with all his fury. "Damn the Shaman!" The clang pierced the night like a death scream. "Damn the treaty!" *Clang!* "Damn the old ways!" *Clang!* "Damn the greedy bastards that started this!" *Clang!* Tears welled up in his eyes and poured down his cheeks as rage overtook him. Sweat beaded up over his face from the exertion. "Damn them all!" His aim slipped and a corner of the deformed block cracked off, spun up, and sliced him across the jaw. He ignored it and just kept crying and cursing and slamming the hammer down as hard as he could.

The blood from the cut mixed with the tears and the sweat that covered his face, formed a fat droplet on his chin, and fell cleanly through a space between the floorboards into the sea.

16

AS HE SWAM ALONG UNDERWATER, Sten slowly realized he was in another mermaid dream. The motion of sliding through the water with only the slightest push with his tail felt so natural he didn't question it at first. Once he did connect, he looked around more carefully, wondering what the dream would show him this time.

He was swimming over the amphitheater in Celidan. He looked down at what should have been the Eye of Rorra, but he couldn't see anything. He remembered Chielle had shown it to him from the stone seats, so he dove and turned to face the center from where he had stood in the diving bell.

He couldn't see anything at first, so he stared intently. He caught a glimpse of rippling water and waited for it to open up into the window that was the Eye. It did not. Instead the ripples coalesced and appeared to be moving right at him. He started to back up, but it was moving too fast and it was upon him.

It was the shape of a mermaid, made of water, visible only by the distortions and reflections of things behind her. Sten was transfixed and before he could move, she reached out and held his face in her hands and kissed him full on the mouth. He felt water rush into his mouth and all around his face as the watery form rushed past and around him. He turned to watch her and she was gone.

His heart was racing, and he found himself breathing hard through his gills, which felt really strange. He had no idea what had just happened. Was that Rorra? Why did she kiss him?

He heard what sounded like distant drums. He spun around, trying to place them, but couldn't. He remembered Chielle describe how she "heard" with her face to get an all-around picture of her surroundings. He paused and felt for the sound. Yes, drums, drums and cymbals, maybe even stomping feet. Feet? Maybe it was coming from the surface. He swam up and found he could track it.

He breached the surface right off the beach next to his wharf. He knew this place was miles from Celidan, but he went with it. The sound was huge and coming from up in the town. What in the world could be making such a racket?

He struggled up out of the surf and onto the beach, trying to quickly learn how to achieve the hunching step shifting his weight on and off his pelvic fins like crutches. He failed to time his weight shift and he threw himself on his face. He looked around and there was no one on the beach to see him. He squirmed around and got himself up over his tail again. He tried to remember exactly how he had seen Chielle do this. She was so fluid in her motion he had never really broken it down. Doing it himself was an entirely different matter. He planted his pelvic fins stiffly and coiled his tail up off the ground and swung his weight under to land on what should have been his thighs, but was now his backwards curving upper tail. It worked!

He only made it a half dozen "steps" up onto dry sand when the source of the noise came to him. A throng of villagers spilled out onto the beach, singing and dancing and pounding drums and shaking noisemakers in what he now saw was an enormous celebration. His first reaction to all these people coming his way was to dive back into the sea. He didn't know if his dream villagers were more or less friendly to Merrow than the real-world ones.

He got his answer when several men and women ran up to him and started cheering and patting him on the back and welcoming him into the merriment. He couldn't tell what they were so happy about, but he was glad they didn't attack him. He looked around and saw several other Merrow dancing and singing in the crowd. The camaraderie took him entirely by surprise.

"What are we celebrating?" he asked a random dancer.

"Rorra's gift!" the man cried over the din.

"What is Rorra's gift?"

The man double took on him. "You're a Merrow. If you don't know, then who does?" Before Sten could ask him further, he spun off into the crowd dancing and singing.

Sten saw Merrow standing on their folded flukes in the sand swaying and gyrating their hips to the drumbeats and handclaps while singing their long warbling songs. Alongside them humans danced faster paced steps to the fiddles and whistles, yet stayed in time with the Merrow music. The blending of the two musical styles was striking and yet felt so right. Like so many things he had seen between humans and Merrow, they seemed to fit together like two halves of a whole.

A woman called his name from behind him that he thought might be Chielle. He started to turn around, but tripped over his tail and fell.

He landed awake in his bed. Being horizontal under covers with legs took a moment to accept. He wiggled his toes just to be sure. He sat up and swung his legs over the edge of the bed. "What was that all about?" he asked his empty room. "Clearly wishful thinking having its way with me."

He saw dawn was just breaking through the window on the far side of his bedroom. Something did not look right about the sky. Or was it the sea? He leaned over without getting out of bed to look straight out but saw nothing unusual. Maybe he was just disoriented from the dream. He got up and started his day as usual. By the time he started thinking about breakfast, the odd feeling was back. He decided to go outside and see for sure.

The ocean was gone. He ran to the edge of the wharf and the sea had dropped to only a few feet of water. The *Back Forty* was tilted over resting on its keel in what couldn't be more than ten feet of water. Even the lowest tide left over twenty. The ramp down to the landing hung almost vertical. There was a steady cold wind blowing off the ocean. The wind was never cold here, and it was certainly never steady off the sea in the morning. It was all so weird he wondered for a moment if he was still dreaming.

"Sten!"

He scanned the choppy waves and saw Chielle bobbing out in front of the wharf. "What happened?"

"It's Rorratonton, the storm of all storms!"

He looked to the horizon but saw nothing. "Where?"

"Out past the horizon, but moving really fast. You have to evacuate the village."

"Did you pray to Rorra last night?"

"Yes, I did, but not for this. Did you pray too?"

"No." He felt the cut on his jaw. "Well, kind of, yes. I think Rorra has decided the humans have to go."

"That's why you have to evacuate," she pleaded.

"That won't help. We can save ourselves, but a storm this size will smash all the boats. Without the fishing fleet, the town can't survive."

While they spoke, Sten kept watching the horizon. He suddenly realized what he was seeing. It had turned black and was moving this way. It stretched as far as the eye could see in both directions. "Holy Atlan," he muttered to himself. "There won't be much left of the town itself."

"It will be here in less than one of your hours."

"That's not enough time to row out to the boats, sail them out and re-anchor them away from the shore, and still make it back to safety."

"Is half a mile far enough?

"I don't know. Probably, depends on the storm surge. Why does that matter?"

"There is a drop off half a mile outside the harbor. The ships' anchors might hold if they stuck below the lip edge."

"You're not hearing me, Sweetheart. There isn't enough time."

"Not for the fishermen, but there is for us."

"What?"

"The Merrow can pull the boats to safety."

"Pull, what? Why would you want to?"

"The fastest way to wipe out fear and mistrust is with generosity."

Sten was struck speechless for a moment. He was so proud of her yet so afraid for her. "Isn't that going to be dangerous even for you? What if the storm hits in the middle of your efforts?"

"The more Merrow we get to help, the faster we'll get done."

"How many do you have?"

"Certainly all the younger generation who don't like the old law. Lots of us have been waiting for the chance to break out of the old ways, and this is it."

"I think you underestimate just how dangerous this is going to be."

"We work as a community, remember?"

She was right. It wasn't in her culture or her personal nature to put herself first. "Chielle, please be careful."

"We don't have time to worry," she answered with a knowing smile.

"All right. Gather up your people. Focus on the fishing boats. You're not going to be able to save every boat in the harbor. I'll convince the town to evacuate the coast. But please don't do any hauling yourself!"

"Gotta go! I love you!" she called as she disappeared under the waves.

"I love you too," he said into the wind.

He looked down and sadly realized Norn's boat, already grounded, was going to be a loss. He ran as fast as he could. He passed Jacio coming the other way, and the boy joined him running down the beach. He saw the fishermen down on the wet pack dragging their rowboats down the very long beach and launching them into the much too shallow water. The soft sand at the wharf end was hard to push through.

"Stop!" he yelled. "There isn't time!"

They didn't even look up. The wind coming off the storm had grown too strong and loud. Finally he and Jacio got onto the hard, wet sand and could run. "There isn't enough time! The storm is too big and it's moving too fast. The Merrow are pulling your fishing boats out of the harbor to safety!"

The men within earshot crowded around him and spoke at the same time.

"They're what?!"

"Who said they could touch our boats?!"

"How do you know?"

"Those boats are our livelihoods!"

Sten tried to calm them down. "Your boats mean the survival of our whole town. The Merrow know that. We may have our differences, but they aren't going to sit by and let us get wiped out."

One of the captains, Dade Bellows, a white-haired man with a dark golden tan, and friend of Selric Boole's, demanded, "How do we know they aren't just going to steal the anchors for scrap metal?"

"Are you serious? Have any of you ever found anything stolen from any of your boats? Those boats sit out in the harbor every night. If the Merrow were the thieves you say they are, why haven't they stolen you blind? They're not thieves."

"We'd still rather take care of our own boats!" insisted another.

"You can try, but by the time you sail against that rising wind and set anchor, you're going to be stuck on board when the storm hits. Do you want to go down with your boat if it sinks? There just isn't time!"

"Why should we listen to you? You're just a fin lover." Captain Bellows fired back.

Jacio surprised Sten by stepping up. "I used to think they were no good thieves too. But I've met a few of them, and they're really good people. You should be glad they are willing to help you after all the hate you've shown them."

Sten was proud of him, and he saw several of the men consider Jacio's words.

Dade wasn't having it. "Are you men going to listen to a boy, the blacksmith's Indru boy?"

"Use your heads, men," Sten insisted. "What would Atlan do? He survived the Great Cataclysm by using his head first and his hands second. Why fight the sea when the Merrow have that covered. You've got better things to do with the short time you've got."

One of the men in the back who had not spoken yet stepped forward. "Sten, what are you suggesting?"

Dade cut him off. "Clete, are you really going to listen to him?"

"Yes, Captain Bellows, I am. Captain Boole showed us where blind hate takes us. If the merfolk are out there risking their necks for us, then we can do better than standing here debating how much we don't trust them."

Sten was amazed. "We need to get these rowboats and all your nets and gear back off the beach, as far back up in town as you can get them. Tell everyone to evacuate the coast. From what I saw up on the wharf, the sea could rush in and flood all the way back to the town square."

Clete turned to the others. "We've got work to do." They all grabbed the rowboats and started heading back up the beach. Dade hesitated and flustered, but then followed suit.

Sten, Jacio and a sailor grabbed the sides of a rowboat and started sliding it up the beach. Sten looked back and saw Captain Bellows, white hair blowing in the wind, and three of his crew running one of their rowboats out into the surf after all.

Chielle swam right passed the red-garbed temple guard, reached up, and rang the town alarm bell with all her might. The guard stared at her with a menacing glare while two others swam up behind her and surrounded her. They did not seize her. The rule was anyone can sound the alarm, but you had better have a really good reason.

Villagers rushed to see what was the matter, but she kept ringing it until she had most of the town in the arena. She figured she would only get this one chance, she needed a response right away, and she would either succeed or fail. She stopped ringing it when she saw her father arrive.

"Please listen up, everyone! We have an important decision to make, and we need to make it right now. Rorratonton will make landfall in less than a sunstone. The humans do not have time to sail their boats out to safety and still make it back to shore before the storm hits and floods Saint Rochel. If we let the storm smash their fishing boats, their village will fail. They will have to abandon their homes."

"Finally, some good news!" someone yelled from the back. She thought she recognized the voice as belonging to Yurum Mool, a loud-mouthed, mean-hearted friend of her father.

She pressed on undaunted. "We have a once in a lifetime chance to do the right thing. If we drag their boats to safety, they will know we saved them, and all this hatred that has grown from their suspicion and distrust of us will end."

At that, most of the gathered muttered objections and criticisms among themselves.

She knew she needed to make her point before she was booed off the stage. "They know how much trouble they are in. They know how badly they have treated us. A lot of them want to reach out to build bridges between our villages, but they can't because we have decided to cut off contact with them. Now, I'm not going to argue whether that's a good idea. Our elders have decided we need to stay away from the human influence. But does that mean we should sit by and watch them lose everything, when it would be so easy for us to save them. Even if we stay separated, they would be forever grateful for our help. They would know how good we are and how much they can trust us. They are part of our world, like it or not. They are part of Rorra's world."

"Then why is Rorra about to drive them into ruin?" someone called out.

"I don't pretend to understand what Rorra is doing. Maybe she is giving us this chance to show how good we are."

The crowd stopped shaking their heads and muttering. Maybe she was getting through to them.

"We need to stay here and secure our own village," someone pointed out. "This storm is too big to just pass over us with no damage."

"It won't take many of us to do this. Rorra has also given us a pod of gray whales who are coming up the coast right now, out of season, ready for us to put to good use pulling those boats to safety."

"How do you know about that?" This time she was sure it was Yurum, and he was definitely hiding back in the third row.

"I just saw them on my way back from Saint Rochel."

"What were you doing there? We're forbidden from making contact."

"Yurum, I thought it only fair to warn them of the storm."

"You saw your boyfriend, didn't you?"

"Yes, I told Sten to tell the village."

The crowd parted and Jeljing himself swam up toward her.

She swallowed hard and pressed on. "How will you all feel if we let the humans lose their homes when we know how easy it would be …"

The Shaman held up his hand and settled to face her. His branch coral crown made his head appear unnaturally elongated. It also accentuated every head movement. "You can stop. You made your point." He winked at her and turned to face the crowd. "Chielle is right. We are above being vindictive. I too am confused by what Rorra is doing with this storm. If we can make good of it by doing the right thing by our neighbors, in spite of how they have treated us, then we should."

He turned to her and smiled. "Go get those whales and save those boats."

She bowed down, grabbed up his hand and rubbed her cheek on it to kiss it. "Thank you, Your Grace. You won't regret this."

She swam out across the crowd, signaling to her brother and their friends to come along. Numerous other young Merrow swam up from their families and joined them. As she swam passed, she saw her mother standing by her father. Chambor Mmava watched her with neither a smile nor a frown. Chielle knew that was her father's wait-and-see look. Gonnakaa, on the other hand, quietly beamed up at her in pride.

17

THYMON FOLLOWED HIS SISTER'S LEAD as she signaled to the other fourteen young Merrow to fan out in front of the advancing whales and not let them pass.

"You have to be nice to them. Firm but nice," she told him.

"Yes, I've done this before. You compliment them, praise them, they like that."

"They're probably pretty scared from the storm. They won't want to stop. Just don't take no for an answer."

The usually clear water was churned cloudy even this far out and deep. Thymon spotted six whales, four big females and two smaller males. He was glad to see there were no babies. The females could get violently uncooperative when they had babies along. He swam up to one of the females and pulled alongside her enormous head. "Welcome beautiful sister," he greeted her in her own language.

She eyed him suspiciously. "Welcome to you," she said steering away from him.

He darted around to her other side. "I need your help. Rorra needs your help. You alone are strong enough to help."

Two other Merrow fell in alongside the forty arm-length whale and stroked her barnacle-scarred gray sides with their hands.

"Storm coming. Must leave," the big gray told him.

"Yes, big storm. We will keep you safe from the big storm," Thymon assured her. "First we need your help, your strong and gentle help."

She slowed to a drift. "You will keep us safe?"

"Yes, there are many of us. We have refuge. You are large and able. We are small. Will you help us?"

"To do what?"

"Push boats."

"How far?"

"Not far. From the harbor to the drop off."

The whale turned toward the harbor as she spoke, guided and encouraged by the Merrow. "How many?"

"Ten. It will be easy with you so strong, so graceful, so gentle." Thymon looked back and saw the other teams had turned their whales too. They were all pointed toward the harbor, and they seemed to be watching Thymon's whale who was in the lead. "You are leader mother. The others look to you to lead."

She kicked and sped up the coast and into the harbor.

Thymon signaled for his partners to swim ahead and prepare the first fishing boat. When Thymon and his whale arrived, they had jumped on board and pulled up the anchor. Thymon was thankful there was still enough depth in the harbor for the whales to maneuver. He guided his enormous charge around behind the boat to nudge against its stern. The boat was longer than the whale, but she had no problem shoving it out to sea. Thymon was pleased with how easy this was going.

He looked around and saw there was another two dozen boats anchored in the harbor besides the ten fishing vessels. Thymon wasn't sure if they would have time to rescue them as well.

The storm did not cooperate. By the time the first boat cleared the lip and dropped anchor, the sea grew choppy with whitecap waves and the wind was howling. He was glad to see another five boats moving into position. He turned his whale back for another boat as quickly as he could coax her.

Back in the harbor, things had become dangerous. The waves were tossing the boats high and low, and it was hard to get his whale to cooperate. His partners barely got the anchor up and had to jump off the boat or be thrown. Thymon put his hands on the stern and pushed. His fellows saw what he was doing and joined him.

"We all work together for Rorra," he chanted.

"We all work together for Rorra," the others joined in.

"We all work together for Rorra," they sang all together.

Finally the whale followed their lead and pushed up against the boat. "Together for Rorra," the behemoth sang as she took over the pushing.

He looked across the harbor and could barely see how the other teams were doing in the dim light under the sky that was now black. Rain started coming down in great sheets. He caught a glimpse of Chielle lining up her whale behind the next boat over. The anchor was up.

A bolt of lightning flashed, and he saw men on board the boat. Chielle did not see them. One of the men had a harpoon and he was running for the stern. Thymon left his team to handle his whale and swam as fast as he could to his sister's aid. He cried out to her above the water, but his voice was lost in the wind. He dove under and yelled her name through the water as he swam, but he couldn't be sure she heard him.

He arrived in time to see the man throw the harpoon. Chielle saw the man and dove under. The whale slammed the boat hard and the man tumbled over the back rail. Thymon dove under looking for Chielle, and found the harpoon lodged shallowly in the whale's side. He pulled it free and circled around for his sister. She wasn't where he had seen her. She wasn't with her team at the boat either.

The man floundered and yelled for help. Thymon decided he could wait. He dove under and peered into the dark water but could not find her. He circled the area twice more, fighting back panic. He surfaced to ask the man if he had seen where she went, but the man wasn't where he had left him.

Frustration, anger, and fear all overtook him. He looked back and watched the whale, guided by Chielle's team, pushing the boat to safety. Thymon felt powerless with the storm so violent and overwhelming. He dove again, continuing to look for his sister.

Sten sat at one of the front tables in The Pied Cock, looking through the shuttered windows at the wagon he had loaded with his most valuable tools. Rain fell from the black sky in a continuous downpour. The wind tore at the tarpaulin he had tied over his belongings. He knew his shack would not survive the beating the storm was giving the wharf. He looked around the room, which was full but not as crowded as he expected, at the others who had come to wait out the storm. The place often smelled of damp. This was the tropics, after all. With the downpour, the usual sap smell of the wood beams was mixed with mud and mold from below the floor boards.

One table was full of the fishermen he had helped at the beach. They all looked really worried and made small talk to distract themselves. Clete Sandsen caught his eye and nodded. Sten raised his glass and nodded back.

Arum Blaine returned to their table and set another beer in front of Sten. "We're going to be here for a while," the constable said humorlessly.

"Could be even longer," Sten countered. "After this, I am probably homeless."

"The town's got a bigger problem than that." He sipped the foam off the top of his own beer. "How are we going to rebuild with no working blacksmith?"

"Damiel's will be open. He's way inland. Besides, I can set up shop anywhere you've got bricks and charcoal. When I first got here, I was working out of one of Norn Tureck's barns."

"That was just over a year ago? You came from up in the northeast, mountain country, right?"

"Yes, a village called Nathanson. Why the sudden interest in my background?"

"Well, I was going to sidle up to it, being all clever, but I guess I'm just not that smooth. I understand Patry Bilboa treated your broken ribs after your fight with Selric Boole. She asked me if I knew about your lash scars. She said she counted fifteen. As the Officer of the Peace here I have a right to know if someone has a criminal past, even if they have paid for it. Fifteen lashes got my attention. Anything you want to share with me?"

Sten looked around the room and no one was listening. "I murdered a man. It was revenge. He killed my little sister. Actually, he raped, killed, and mutilated her. I was responsible for her after our parents died. She was sixteen. I was twenty-four. I was found guilty, because I was. No one could prove the killer did it, but everyone knew he did. The judge went light on me instead of hanging because he agreed the killer had it coming." Sten was surprised at how calmly he could talk about this most painful time of his life. Maybe he wasn't as nervous telling Arum as he had been telling Chielle.

"I thought I paid my debt to society and should be able to go on with my life. Nothing was ever the same after everyone I grew up with thought I was capable of murder. So I left. I made my way all across the continent over the next two years before I finally felt like I could make a fresh start here."

Arum leaned back and stared at him dispassionately all through his story. Sten had seen that look before, that taking-it-all-in, non-committal look the lawman had. "That explains a lot of why you are so driven for justice. When you got so fired up about the Merrow being mistreated, I thought that might mean you knew a thing or two about the law."

"I've been on the receiving end of the law."

"That's right, when Roff Collum got his lashes for shooting that merman, you said he should pay the price like a man and be done with it. You paid your price, but it didn't work out so well for you."

"I hoped for better here."

The building shook and groaned against the wind. Sten looked back out the window.

"We'll be fine," Arum dismissed.

"I'm not worried about us."

"You've told me what a smart girl your Chielle is. She knows that ocean better than any of us ever will. You've got to assume she'll be fine. Otherwise you'll just stay up all night sweating it, which will make no difference."

"You have an amazingly detached sense of things, you know that?"

"I don't let things get to me, if that's what you mean."

"You'll have to share your secret with me sometime."

Arum squinted on a thought. "I know it's not my place, and the last time I said something stupid about the Merrow you let me have it out in the street."

"Even so, you feel compelled to stick your foot back in your mouth?" Sten said with a smile.

"I guess so." He grinned and shook his head. "You seem awfully smitten with this girl in a very short time. Are you sure she hasn't enchanted you? Mermaids are supposed to have siren powers over men."

Sten saw this coming and chuckled. "You know, as ignorant as that is, I can't get mad at you because I asked her the same question. No, they actually can't use their voice or any magic to enchant a man. That really is just a myth. No, I fell in love with her the old-fashioned way, for all the right reasons."

They were interrupted by a roaring sound that seemed to come up from below the floor. Sten looked out the window and saw water flooding up the street from the ocean. It came in waves, just a few inches at first, but soon there was a couple of feet of standing water filling the street. Many of the bar patrons got up and looked. Paulbert Caron came running up, pony tail wagging, with an armload of towels which he kicked into place across the bottom of the door.

"This street has got to be, what, twenty feet above highest tide?" Sten figured out loud.

"That's some storm surge," Arum agreed.

Everyone sighed relief when the water stopped rising and seemed to recede slowly back to the sea.

Sten shook his head and rolled his eyes with a great exhaled sigh. "What is it?"

"Here I am sitting, waiting for the storm to pass, unable to do anything to save the town or help the Merrow save the boats. Just sitting here going with the flow of things, trying to have faith that things will turn out all right," he said with exasperation. "That's the Merrow way of doing things. They trust in Rorra, their sea goddess, and wait to see what Rorra will give them. At this same time, Chielle, the love of my life, is out in the hurricane dragging fishing boats to safety. She's taking control. She's seizing the opportunity. Isn't that supposed to be the human way, the way Atlan taught us?"

"You have a problem with this? Would you rather be out in the ocean fighting a hurricane?"

"No. Well, yes, but that's not the point. The irony is just making me crazy. I'm so frustrated. I can't stand this."

"You should take this as a lesson. She learned assertiveness from you. You should learn patience from her."

Chielle looked up and was shocked to see a man on board. She was further horrified to see the white-haired sailor haul back to throw a harpoon at her and she dove under the stern of the boat. Her whale also saw the man and kicked mightily, plowing the boat so hard it lifted the back out of the water. She turned around to see what the whale was doing and the boat slammed down on top of her, knocking her unconscious. With all of the air forced out of her lungs, she sank heavily into the dark waters.

18

Chielle was walking through the snow again. She found the scrunching sound of snow underfoot very satisfying, and she stomped her fur boots a little harder with each step to make more of the delicious noise. She had come to love the feeling of pushing off with her feet against the ground. She still didn't like how her knees only bent in one direction. She kept wanting to move them to the side or in curves. Still, as long as these dreams kept giving her the chance, she was going to take it for all it was worth.

She was walking across a field of snow with no clear destination. It was pleasant enough, with her bundled up against the cold, the sun high in the clear blue sky over the untouched smooth snow, the smell of crisp, clean air in her nose. She didn't worry herself about where she was going. Best to let the dream take her and show her what she needed to see.

She took a step and it sank lower than she expected. She figured it was just a dent in the ground below, so she took another step. This one sank even further. She stepped to the side to find level footing, and the bottom fell out with an alarmingly loud crack. Her steps knocked open a fissure in the ice below the snow and she barely had time to catch herself with her arms on the snow. She looked down into the dark crystal blue gap and fought back panic. She pushed her booted feet against the slippery walls of the crack but could not get any traction. She tried to wedge her legs against opposite sides of the crack to push up, but this pulled her body away from the one side she was hanging onto. She felt her grip slipping and she clawed at the snow, but it was too late. She fell into the crack, sliding down the walls of ice until her body wedged tight. She looked up and saw she was at least ten cubits below the surface.

She had no idea how she was going to get out. Panic set in as she frantically looked around for any option and found none. "Help!" she yelled. Her voice rang off the walls, but she doubted the sound made it out of her prison. "Help!" She had no tools in her clothing. Her only consolation was her clothing was thick enough to protect her against the bitter cold of the ice all around her. "Help!"

She considered taking her coat off and wedging it below her. Even if she could stand on it, the surface was too far away for her to reach it. "Help!"

Minutes went by. She wondered if anyone would even think to look for her. She was new in town. The thought squeezed the last bit of hope out of her. She hung her head and started to cry.

Something moved next to her. She jumped, fearing something alive and dangerous was in the crack with her. She looked up and it was the end of a rope, a rope hanging down into the crack.

"Hello down there!" A man's voice called from the surface. "Are you all right?"

"Yes, I'm not hurt, just stuck. Can you pull me up?"

"I'm an old man, so I'm not sure I can pull you. I'll hang on, and you climb."

She twisted around and got a good grip with both hands. "Are you ready?" she called up.

"Yep, I've got you."

She pulled and tried to kick with her feet, but again, they slipped off the walls uselessly. She took a deep breath and pulled with all her might, dragging herself up. She got her hands down to her chest and then flashed one hand up to grab some more rope.

She had never climbed something hand over hand before and it took a moment to figure out the motion.

In the back of her mind she became aware that she was not holding a rope, but a chain. Her feet were not hanging uselessly, but rather her tail was throbbing in pain and not moving. She tried to bend it and stiffening pain racked up its length. Her head hurt too. She blinked and the dark blue ice faded to dark water, brown from the churned bottom. The hardness of the ice walls gave way to the violent surging of the tides around her. She looked down and saw an anchor holding the chain steady enough for her to hold on. She looked up and saw a boat at the other end being tossed around. She remembered where she was and realized how quickly she needed to get to safety. Her hands had already pulled her halfway up the chain. She didn't know how long she had been knocked out. The storm surge could arrive at any moment, and she would be swept up onto the shore like so much kelp. Being hurled onto the buildings of the waterfront was not something she wanted to think about.

Time to go.

As soon as the rain and winds relented enough, everyone in the pub ventured out to survey the damage. Sten ran for the shore. The water in the streets was still running back into the sea, and he had to watch his step as he overran the runoff. As people ventured tentatively from storefronts, Sten noticed someone jogging along behind him. It was Clete and the other fishermen from the pub. He knew what they wanted to see.

As he neared the shore, he was taken by the smell of rot. When he turned out onto the beach, he could see why. Great heaping piles of seaweed had been thrown up onto the buildings facing the beach. Many buildings were caved in or had their roofs smashed by the force of the water. People were inspecting the damage, but no one appeared harmed. He was glad to see folks had cleared out in time. As he scanned the debris, he was even happier to see no Merrow bodies thrown ashore.

Several boats were tossed and broken on the beach. The fishing boats were not among them. The light rain and the dark skies made it hard to see very far, but he could make out boats moored outside the harbor. The Merrow had come through.

Yet there was no sign of the Merrow. He stood on the beach with his fists clenched, barely able to contain his impatience and dread. Where was she?

The fishermen who ran up behind him spotted their boats safe outside the harbor and began cheering and yelling. Clete ran up and grabbed Sten in a bear hug. "I'm sorry we ever doubted you or your merfolk."

"I'm just glad they pulled it off. I wonder if Captain Bellows made it back safely."

"We'll find out when we row out to fetch the boats once the sea calms down." Clete looked out again at the ocean which was choppy but no longer threatening. "I hope your girlfriend is all right."

Sten was surprised and smiled at him. "Thank you for that."

What had been a trickle of people coming to the beach was now a steady stream of concerned onlookers. The town's three dozen fishermen were gathering on the wet sand near the surf, pointing and clasping each other on the shoulders. Sten looked over at the wharf. The pilings were still intact, but a lot of timber was torn away. His shop had some walls standing, but it was clearly thrashed.

The fishermen called out and Sten turned to see them pointing into the surf. He didn't see them at first, then he spotted heads bobbing behind the breakers. Swimmers, yes, the Merrow had come to see what the storm had done. Sten ran down to the water's edge. "Welcome!"

Clete stepped up beside him. "Yes, please come ashore! We want to thank you for saving our boats!"

Very tentatively, a handful of young Merrow men came up out of the waves. Clete and Sten shook their hands. "Thank you all so much for saving our fleet," the fisherman started. "How did it go? Was it dangerous? Was anyone hurt?"

"It was scary toward the end with the last few boats," explained a tall, lean Merrow man. "The storm came up strong and tossed your boats around like toys. I've never seen anything like it."

Sten was taken with how normal he sounded, just like any young man after a big adventure. He was glad the fishermen were seeing how approachable he was.

"I think there were some injuries. We had whales helping us."

"Whales?" Sten was amazed.

"It was Chielle's idea to use them."

"Where is Chielle?"

"I don't know." He looked around at his fellows who were talking with villagers. "I'm sure someone has seen her."

Sten held his hand out. "By the way, I'm Sten."

"Oh, you're Chielle's Sten. Glad to meet you. I'm Kriish. I'm a friend of Chielle's brother Thymon."

"I know Thymon. We once shared a quill together."

Kriish looked rather shocked.

"Maybe I shouldn't have mentioned that," Sten said with a shrug.

The clouds were starting to thin and break up, letting in late afternoon light that made it much easier to see on the beach. The villagers had all come down on the sand and were checking out the stranded, broken boats and meeting the Merrow. Sten saw this but he didn't think about what a great step this was. He was too distracted. Kriish has said there were injuries.

He shook Kriish's hand, "It was very nice to meet you. If you'll excuse me, I have to go do something." He started walking down the beach, looking at each of the Merrow who had come on land. He did not try to assure himself, as Blaine had tried, that she was certainly capable enough to not get hurt. The more faces he saw, the more nervous he became.

He saw what looked like two Merrow attached to one another coming up out of the waves. He ran to the water's edge and saw it was one carrying another. When they cleared the breakers, he saw it was Thymon carrying Chielle.

Sten ran out into the water. "Chielle! Thank Heavens you're all right. Wait a minute. You're not all right. Can't you walk?"

She turned around in her brother's arms and hugged Sten. "Hello Sweetheart."

He hugged her back and took her from Thymon. His ribs spasmed with the sudden weight. He ignored it. "Have you broken something? Are you in any pain?"

"She won't admit to any pain, but it obviously hurts too much to swim or walk," Thymon explained.

Sten stared at her with such excitement and such relief he found himself breathing hard. Just holding her in his arms, being able to protect her when he had just felt so helpless, he couldn't think straight to ask the next question.

"Oh dear, are you all right Sten?" She held his face in her hands and looked into his eyes. "You look like you're going to faint."

"I'm just so relieved. You can't imagine how happy I am to have you here. How were you injured?"

"A boat got lifted up and it fell on me. I was knocked out and when I came to my tail was badly bruised. I don't think anything is broken, but it hurts a lot when I try to use it."

He leaned in and rested his forehead on hers. "I've got you now."

"It took us a while to get up onto the beach," her brother added. "All the water running off the land is creating some really strong riptides. I wanted to take her home to treat her, but she insisted we come ashore first."

"Your friend Kriish said you wrangled whales to help push the boats. That's amazing."

"It was one of the whales that lifted the boat that landed on me. They're really strong."

Thymon wasn't going to leave that alone. "I saw what happened. The whale defended you. I pulled the harpoon out of the whale's hide."

"Whoa, harpoon?" Sten jumped in. "What happened?"

"One of the boats had sailors on it, and one of them tried to harpoon Chielle when she lined up her whale. I saw what was happening and I swam over as fast as I could, but it was too far. The sailor threw the spear, and the whale dove under it and into the back of the boat. Chielle swam under the boat, but then it came down on her. She sank to the bottom and I couldn't find her for the longest time. It was very scary."

"Did the sailor have long white hair?"

"Yes," Chielle said.

"Dade Bellows."

"You knew him?"

"I tried to stop him."

"He fell into the sea and perished," Thymon explained. "The other sailors are still stuck on that boat."

Sten walked up onto the sand carrying her, headed for a group of very noisily happy men and Merrow. He noticed a group of villagers headed down the beach toward the reveling fishermen as well. "Sweetheart, I want you to meet the fishermen whose livelihoods you just saved."

"Clete Sandsen, this is Chielle Mmava and her brother Thymon. It was Chielle's idea to re-anchor the boats outside the harbor."

He shook her hand vigorously. "That's fantastic! We can't thank you enough!" He turned to the other fishermen who were trading stories with the other Merrow. "Men! This is the little lady who thought of towing the boats to safety! Can I have a three cheer?"

"Hip, hip, hurray! Hip, hip, hurray! Hip, hip, hurray!"

Chielle lowered her head, embarrassed by all the noisy attention.

Sten saw the group of villagers on the other side of the revelers taken aback by the cheer. They spoke among themselves and then left as a group.

Sten explained to Clete. "Chielle was injured saving Dade Bellows' boat. Unfortunately, Captain Bellows fell overboard in the rough seas and drowned. His men are still on their boat."

Clete nodded. "We'll go get them presently." To Chielle he added, "I'm sorry you got injured, miss."

"Thank you. I'll be all right," she assured him.

Sten tracked the moving group of villagers as they made their way back to the debris-strewn waterfront walkway. He saw lots of shaking heads and waving fists. Not everyone was pleased with the celebration.

His eye was caught by someone climbing up the poles of what used to be the welcome sign over the wharf. The recently repainted wooden unwelcome sign was entirely blown away by the storm. He pointed to them for Chielle to see. While they watched, two men shimmied up the poles and hung a cloth sign across the gap that read, "Welcome All."

She gave him a big congratulatory hug.

Patry Bilboa waded through the crowd that had collected at the end of Main Street, looking out over the waterfront. She absently noticed the exquisite bustled red dress in front of her and deduced it had to be Vanda Rymerand. She tapped the young woman on the shoulder. "Isn't this quite the turn of events?"

Vanda turned back and scowled. "Indeed."

"I am as surprised as the next person, but I have to say, I am pleased they rose to the occasion." Patry noticed that her words were not having the effect she expected. In fact, the more she spoke, the angrier Vanda seemed to become. "The fishermen seem to be having a party right there on the beach. I assume the merfolk succeeded in saving their boats."

"I'm convinced it's a trick," the young blonde growled through clenched teeth. "There is no way those fin have that kind of integrity."

"Vanda dear, if I may say so, your anger seems bigger than any lingering suspicion. Do you know something we should all know?"

"Only that they are thieves. Always have been and always will be. That strumpet Chielle they are all cheering about stole my Sten right out from my grasp. Can you imagine that? Sten with a stinking fin, over me? Who does she think she is?"

Patry was relieved to hear Vanda's anger was simple jealousy. For a moment, she worried if Vanda had discovered some hidden agenda. While the young woman railed on about her would-be paramour, Patry noticed a glittering bauble on a chain around Vanda's neck, bouncing between her breasts pressed up by her low-cut bodice. "Yes, yes, dear, men are remarkably fickle that way, I'm sure. If you will excuse me, I need to ask you about your beautiful necklace."

Vanda held it up to show it off.

Patry was stunned silent.

"Isn't it exquisite. I believe these are all real diamonds and rubies. Mama gave it to me just before she passed away. She said it was her 'closest held treasure,' whatever that meant. Clearly one of a kind. It is certainly my favorite."

Patry could not bring herself to speak. She held back a tear and took a deep breath to steady herself. "Yes, it is lovely. If you'll excuse me, I have something I must do." She pressed her way through the crowd and marched out onto the sand.

Stomping through the sand, she could not hold back any longer and she broke down crying. "Selna Rymerand, how could you! We're you so jealous of our friendship you had to tear it apart with theft and lies? I trusted you. I trusted you!" She stopped walking, bent down and clasped her face in her hands. She started sobbing, overcome with anger and regret. "You, you monster!"

She sniffed a great inhale and stood up straight. "I may not be able to curse you to your face, but I can certainly make amends. She wiped her tears away and resumed marching down to the water.

It wasn't hard to find Chielle. For some reason Sten was cradling her in his arms. Maybe he was just glad to see her. She stepped through the sailors milling about. "Chielle, my dear. congratulations on a job well done!"

"Mrs. Bilboa, what a pleasant surprise."

"Hello Patry," Sten greeted her.

"Hello Sten. Chielle, I have to ask you a favor. When you next see your mother, could you please tell her I need to see her as soon as possible? It is a private matter and quite urgent."

"Of course, I'll be glad to."

"Thank you. Tell her I will come wherever and whenever works for her."

"I will. Is everyone all right?"

"Yes. In fact, things are going to be much better from now on."

Sten watched her trudge away back into town. "You told me your mom and Patry used to be best friends. This sounded hopeful."

"It did. We'll see."

They were interrupted by a commotion down at the water's edge. The fishermen and their Merrow guests parted to allow Jeljing, the Merrow Shaman and his entourage to stride ashore. The leader's elaborate coral crown and wide, colorful, beaded collar had been impressive in the town square. It was rather intimidating in person, making him appear a foot taller and a foot wider. Sten braced himself for what he was sure to be bad news. Aside quietly to Chielle, who was still in his arms, he asked, "How do I address him?"

"Your Grace," she whispered back. "Let him speak first."

He pulled up to stand on his fluke while his guards did the same behind him. "Mister Holdsmith and Miss Mmava, this was not a normal storm, was it?" He asked rhetorically. "It was almost as if tensions between our two peoples had built into a typhoon. What would you know about such things?"

"The storm was a gift from Rorra," Sten declared.

He felt Chielle stiffen in his arms.

The Shaman raised an eyebrow. "Your village is badly battered, yet you think this was a gift?"

"The town can be rebuilt. The goddess gave us a chance to rise above our differences, a chance for humans to remember how good the Merrow really are."

The eyebrow came down and his gaunt old face stretched into a grin.

Sten decided this was his one chance. "The Merrow risked their safety to show their good will. To make this peace last, please let the humans show our good will in return. Let us exchange gifts with your people. No one lacks for anything with an abundant sea and land. That goes for steel too. No more smelting in volcanoes out of desperation. It is only right to give when there is need. You live your lives by this truth. Let us show you that we believe that too. We can overcome greed if we are given the chance to do the right thing. You call it mutual giving. We call it trade. It will keep both of us away from fear and hate."

The Shaman looked around the beach at the humans and Merrow standing side by side, paused in the midst of open celebration. He looked Sten square in the eye. He raised his hand and swept it over the attentive crowd. "Only if, and only for as long, as trade fosters more of this."

Sten reached up with his right hand while still supporting Chielle's tail with that arm, and shook his still outstretched hand. He caught the shocked look on Chielle's face out of the corner of his eye. Well, he was bound to breach some formality at some point. "You won't regret this, sir."

Arum Blaine stepped up unexpectedly from somewhere behind Sten and greeted the Shaman. "Your Grace, welcome ashore. Please allow me the honor of treating you to some of our hospitality."

Sten was amused at Arum saving him from his embarrassment. His amusement was short lived. Right behind Jeljing's exiting entourage was a stern looking, barrel-chested Merrow in a dark blue tunic that somehow reminded Sten of Chielle and Thymon. "Oh," he muttered when he realized why.

"Daddy," Chielle started, "this is Sten Holdsmith. Sten, this is Chambor Mmava, my father."

Her father folded his arms over his thick chest. Sten couldn't stand letting an awkward silence ruin this moment, so he stepped right up. "Sir, I am delighted to finally meet you. I wanted to meet you when I visited your beautiful town last week, but I couldn't stay very long."

He eyed Sten up and down. "I expected you to be taller. Everyone talks of this crusader for justice who is going to bring peace to the two villages. This adventurer who risks drowning to see Celidan with his own eyes. This compassionate friend who my youngest daughter has fallen in love with. I thought, surely a man worthy of so many accolades must be a giant among men."

"Daddy, he is. His people recognize him as a hero."

"I can see that. I see you, Sten Holdsmith, as the man who inspires my daughter to do crazy things, like pushing boats to safety in the middle of a typhoon. I can see she was injured in the effort, otherwise you wouldn't be holding her like that. You follow your heart. I was prepared to not like you, but I see I have no reason."

Sten wasn't sure if he should be encouraged by this or not.

"Our village took damage from the storm as well. We are going to need the talents of all our people to help with repairs, including Chielle."

"Does that mean you are no longer banning me from seeing Sten?" she asked a little too quickly.

Chambor continued talking to Sten. "I cannot control my headstrong daughter, so I am hoping you can at least keep her from harm. I will release her from the ban to see you, but I need your assurance that you will not let her take any more risks like this."

"Thank you, Sir. It will be my honor to protect your daughter from herself, and anything else that threatens her."

Chielle wiggled her tail to get their attention. "Hey, you two! I'm right here."

Sten smiled at her. "Thank Rorra for that."

Sten looked back and saw Sooreet standing at her father's shoulder. She nodded and raised her eyebrows at him dubiously for just a moment.

"Sten, this is my big sister Sooreet."

She extended her hand and Sten shook it. "Very glad to meet you. Did your mother come as well?"

Sooreet smiled politely. "It is good to meet you too. She said she would be here."

The clear, hollow sound of a fiddle cut through the drizzle and the muffled din of people talking. Sten craned his neck to see and indeed some men were dancing to the fiddler on the hard-packed wet sand next to the lapping waves. The song was a reel, a relatively calm dance tune that Sten agreed would be a good way to introduce step dancing to the sway-minded Merrow. The Merrow were watching the bouncy steps intently.

One young Merrow man with a bandaged arm hunched into the dancers, stood up on his fluke, and began clapping his hands in half time to the music. He then swayed and gyrated in time with his clapping.

"Go Serool!" Thymon called out.

Sten was surprised at how well the two dance forms blended, one lots of small steps and the other no stepping and all swaying on a planted tail. What amazed Sten even more was how he had seen this blending before, in the dream he had last night, the dream he had dismissed as wishful thinking.

"What is it Sweetheart? You look like you just saw a ghost."

He shook his head absently and grinned. "No, not a ghost, a goddess. Rorra showed this to me, to tell me everything would be all right."

"In a dream?"

"Yes."

"Sten, when you were a boy, did you ever fall into a crack in the ice and need to climb out with a rope?"

He double took and gasped. "Yes! Did you dream about that?"

She nodded and said, "I think your memory saved my life out there in the storm."

Sten wasn't sure what to make of that, so he just hugged her closer.

They did not see it, but Serool paused in his dance and frowned when he saw them embrace.

Other Merrow started singing a high-pitched chant that went with the swaying dance and clapping, and again complemented the more rapid violin playing. Another human added a penny whistle and another a boran drum. In no time more humans and Merrow joined in the dance as well, and the revelry became contagious. It was a beautiful moment Sten never thought he would see. His breath caught in his throat.

Chielle pointed past the dancers. "Look, there's my mom."

"Oh, good. I'll finally get to meet her face to face and thank her for patching me up."

She started to call out to her, but Sten stopped her. "Hang on. Look over there," he said pointing. That's Patry Bilboa, and I think she's found your mom."

They watched as Patry pushed through the crowd to Gonnakaa. Patry did most of the talking.

"That looks pretty intense," Sten observed. "I wonder what they're talking about."

"I might know. I'll ask Mom about it later."

Patry suddenly abandoned her usual collected demeanor and started pleading. She looked really upset, maybe even crying. Gonnakaa threw her arms around the woman and started crying with her in an embrace that Sten thought could only mean forgiveness.

"Looks like some of the wounds dividing us go pretty deep."

Chielle squeezed his shoulders and pressed her cheek against his chest. "Mrs. Bilboa said it herself. Things are going to be much better from now on."

19

T HE FURTHER STEN WENT OUT ON THE WHARF, the more timbers were missing from the walking surface. He steered the handcart around the holes as best he could. By the time he got to the remains of his shop, he had to carry the cart while stepping from beam to beam.

The tide was strangely high, only a few feet from the top of the wharf. The water lapping at the pier pilings, usually a distant rhythm of life on the wharf, was loud and unavoidable. What a difference from the day before when the storm had pulled most of the water out of the harbor.

A warm wind blew grey clouds around while small patches of blue let the sun peek down. Sten was glad it wouldn't get too hot since it was very humid.

The sea gulls were back from wherever they had hidden. They mostly ignored his approach, as they always did. The barking of the harbor seals around the pilings was absent as was their smell. All he smelled was damp wood and the sea. The place seemed strange without that smell.

The floating landing and its ramp were nowhere to be seen, ripped away and sunk. Norn's poor boat, The *Back Forty* was also missing and lost. The walls of his shack had more panels missing than intact. The thatched roof was nearly gone. A whole day after the storm ended, everything was still sopping wet.

He stepped inside and shoed away a couple of curious gulls. "Playtime's over, guys!"

The brick hearth had collapsed when the beams beneath it shook. He stood there imagining what that must have looked like. The smell of the hearth, so much a part of being home, was gone, replaced by the dull smell of wet ashes. He was glad he had grabbed most of his smithing tools, since it would have been a mess digging things out of that pile, assuming they had not fallen into the sea.

He was amused to find his pots and pans still in the cabinets.

His living quarters were the worst. Two of the outside walls were gone, and where his bed and sitting area had been, he was greeted by a clear view of the sea below.

"Oh, Sten," Chielle sighed behind him. "Your home is destroyed."

He hadn't heard her come up behind him. She must have hopped up onto the deck with the sea level so high. He smiled back at her from the doorway. "The storm took the bed where we first made love."

She stepped up beside him and looked. She whistled at the sight, without blowing out any air in that way that only Merrow can. She was wearing some kind of wig woven from yellow threadlike sea grass. It covered her gill fringes and hung down over her shoulders.

"What are you wearing?"

She flipped the ends around. "Do you like it?"

"It's pretty. You did a beautiful job weaving it. It looks almost like human hair."

"Exactly," she beamed.

"Can you breathe all right? I mean it covers your gills."

She looked annoyed. "Yes, I can breathe fine."

"Did you make this for me?"

"You don't like it, do you?"

"Yes, I like it. It's just different. I want you to know I love the way you look normally. You don't need to change anything for me."

"I know. I thought it might be easier for you to, I don't know …"

This awkwardness wasn't like her. "Something's bothering you. What's got you thinking you need to look more human?"

"It must have taken you some time to accept how different I am from you. I know it took me a while to get used to all your hair. Hair seems to be such a big part of being human, I thought maybe I should have some too."

He paused and chose his words carefully. He had been working up his nerve to start a conversation about their relationship, but this was not how he had pictured it. "It didn't take me long at all. I started falling in love with you as soon as I got to know you."

"Well, I don't like that you have to think of me as a departure. I thought you might like to see me more like the women you've known."

Sten snorted. "Sweetheart, you are more woman than anyone I have ever known. I love you just the way you are."

"You shave for me."

"That's true."

"I've seen how much trouble shaving is. You cut yourself almost every time," she said.

"You're right. I am touched that you made the wig for me. We talked about how the townspeople will accept you. The wig might make a difference to them. As long as you know you don't need it for me. I love you just the way you are. You are beautiful. You know that, right?"

She looked down, and he expected her to peek up at him in that coy way she often did. Her eyes stayed down. "Yes, but I'm afraid."

"Afraid? You, who just stood up to the whole of Merrow tradition to save us all from a typhoon? The heroine of my life is afraid? Of what?"

"That someday you will tire of how we can't make love properly."

He had not expected that. "What, do you think I'm going to leave you for a human just because she has the plumbing I fit into? Sweetheart, every woman I have ever known has had the right anatomy for that. None of them have ever been the right person for me. My goodness, we share dreams. You are my soul mate. You've got that over anyone else, regardless of species."

"I believe you when you tell me you love me. I know your promises are good. I don't want you to promise something that will make you unhappy."

"The only thing that would make me unhappy would be losing you." He paused and smiled lovingly into her eyes. Something else was still upsetting her. "What is it, really?"

She swallowed hard. "My brother's friend Serool."

"The dancer with the crazy moves last night?"

"Yes."

"Did I see him giving you the eye?"

He completely caught her off guard. "Um, I don't know. I didn't see that."

"Do I have a rival?"

"Goodness no! I mean … no. Not Serool." She shook her head. "No, he told me that a few days ago, he was up in Saint Rochel, you know, to keep an eye on things."

"While wet and invisible."

"Yes, that. He says he saw you and this really pretty woman in the pub. And you gave her a gold ring."

Now Sten reeled. "What? Oh man, the wet spot on the window. He must have leaned into it. No, that's not what happened at all. Vanda is an old girlfriend of mine, from months ago. She's very brash, and she had me take the ring off her finger 'cause it was stuck."

"Does that mean you aren't seeing her anymore?"

"Oh my lord, no. She's a terrible bigot. If Serool had stuck around for just one more minute, he would have seen me tell her about you and she stormed out furious. Is that what this is all about? Believe me, Vanda is the last person you should consider competition. Living in a small town, sometimes you have to deal with ex-partners."

"That's true," she said with a nod. She still did not look at ease. He gathered his courage. This really had not gone as he planned, but the right moment is the right moment, planned or not. "Now, I will admit there is one part of your mermaid anatomy that did cause me some concern, and that was your webbed hands."

"What do you mean? You said you liked how soft my webs are."

He walked out to his cart and dug out a satchel. She followed as far as the door. Was this the right time? Is there ever a right time? His heart was pounding and his throat was tightening. She was fragile now, with fears he didn't want her to ever have again. He could think of no better way to put those fears to rest, once and for all. "That's true, but you can't wear a ring on your finger."

He handed her a small wooden box, which she took and opened. The polished silver filigree bracelet gleamed in a ray of sun that ducked in through the broken shack. The metal swirls formed the letter "H" at the center. She took it out and stared at it intently. She looked like she knew this meant something important, but wasn't sure what. "When I wear this, everyone will know it's from you, right?"

"Exactly."

She pointed to the woven shell bracelet on his wrist. "Like that one."

He laughed. "Yes. You know, I am so dense, it took me forever to realize how much this really means."

She brightened with the happy connection, "And, this … marks me as yours?"

He knelt down on one knee. "Chielle Mmava, will you marry me?"

She sucked in a surprised breath and shifted her wide-eyed stare from the bracelet to his face, and just froze. He noticed she had stopped breathing. A long moment went by.

He laughed. "I know you can hold your breath a long time. You haven't answered my question."

She caught herself and blinked furiously. "I … I … I'm speechless." She hastily slipped the bracelet onto her wrist and blurted out, "I wasn't expecting this. Yes. Oh, yes! By the depths and waves, yes!" She flung her arms around his neck and hugged him tightly to her breast. "Yes, I will marry you Sten Holdsmith. I will be your loving, devoted wife for the rest of my days."

He stood up and she leapt into his arms. He grabbed her around the waist and spun, swinging her tail around and around.

She kissed him on the lips and rubbed her face against his with slow deep affection. "Oh, Sten."

"What I'm offering won't be an easy life. Especially for you, since I can't live in the water the way you can live on land."

She buried her face in his neck and squeezed him tightly. "I know. I've thought about that." She loosened her grip and looked up at him. "I have thought about what life would be like with you. I never expected you to ask me to marry you, but I have certainly fantasized about it. I know we can make it work. I love you too much not to do whatever it takes."

She paused to digest. "Here I had myself all worked up, pouring out all my doubts, and all this time you had this here on your cart?"

"I was waiting for the right moment."

She held up her arm and admired the bracelet. "Oh, Rorra be praised for bringing me to you."

Sten grinned. "I agree." He set her down.

"I can't wait to tell Mother. Oh, dear, what about my father?"

"Have you forgotten that he made me promise to protect you yesterday? I was rather shocked, to tell the truth."

"That was huge, wasn't it?"

"I'm hoping that's only a handshake away from giving me permission to marry you."

"Marry me," she repeated gleefully, bouncing on her folded tail. "I can't believe it." Her broad smile faded. "Wait. How can we get married? Who will marry us?"

Sten grinned again. "I already thought of that. I have friends in high places."

She grinned back. "The High Lord? Would he do that?" She interrupted herself again and frowned. "Would my people acknowledge a marriage held by men?"

He tenderly smoothed her wig tendrils and gill slits. "So many questions, you worry too much. I've thought this through. I happen to know the High Lord held court with your Shaman this afternoon, to talk about how our peoples can get along better. I'm pretty sure they will jump at the chance to jointly officiate a wedding that cements the peace they both want so badly."

She lowered her head coyly and looked up at him.

He was thrilled to see that look was back.

"Clever you. You have made me the happiest girl in the world. Both worlds."

ABOUT THE AUTHOR

Jay Hartlove is the award-winning author of the urban fantasy "Goddess Rising" trilogy (*Goddess Chosen, Goddess Daughter,* and *Goddess Rising*) and the fantasy romance *Mermaid Steel*. He is also the playwright, director and producer of *The Mirror's Revenge*, the musical sequel to the "Snow White" fable, which had its theatrical run in the San Francisco Bay Area in August 2018 to rave reviews.

His stories are filled with conspiracies and the supernatural, gods, dreams, angels, and hidden connections. His creative motto is "Dark Secrets Revealed". He loves to take stories where the reader does not expect, with sympathetic villains, heroes with very dark pasts, and lots of plot twists. He was selected as one of the "50 Authors You Should Be Reading" by *The Authors Show*.

Jay is a former competitive costumer, having won Best in Show at both San Diego ComicCon and WorldCon. You can read more about Jay's creative adventures, including much of the research he put into his books, at *jaywrites.com*.

ALSO BY JAY HARTLOVE

GODDESS CHOSEN

Book One of the *Goddess Rising* Series

by Jay Hartlove

The man who would beat the devil isn't a hero, but a ruthless madman.

GODDESS DAUGHTER

Book Two of the *Goddess Rising* Series

by Jay Hartlove

How far can you genetically alter someone before she becomes someone else ... before she loses her soul?

GODDESS RISING

Book Three of the *Goddess Rising* Series

by Jay Hartlove

Saved by a goddess ... but only as a tool for revenge?

Available from Paper Angel Press in
hardcover, trade paperback, digital, and audio editions
paperangelpress.com

nd-product-compliance